For Otis

About the Author

Ann Hammerton was brought up in Nottingham where her parents both ran successful businesses.

After a private education and music college, her career as a professional singer included musicals, reviews and recordings, both in the UK and abroad.

Some years followed working in advertising, marketing, trading and property. At the age of fifty-five she moved to France, there to become fascinated with old stone properties which she renovated.

She returned to England in 2007, writing having become her main interest. She now lives in Eastbourne where she continues to work on ideas for further mystery novels.

The Brigstone Man

Dedication

This book is dedicated to my friend Isobel Dunlop, without whose unwavering support and encouragement I may never have continued with my writing, and my grateful thanks to my good friend Bill.

Ann Hammerton

The Brigstone Man

AUSTIN & MACAULEY

A CIP catalogue record for this title is
available from the British Library.

ISBN 978 1 84963 082 5

www.austinmacauley.com

First Published (2011)
Austin & Macauley Publishers Ltd.
25 Canada Square
Canary Wharf
London
E14 5LB

Printed & Bound in Great Britain

The Characters

SALLY WINCOTT	A twenty-six year old advertising executive
JOHN TAYLOR	Sally's live-in partner, a BOAC airline pilot
DR JOSEPH JORDAN	An American professor of Anthropology and Sally's natural father
PIERRE SOULAYA	A renowned Lebanese archaeologist and old friend of Jo
GEORGE APOSTOLONIS	A Greek archaeologist and metallurgist
D I MCGREGOR and D S JONES	Police officers investigating Jo's murder
CHRISTIAN	A French Dominican monk and Sally's unknown half-brother
AURORA SOULAYA	Pierre's feisty daughter
MARIE	Pierre's post-graduate student assistant
ALEX MCCLOUD	The son of Jo's successor at the Minnesota university and Sally's new lover

JULIE	Sally's P A at the advertising agency
FELIX	Sally's black and white cat who gets very fed up with being shoved in and out of the cattery

Chapter One

London 1972

The phone rang just as Sally's left foot touched the bathmat.

"Damn!" she muttered, as she reached for a towel to stumble dripping into her bedroom. She lunged for the phone before it clicked over to the answerphone.

"Hello?" she said brightly.

"May I speak to Miss Wincott, please?"

"Yes, speaking," replied Sally.

"This is the Bankside Hospital, Miss Wincott, and we have your father here," a woman announced.

"What? I haven't got a father. You must have the wrong number."

"You are Sally Wincott?"

"Well yes, I am, but my father died some years ago."

"I am sorry, Miss Wincott. I understand this must be a shock for you, but the gentleman we have here is asking for you."

"There must be some mistake. I must go now, I'm sorry but I'm waiting for an important call."

"Please don't hang up, it really is important, Miss Wincott. Dr Jordan was knocked down on a pedestrian crossing, and had a heart attack when he was brought here. He is extremely agitated, and insisting that we contact you."

"But damn it, I don't know any Dr Jordan!" Sally was feeling more than a little annoyed.

"You must come to the hospital, Miss Wincott, before it is too late. He is in a critical condition. If he isn't you father, how can it be that he seems to know all about you and where you live?" The hair on Sally's wet arms stood on end as she shivered clutching the towel around her.

"Oh, all right. As you're not far away, I'll come to see him, but I really have no idea who he might be."

"Thank you, my dear. It's the right thing to do. Come to Casualty and ask for Sister Fraser; I'll be waiting for you." And before Sally could change her mind, she had hung up.

"Damn and blast it!" Sally shouted at the dead phone. Why did I answer it? Now I'll have to go traipsing off to see some strange man who's probably dying, and what good will it do? I don't know anything about my natural father, except that he knew my mother in France. I must be mad! What if he is some sort of crank who found my name in the phone book? Even supposing he is my real father, would I really want to meet him? Still muttering angrily she tripped over the bath towel and trod on Felix, her black and white cat.

"Meeeow..." he yelled.

"Oh Felix, I'm sorry, but I wish you'd stop getting under my feet," she said, scooping him up into her wet arms to set him down on the sofa.

Quickly pulling on a pair of jeans and a sweater, Sally grabbed her handbag and was just leaving the flat when the phone startled her once more.

"Hello, Sal!"

"John! You just caught me. I was on my way out."

"I called a few minutes ago, but you were engaged. Where are you off to anyway?"

"Oh, John, you'll never believe it, but I've got to dash round to the hospital to see someone."

"Why, what's happened? Are you all right?"

"I'm fine, just a bit perturbed," she replied. "The hospital called to tell me that my father is there asking for me."

"But your father's dead, isn't he?"

"Exactly," agreed Sally. "But some man has had a heart attack and is saying that I am his daughter, and I've got to go to see him. I know it sounds crazy, but I felt I had to agree."

"But Sally, he can't be your natural father, you don't know

anything about him. Are you sure you should go? He may be some nutter."

"Don't worry, Darling," laughed Sally. "I'll be back soon, and I'll tell you all about it when you arrive."

"I'd come with you, Sal, but I won't be there for about an hour. Do be careful, won't you?"

"Of course, silly. See you soon. Bye," and blowing a kiss down the phone she hung up.

Stepping out into the darkening street, Sally walked quickly round the corner towards her car. It was Sunday evening and people were returning from their weekend out of town. There were cars cruising slowly around the square, jostling for parking spaces, so rather than lose her spot, Sally decided to take the tube to the hospital.

Sally Wincott was an attractive girl in her late twenties. She was tall and slim, and wore her dark blonde hair swept loosely back from her face. She was unmarried, although there had never been any shortage of boyfriends. She had been adopted as a baby by a couple already in their fifties, and they had been her only family. All that she had been told about her natural parents was that her mother, who had been living in the South of France during the war, had fallen pregnant and returned to England where she had died soon after Sally's birth. Sally had never given a thought to her origins. She had adored her adoptive parents and was heartbroken when they both had died soon after her eighteenth birthday. Her stable and loving upbringing and private education had given her confidence and maturity beyond her years, and she had progressed rapidly in her career to become the youngest account director in the advertising agency where she worked. Honest and outspoken at times, her not infrequent gaffs would sometimes embarrass and hurt her entourage, but she had a great sense of humour and was loved and respected by her small circle of close friends.

The hospital was a dreary looking red brick building, surrounded by a large estate of council flats. Sally followed the signs leading to the Casualty Department, and asked for Sister Fraser.

"Ah, my dear, I'm so glad you decided to come," said the plump, bustling woman as she led Sally down a dimly-lit corridor. "We had to move him to Intensive Care, but he's rallying pretty well. He seems such a nice gentleman, and he'll be so pleased that we found you."

"But honestly, I don't know what I'm doing here. He can't possibly be my father; my real father probably doesn't even know that I exist," said Sally.

"Don't worry my dear, I think you'll be surprised when you see him. I believe I can see a likeness just by looking at your face."

"Oh, Lord!" muttered Sally as she entered the ward. What on earth will I say to this man?

There were four beds facing her. Each holding someone hooked up to drips with cables attached to various life-support machines.

"Here we are," sung Sister Fraser as they approached one of the beds. On it lay a man, perhaps in his mid-sixties, with tubes spilling out of his mouth and nose. He was quite a handsome, distinguished-looking man with silver white hair, but his gaunt face bore the ashen pallor of death. He seemed to be sleeping, but as Sally approached to look at him, he eyes popped open and met hers. She jumped back startled, her heart beating fast. Hell! She thought, clutching at the metal bar at the side of the bed. She felt scared and she didn't know why. She wished the floor would open up and swallow her. She wanted to turn and run away from the strange situation which seemed somehow to pose a threat to her well-ordered existence.

The television was on when Sally got back to her flat. John was stretched out on the sofa watching a film, with Felix curled up on his feet.

John Taylor was a forty-five year old airline pilot with British Overseas Airways, and regularly flew the London Bahrain route. He had met Sally at Heathrow where she was meeting a client. Her client had missed his plane and would not be arriving until the next day, so she and John had dined together before parting with each other's phone numbers. A month later, John had moved into Sally's flat. John had married fourteen years earlier, and had two children, but a bitter divorce had split the family, and the children now lived with their mother in the country.

"Hello, Darling," greeted Sally, as she struggled out of her coat. She ran across the room and threw her arms around him.

"Oh Sal, I missed you," said John. "Don't run out on me again." Sally laughed, relieved to feel his strong arms around her once more.

"I'm sorry Darling, but I wasn't very long, was I?"

"No, but tell me what happened. What was he like, this mystery man?"

"Just let me get a glass of wine, and I'll tell you," she replied.

Sally pulled a chair over to the sofa and sat down. Then she recounted how she had jumped out of the bath to answer the phone, thinking it was him, only to have the summons to the hospital.

"So why did you agree to go?" asked John.

"I don't really know. It was strange. She was so insistent. Sister Fraser was her name, and she made me feel sort of guilty. She gave me the impression that he was dying and was desperate to see me, so I just felt I had to go. I mean, what if he does turn out to be my father, how would I feel if I had refused to see him before he died?"

"Oh come on, Sal, we both know it's hardly likely to be true. Good Lord, if he is your father, why has he never tried to find you before?"

"I don't know, I don't know what to think; especially after what he told me."

"What? Then tell me, Sal," he urged. Sally sighed.

"When I got there, the nurse took me to the Intensive Care ward, and there was this man, looking dead already. She said that he'd been knocked down by a hit and run driver, and then had a heart attack in hospital. Then she left. I sat by the bed wondering what on earth I should say, but his eyes were closed and I thought he was asleep. I was just wondering if I could creep away, when his eyes popped open and stared straight at me. I nearly jumped out of my skin. They were steel blue, and were piercing right through me!"

"Good Lord! What happened then?"

"He sort of beckoned me to move nearer, then touched my cheek and murmured, 'Nancy', my mother's name. then he gave me this," and Sally opened her handbag to pull out a crumpled scrap of paper.

"I'm not supposed to tell anyone about it. It's supposed to be the key to some incredible mystery, and it's got some numbers on it. He said that if anything happened to him, I was to send the letters immediately by courier."

"What letters?"

"I suppose they must be hidden somewhere. Perhaps he's a secret agent, or some sort of industrial spy."

"What on earth are you getting mixed up with Sally?" asked John, concerned.

"Listen, John; it may have been the delirium of a mad man, or it could be serious. He told me that there were people in high places meaning, I suppose, the government, who would stop at nothing to prevent the knowledge it represents from being made public. He said it would completely change history, and even that my life could be in danger if anyone knew who I was, and what he had given me. He said I am the only person he can trust to pass on the knowledge. It really sounded quite terrifying, and I hope he is mad, even if he is my father and has made the whole thing up." And trembling Sally climbed up onto John's lap.

"Steady on, Sal! Of course he's bonkers. You mustn't go getting upset over a cock and bull story from a complete stranger. It's too far-fetched to be true."

"I know, but I've got a horrible feeling. There was something about him that rang true, and despite being frightened, I really did feel drawn towards him. It's all so weird."

"What else happened?" asked John.

"Well I was sort of dumbstruck. I could barely stop myself from laughing. It was embarrassing. I was sure that he must be mad, and that if I could be taken in by the idea that the scrap of paper I held in my hand could change history, then I must be potty too. I stood up to leave, but as I turned away, he caught my hand, murmuring that he had something else for me. It was this," and

Sally handed John a small, framed photograph.

"Who are they?"

"It's my mother, with him I suppose. There's a palm tree there, so perhaps it was taken in the South of France."

"She was pretty, wasn't she, and does that look like him?"

"It's difficult to tell," Sally replied. "It's so badly faded, but it could be him."

"But Sal, even if it does show that he knew her, it doesn't prove that he's your father, does it?"

"I know. But it's nice to have. I've never seen a picture of her before."

"Then there's one mystery solved," laughed John, giving Sally a big hug.

It was almost one o'clock when Sally disappeared into the bathroom for a shower, while John picked up the glasses and carried his supper tray into the kitchen. The phone rang as he turned on the sink tap.

"John Taylor," he replied, picking up the wall set.

"May I speak to Miss Wincott, please?"

"Miss Wincott is not available," replied John. "And don't you think it's rather late to be calling?"

"I'm sorry, but it is important. I'm calling from the hospital. Miss Wincott came here earlier to see a patient."

"Ah, you must be the lady who called before?"

"That's right, it's about her father, Dr Jordan," replied Sister Fraser.

"Yes? I know all about it. You may leave a message if it can't wait until morning," said John impatiently.

"I am sorry, but as he gave her name as his next of kin, I have to let her know straight away."

"Let her know what?"

"Dr Jordan passed away half an hour ago."

"Oh well, that's that then, isn't it?" remarked John, feeling slightly embarrassed. "Thank you for calling Sister. I'll give Sally the message." And he hung up. Thank God for that, he thought. Perhaps now Sal will forget all about it.

Sally slid into bed beside John.

"What a night! How on earth will I be able to sleep after all that."

"You will Sal. Your so-called father, Mr Jordan, is dead."

"What?" shrieked Sally, sitting bolt upright. "Was that the telephone I heard?"

"It was. Your friend Sister Fraser rang to tell you that he died half an hour ago. So now my dear you can put that little episode out of your head and go straight to sleep."

"But how can I? It's even worse now, because I'll never know if it was true or not." John pulled her down under the duvet.

"Come here, silly. None of it was true, and he wasn't your long lost father, right? Now shut up and go to sleep." And he buried her mouth under a long, hard kiss.

Chapter Two

Dr Joseph Jordan swung round in his armchair to look out of his office window at the Mississippi below. He had spent a tiresome morning finishing off a pile of reports, signing letters and memos, and clearing out his private files. His only remaining task was to prepare for the final briefing with his colleagues of the past fifteen years. As head of the Department of Anthropology at the University of Minnesota, he had presided over a wide variety of work, concentrating mainly on the origins of indigenous inhabitants of the American continent, and now, at the age of sixty-two, he faced what was to him the depressing reality of retirement.

Turning to gather up the last bunch of files on his desk, he noticed a small piece of paper as it fluttered to the ground. "Oh dear," he muttered, as he bent down to retrieve a piece of blue notepaper. Fumbling in his jacket pocket for his reading glasses, he immediately recognised the neat handwriting. It was from his great friend, Professor Pierre Soulaya, at the American University in Beirut. It was dated two months earlier, but he had forgotten all about it. He had told Pierre of his impending retirement, and Pierre had written, begging him to join him in London, where he was planning to spend some time working on research into early astronomers, and the apparent connection in the building of the pyramids and some of the huge megalithic constructions elsewhere.

Joseph had worked on some of the ancient sites in Peru, as well as the great city of Tihuanaco in Bolivia. Of course, that's it! That's what I should do. Silly me thinking my life was over. And he strode purposefully from the room.

Later that afternoon, Jo put through a call to Beirut. Pierre

Soulaya was at home in his apartment in Lyon Street when the phone rang.

"*Bon Soir Pierre*, it's Joseph from Minneapolis."

"Ah Jo, what a surprise! How are you, my friend?" As always, Pierre's English was impeccable.

"I'm very well, Pierre, although feeling slightly guilty. I have just found your letter."

"My letter?"

"Pierre I am so sorry for the delay in replying, but I have been rather busy, finishing off here."

"No problem, Jo, but are you a gentleman of leisure now?"

"Not quite. I have a few more meetings, then I shall be one of the great unemployed." Pierre laughed.

"That I don't believe. I bet you have a thousand projects up your sleeve, don't you? And what about that book you told me about. Is it finished yet?"

"Not quite, but I think I'll put that on hold for now. That's why I am calling. Are you still going to London, Pierre?"

"Of course. Are you interested?"

"I certainly am. I'll book a flight tomorrow, and will stay at the Hotel Russell as usual. Let me know when you will be arriving."

"That's wonderful, Jo! I can't wait to get started on my West Country site."

"You're not thinking of Stonehenge, are you Pierre?"

"Wait and see," was Pierre's reply.

A week later Jo flew to London. His academic wife had died the year before after a fruitless partnership lasting over thirty years, so he was free to travel whenever he could get away. Checking into his hotel, he found Pierre's telex waiting for him. Pierre would be arriving in two days' time, which gave Jo a little time for sightseeing.

One morning strolling down Brompton Road after a brief recce around Harrods' famous food hall, he noticed a woman on the pavement ahead of him and became aware of a familiar walk. There was something about her back that reminded him of someone in the distant past. At Brompton Oratory the woman stopped and turned to cross the road, and in that split second a name flashed through his head. Nancy! How extraordinary to think of Nancy after all these years? Jo stood watching the woman for a few seconds. Then, resisting the temptation to catch up and speak to her, he continued on his way to the Natural History Museum. That evening, in his hotel room, Jo recalled his feelings when he'd watched the woman ahead of him on the road, and his mind went back to Nancy.

It had been 1945. Paris was liberated and the war in Europe was over. Jo's unit had been demobbed and, after an exhausting week of celebrations in Paris, he had hired a car and driven South to Toulouse, planning to explore the country down as far as the Pyrenees, and to see the great walled city of Carcassonne and the Cathar castles.

He had met Nancy at a café near the Place du Capitole. She was a pretty English girl whose French husband had been shot with his Résistance group, and she was in Toulouse looking for a job. The lonely girl had accepted Jo's friendship unquestioningly, and they became lovers. When Jo left Toulouse to continue his journey, Nancy went with him.

Nancy had gone to France in 1938 to work for a wealthy family with vineyards in the valley of the Aude, but she had become involved with Jean Françoise, the son of the house, and had fallen pregnant. When Jean and Nancy had walked hand-in-hand into the house one evening to announce to his parents that they were married, his father was furious, And Jean had stormed out and joined the local Résistance movement. Nancy's baby, a boy named Christian, was born the day after Jean Francoise was killed, but his family would have nothing to do with him, considering him a mere bastard, so it was arranged that he should be adopted by a childless couple who worked on the domaine. Nancy had stayed on until the end of the war, treated almost like a servant then, one night, she had packed her bags and caught a train to Toulouse, determined to make a fresh start.

Jo and Nancy had been together for some weeks when one evening, sitting in the crowded square in Carcassonne City, a cry from a passing group of tourists startled them.

"Joseph, Jordan, what the hell are you doing here?"

"Great Heavens!" exclaimed Jo, jumping up from his chair. "I didn't know you were coming this way, Mike. Can't I ever get shot of you?" The tall American, his white teeth almost dazzling in his tanned face, had moved over to place his hands on the back of Nancy's chair.

"Hey Jo, who's the lovely lady. Aren't you going to introduce me?" Seeing Nancy's unease, Jo placed a protective hand on her arm.

"Nan, this is my great buddy, Mike Steward. We were in the same outfit in Paris, and he's quite harmless."

"Hi Nancy!" said Mike, grabbing her hand.

"How do you do," mumbled Nancy, blushing as she disentangled her hand.

"So where do we go from here? There must be something jumping in this joint," said Mike, pulling up a cane chair next to Nancy. Jo smiled at his friend's usual enthusiasm.

"I doubt it. Let's meet up for breakfast in the morning, Mike."

The following morning Mike found his way to the chateau where Jo and Nancy were staying. They spent a wonderful day together, laughing about their time in Paris with their army intelligence unit, and reminiscing over their years together in college in Massachusetts, where Jo hoped to return to complete his doctorate. They stopped at numerous vineyards tasting the local wines, ate a gargantuous lunch at a rustic auberge, and ended up on the steep climb to the ruins of the last Cathar stronghold at Montsegur, totally spent. The sun was beating down and Nancy was refusing to walk another step. With their supply of bottled water almost exhausted, they sank down in the thorny garrigue and fell asleep sheltered by a group of rocks.

Waking suddenly, a large hornet buzzing dangerously around his head, Jo sat up and glanced across at Nancy. She was lying curled up, her head resting on a makeshift pillow of shoes and sweaters, and he knew in that instant that he loved her. She looked so frail and helpless lying there on the rocky ground, that he longed to scoop her up and carry her home to America. The sun had lost its powerful rays and a slight breeze blew up. It was time to go.

They spent the night in a village house in Belesta, welcomed by a kindly woman in black who seemed overjoyed to fuss over the three strangers. Over a huge, steaming dish of cassoulet, she told them her husband had left for the high pastures with his sheep for the summer. They continued eastwards the next day, passing green oak forests and rushing gorges. Nancy and Mike became close, and talked almost non-stop, and it didn't take the outgoing Mike long to squeeze out the whole sad story of her life in France. She was more at ease talking with him than with the more serious Joseph, who seemed not to notice. He was more concerned with the day's route, determined to see more of the great hill-top fortresses that lined the frontier between France and Spain.

That evening they drove into Perpignan, where they parted company. Mike was continuing South West to walk the mountain passes used earlier by hundreds of Spanish royalists escaping the civil war, while Jo and Nancy were returning to Toulouse.

It was only two days later, when Jo awoke alone in his hotel room, to find that Nancy had gone leaving a brief farewell note. He couldn't believe it. He felt sure that she loved him. What on earth had possessed her to take off without any warning? And what future lay ahead for her, alone in Toulouse with no money?

He felt terribly hurt and angry, and determined to find her. The receptionist at the hotel told him that she had asked him to call a taxi, but he had no idea where she was going. For days Jo scouted around Toulouse, searching the cafés and bars, and even asking at the larger shops, but to no avail. He left letters for her at the hotel and at the British Consul, giving his home address, then, reluctantly, a week later, he flew back to America. It was time to take up his normal life again.

In Boston, several months later, whilst thumbing through his mail one morning, Mike found a letter from Paris. It was from Nancy. In it she confessed her love for Jo, but explained that she had left because she was pregnant. She was afraid that if he found out that she had had another child, she would be left alone again. Wondering whether it would be wise to tell Jo, he postponed the idea for the moment. He was about to sit his final exams for his law degree. He would write to Jo later.

Pierre Soulaya was staying in a furnished apartment in London, as his wife had accompanied him for her annual shopping trip. He had arranged to meet Jo at the British Museum, where he planned to spend several days reviewing some papers in The Reading Room.

The two friends greeted each other warmly. Pierre Soulaya was a world-renowned archaeologist, and as their two spheres of work had often overlapped, they had developed a strong working relationship.

Pierre explained that his current interest lay in the quest for knowledge about the earliest astronomers, and in finding a connection in the building of prehistoric monuments worldwide.

"You know Jo, there are several schools of thought about how such enormous constructions could have been erected," remarked Pierre, as they sat down at a table to await the documents he had ordered. Jo nodded.

"And it is obvious that to lift such huge blocks of stone would have needed thousands of men, using goodness knows what method to do so. Then there is the added problem of transporting the stone to the site, often from distant regions."

"Just so," said Pierre. "We know there are those who believe that it was not men at all who built the pyramids, but some totally different race of intelligent beings from another planet, or even 'Gods' from the heavens!" Jo laughed.

"However, even if pre-historic man had been able to manipulate such huge boulders, he must have possessed some advanced mechanical knowledge, which makes no sense when you remember that even the wheel wasn't invented then!"

"There may be another possibility," said Pierre, as he rummaged through his papers. "What if they were somehow able to forecast the movements of the Earth; to know exactly when a volcano would erupt, an earthquake would occur, or a tidal wave would flood the land? After all let's not forget that the earth was younger then, and large eruptions may still have been occurring in places. Let's say, for arguments sake, that they worked out mathematically that a mountain would be formed at a given time and place, and that the surrounding land would be lifted up several hundreds of kilometres higher. They could then have used that knowledge to raise whole settlements like Machu Picchu, could they not? But that is ridiculous because it would mean that they possessed mechanical and geophysical knowledge far beyond our understanding, whilst Mesolithic Man is still believed to be a small-brained hunter! However, I do believe, Jo, that it's worth considering that if the earth was moved on its axis, perhaps having been clobbered by a stellar explosion, or a shower of meteorites, its final position may have been affected by the resulting movements of the Sun, or other planets. Could they perhaps have found a way to harness those magnetic forces?"

Jo thought it was time to interrupt.

"And not forgetting that early civilisations in Greece, Egypt and Peru worshipped the Sun and Moon. Look at the similarities in the positioning of the stones, and the hieroglyphics in the pyramids, the temples in South America and Stonehenge, etcetera."

"This is exactly why I feel the need to study the ancient astronomers to find a connection," said Pierre. "I am sure that you are aware that following the tests that have so far been carried out on the stones and earthworks, the explanation for the building of these huge structures lies obviously several thousand years earlier than was previously thought. That is to say, in the Antediluvian period, before the great floods!"

"Great Heavens!" exclaimed Jo, as a bulky pile of manuscripts arrived at their table. "Are they going to keep this place open for us all night, Pierre?" Pierre laughed.

"That would be wonderful, wouldn't it? Oh, and by the way Jo, my team from the university is already on the Wiltshire downs, mapping out an area that I spotted from one of the photographs we took last year."

"How exciting! What are you hoping to find there?"

"It seems obvious that there is some sort of ancient construction there, but plans for an industrial site have been approved, so we don't have much time," replied Pierre.

A couple of hours later, having scanned through the indexes of the top batch of documents, and discarding most of them, they left the museum for a quick lunch at a nearby restaurant.

On his return to his rented apartment the following evening, having spent the day at the museum with Jo, Pierre found a message from Marie, the post-graduate student leading the dig in Wiltshire, asking him to call her. His wife thought Marie had sounded excited, and it appeared that they had found something. After an interminable wait on the telephone, Marie's breathless voice greeted him.

"Professor, I'm sorry! They had to find me. We were eating dinner outside."

"Good evening, Marie. Tell me, do you have some news for me?" asked Pierre.

"*Na-am*, I do. It seems to bear out what we thought from the photographs. There is definitely a large construction there, consisting seemingly of huge granite slabs. We have uncovered what appears to be an enormous flat platform, and judging by the strata, it must be very ancient."

"Good girl! And are you measuring and mapping it?"

"Of course, but first we have to finish uncovering and cleaning it. It is a big job and will take a little time. Then Pierre, I think we should send off some samples for testing, because it must be over a thousand years old. When can you get down here?"

"I can be there in a couple of days, and I shall be bringing Dr Jordan from Minneapolis with me. Can you book us a couple of rooms, Marie?"

"That is good news. I will book your accommodation at the Bear Hotel."

"Thank you Marie; and by the way, well done! Keep up the good work, and let me know if you need any more equipment, won't you?"

"Of course, and thank you. I shall look forward to seeing you, Professor. Good night."

"Good night, Marie, and thank you again," said Pierre, before turning to his wife. "Shall we go to eat something now?" he asked.

Over dinner his wife told him that their daughter, Aurora, would be arriving at the weekend, which eased Pierre's conscience over leaving her in London while he was down in Wiltshire.

The following evening Pierre invited Jo to join him and his wife for dinner at a fashionable Arabic restaurant in Piccadilly.

The table next to them was occupied by a group of affluent-looking Americans, and when one of them stood up in mid-conversation, Jo thought he recognised his voice. As the man passed their table, Jo was surprised to see that it was his old wartime buddy, Mike Steward, who was in London for an international lawyers' convention, and was staying at Grosvenor House. After greeting each other warmly, they arranged to meet the following day.

Having left Pierre to finish off reviewing the last batch of papers at the museum the next morning, Jo set off to meet Mike in a Soho restaurant. Mike was by then a successful company lawyer with his own practice in New York, still full of zest as Jo remembered him, although now wearing an aura of wealth and success.

When their conversation turned back to their Pyrenean hike with Nancy, Mike suddenly remembered the letter she had written.

"Were you in love with her, Jo?" he asked.

"I think I was. It was on that hill that I realised what she meant to me."

"She and I got on really well," said Mike. Jo laughed.

"I know you did, but it didn't worry me. I was never the jealous type. She was such an innocent, friendly girl, it wasn't difficult to love her. She left me you know, just after we got back to Toulouse. I woke up one morning and she'd gone, just like that. I was heartbroken."

"Didn't she give you any explanation?"

"No. I just found a note thanking me, and asking me to forgive her, that's all. Of course I looked everywhere for her, but it was no good, and eventually I had to go home."

"Well, Jo, I think I may be able to throw a little light on that mystery," said Mike.

"Really? But you'd already left, hadn't you?"

"I had, but she wrote to me in Boston sometime later."

"Great Heavens!" explained Jo, sitting up. "She never once wrote to me, and there was I worrying myself silly over her. What did she say?"

"I'd give you the letter if I had it. I did keep with for a while, but I do remember what it said."

"Well come on, Mike, don't keep me in suspense," urged Jo, laughing at his reverberating youthful sufferings.

"She said that she left because she was pregnant."

"What? What reason was that to go off and leave me? Good God I would have married her like a shot. I loved her!"

"It wasn't that simple, not for her. She had been married in France, and her husband was killed in the Résistance."

"Yes yes, I knew all of that. But that was no reason to leave me."

"It wasn't just that," continued Mike. "She'd already had a baby, born after her husband was killed, and it was taken away for adoption. She was afraid to tell you."

"Why on earth? What difference would that have made?"

"It was a terrible time for her. Her husband's parents refused to acknowledge the child, and arranged the adoption, as she couldn't keep it on her own. She was afraid you wouldn't understand, and that she would be left alone again, so she decided to disappear before you found out."

"Oh, the poor child," muttered Jo. "She must have been terribly unhappy. What did she do? Did she tell you?"

"I don't know if she had the baby, but she did say that she was returning to England. That's all she said in the letter."

With their past memories dealt with, the two men turned to lighter conversation and the lunch ended.

Later, back in his hotel room, Jo, trying to recover from the shock that he might after all be the father of some unknown person in England, determined to clear his mind ready for his visit to the dig site the next day.

Chapter Three

In a dilapidated cottage on the Gayda Domaine in the French Languedoc, Christian pulled off his muddy boots and sat down at the kitchen table to await the evening soup. He had grown into a gangly, spotty-faced fifteen-year-old. As the only child of a hard-working, middle-aged couple, struggling to live off their small parcel of land, his childhood had been hard. He had helped his mother with the poultry and goats, attended the village school, and was now obliged to work with his father in the fields, where he grew sunflowers, a little corn, and vines for the domaine. He was a shy, stuttering loner, and his only friends were his mongrel dog and the mentally retarded boy who lived down the lane. Even at school, he was treated as an outcast because he was so withdrawn.

After supper that evening Christian's father announced that he would take him up to the mountains the next day, as he had something to show him. This was a pleasant surprise as he had hardly even taken Christian out in his car. Their only outings had been to the market once a week, and to the big supermarket in town once a month.

Awaking early the next morning and feeling almost excited, Christian dressed quickly in his clean jeans and a new sweater his mother had knitted for him. Less than an hour later, driving slowly down the road towards Axat in the battered old Citroen, his father turned to him.

"Now look boy; this may come as a bit of a surprise for you, but it has to be said."

Christian, startled out of his usual daydreaming, wondered what on earth was coming. His father was a kind although dour man, and rarely spoken to anyone, let alone to him.

"What is it, Papa?" he ventured timidly, wondering if perhaps he was about to be sent away to work.

The old man pulled in at a layby and, still clutching the steering wheel, turned towards Christian.

"Well the fact is, son, that I am not your real father." Christian's mouth fell open.

"But Papa, who is?"

"You see, Boy, that's exactly why we are here. I am taking you to see the place where your father died."

"Oh, so he is dead then?"

"Yes, Christian. It was a long time ago, in the war. He was a hero, your father, and he was killed by the Germans."

"Wow, a hero!" exclaimed Christian.

"Yes, he was with the Résistance. They did a lot of good. They blew up bridges and stopped the German trains, and they killed a lot of the bastards too."

"Wow!" gasped Christian again, his chest filling with pride. "What was he like, my father? Did he look like me?" The old man smiled.

"Not exactly, but he was a handsome man, and very young. I remember when it happened, it was terrible. There were four others from the village with him, none of them much older than you are now, and they were all shot." Christian turned away, tears brimming in his eyes.

"Poor Maman! So did you marry her after that, Papa?"

"No Christian, you don't understand. Your mother was an English girl." The tears started to run down Christian's face.

"Do you mean that I don't have a Maman either?" he sobbed.

"Of course you do, Son," replied the old man with difficulty. "Maman loves you just as much as if you were hers." And unaccustomed to such emotion, he held the sobbing boy tightly against his ample chest.

The old car chugged uphill for a further thirty minutes then rounded a corner to run along the top of a windy ridge. Someone had erected a small stone pillar where the massacre had taken place, and engraved on it in black were the names of Jean Françoise and his four companions.

Christian looked silently around, trying hard to picture what might have happened up there by the side of the road. It was a high, wild place, but strangely beautiful backed by towering snow-covered peaks, and he thought that perhaps it was not such a bad place to die as it was so near to Heaven. He joined his father who was picking some wild orchids to lay by the stone.

"I love you, Papa," he stammered, squeezing the old man's hand as they turned to leave. Then they drove silently home, both wrapped in their private thoughts.

For the next few days, Christian spent as much time as he could in the house with his mother, desperate to know about the other mother who had given him up, but afraid to ask for fear of hurting her. A million questions turned round in his head. What was she like, this English woman, and what was she doing in France? Why did she leave him and where did she go? All that his father had told him was that she was a servant girl with no family, and was working for the parents of Jean Françoise at the big house.

He began to frequent the village church more often, peddling down on his rusty bicycle whenever he could get away. Perhaps God could provide the answers he needed. The local priest, surprised to find him there so often, befriended him, and the following years found him often in the priest's house where he had a sympathetic listener. For the first time in his life Christian felt able to talk openly with someone, and his confidence began to grow.

When Christian was eighteen years old his mother died, and his old father followed soon afterwards. Although it was all he'd ever known, Christian had no wish to work on the land, eking out the same miserable existence that his parents had known, so the cottage and the land were sold at auction. His inheritance gave him hitherto unknown confidence, and he determined to use it to escape to a new life. He had dreamed of one day becoming an engineer, closed up in his room, doodling strange-looking machines on scraps of paper, but now he knew that he had to first spend some time searching for answers to the nagging questions that so bothered him. He had to find out more about his natural mother and his origins. So, one morning he bravely set off for Toulouse, where he boarded a plane for London.

How he did it he never knew. He had never travelled anywhere beyond Limoux, his nearest town, and the one trip to the mountain with his father. But he wasn't afraid. Like a chained-up farm dog suddenly let free, he was totally unaware of the dangers and pitfalls lurking in the world beyond. It was all one huge exciting adventure, and he relished every moment. How calm and confident the other passengers all looked. This was how he wanted to be; a modern, sophisticated man of the world!

Christian's first problem arose on his arrival at Heathrow Airport. He had thought he would be in the middle of London, but instead found himself miles away in a separate town! Luckily for him, there were other French passengers disembarking from his plane, and it was soon explained to him that he had to catch a bus into London. One other young man on the bus was returning to work at a restaurant in Soho.

He told Christian that there were several French restaurants there, and that he might be able to find a job. Christian knew nothing at all about restaurants, but decided that, as he couldn't speak any English, it might be a good idea. Two days later, he was washing-up in the back kitchen of a small café in Frith Street, and sharing a sleazy room over a betting shop with one of the waiters. His life in London had begun.

Christian had only one and a half days off each week, the one full day being Sunday, when the café was closed. This only left him with one half day to devote to the search for his mother, and he had absolutely no idea how to go about it. All that he knew about her was her name and her date of birth, which were written on the adoption papers he had found in an old tin box under his mother's bed after her death. It took him several weeks of halting enquiries before he found out that in England, the records of births, marriages and deaths were kept at St Catherine's House near the Strand. He decided that she would probably have returned to her home in England after giving him up, so he thought that if he could find where she had been born, he would find her. Thus, once a week, on his half day off, Christian set off by bus to Holborn and walked down Kingsway to St Catherine's House, where he spent frustrating hours sifting slowly through the heavy, dusty volumes of registers.

He got the hang of it after several visits, and finally hit upon the right entry, then, eagerly filling in an application form, and paying a fee of almost half his wages, he was obliged to wait for a copy of her birth certificate. For the next few days he could think of nothing other than the day when he would knock on her door and they would be reunited, happy and confident that it would happen soon. But it was not to be.

Nancy's family had lived in Wolverhampton in the Midlands, where Christian journeyed by train on several occasions. He had found the house, but it had been sold years earlier, and the occupants had never heard of Nancy's family. He enquired at the local shops, at the library, and at the Council offices, but all to no avail. Her parents had died years earlier, and nobody had heard of Nancy. On his last visit, he thought of trying the local school, and the secretary there kindly searched through the old attendance files, there, at last, to find Nancy's name. Well, at least she existed, mused Christian, feeling that perhaps he was getting somewhere. But it was a hopeless quest. Nancy had left school at sixteen, and must have gone to work in France some years later. There seemed to be no trace of her after that. To search for her current whereabouts seemed futile, and feeling deflated, Christian, who was by now a waiter in a restaurant, began to think about returning to France.

It was about a week later that Christian remembered seeing that marriages and deaths too were registered at St Catherine's House, and wondered why he hadn't look through those. Surely she must have married when she came back to England, he thought, and filled anew with enthusiasm, he set off on the search again. But there was no trace of a marriage. That left the death records, and feeling despondent, he started ploughing through the heavy books again.

In the register for the second quarter of 1947, he found her. She had died in Hackney at the age of twenty-one. Christian's search was over, and before returning to France he obtained a copy of her death certificate.

Christian who was so overcome with disappointment that he would never know his real mother, hardly looked at it. On it in clear script it was written that Nancy had died in childbirth.

Chapter Four

Jo hired a car in London and drove down to Marlborough where he met Pierre, who had travelled down by train. Arriving at Brigstone Down, they were warmly greeted by Marie with Henri and Naseem, the other two Lebanese students.

"My goodness, you are doing well!" remarked Pierre, as he strode onto the site.

"Isn't this interesting," added Jo, pulling his spectacles from his breast pocket. "It's enormous! What do you think it can be?"

"Look at the density of it here; it's almost two metres deep," remarked Pierre. "Let's go into the can and see what Marie has come up with."

Marie explained that the slab seemed to cover an area of about 324 square metres and appeared to be of the same consistency throughout. It was obviously ancient, but its purpose remained a mystery.

"There is a lot of work to be done, and Henri is making a start on the calculated northern perimeter, as I feel that there may be other constructions surrounding the slab," she told Pierre.

"Why do you think that?"

"Well, whatever the purpose of such a huge man-made platform, there would surely have been some sort of auxiliary structures of shelters for the people using it."

"I agree; but this looks like an enormous job, Marie. Aren't you going to need more people?"

"I don't think so," she replied. "We have eight to ten local people, and the loan of a small digger if we need it, and I am recording everything and scanning the fissures, so we are all right for the moment, thank you." Then satisfied that the work was proceeding as well as possible, Pierre and Jo set off to inspect the site.

They were halfway down the eastern limit, when Pierre stopped to retrieve something that had lodged in his shoe. It was a small piece of metal, and brushing the earth from it, he held it up to the light.

"What is it?" asked Jo.

"It looks like some sort of bolt, and I think it's iron. It's quite heavy, see?"

"It must be modern to be so near the surface," remarked Jo. Pierre was turning it over in his hand.

"There's no corrosion, and yet I'm sure it's made of iron. It looks very like the door bolts we found on Delos."

"Good Lord, don't let's get side-tracked, Pierre. We haven't yet found any evidence of a connection with Stonehenge."

"All the same, Jo, we do know that rustless iron existed in ancient times; it has been found at a number of sites. So I think we will send it to Athens for testing."

"Why Athens?"

"That's the metallurgy laboratory that I've used since I worked with George Apostolonis in Alexandria. I send everything there."

"I didn't know you had worked with him, Pierre. You must tell me about it some time."

"I will, my friend, but first, let's get back to Marie."

A sudden shout from Naseem sent them hurrying back towards the centre section, where he was working with one of the volunteers.

"*Shu hada, Naseem*?" asked Pierre, lapsing into Arabic. Do you have something interesting?"

"*Na-am* Professor, *shuf la hone*?" Naseem was pointing to a black mark on the ground. Pierre sank to his knees for a closer look.

"It's I think calcination, and it does seem deep," said Naseem, pointing with is trowel. He was struggling with his English.

"Mmm, it does look like a scorch mark," remarked Jo as he joined them.

"There's more over here," shouted one of the girl helpers,

working some yards away. "It's curving round. Maybe there's a circle." Sure enough the mark seemed to be part of an arc.

"Now this is interesting," remarked Pierre, as they gathered round. "Let's take some pictures, then we must see how far it goes."

Jo was scratching into the blackened stone with a probe.

"What I don't understand, is what could have burnt so deeply into what appears to be solid granite? I had to be something of an extraordinarily high temperature."

"Perhaps a meteorite?" suggested the girl.

"Perhaps," agreed Pierre. "Although that wouldn't explain the apparently untouched centre section, which would have gone. Well, obviously now we must continue to excavate the central area to see if there really is a circle, and that will take several days."

"I'll send off some carbon scrapings for analysis," said Marie, who had joined them.

"Well done," said Pierre, and feeling confident that they were now getting somewhere, they returned to the caravan to look at the day's findings.

It took two days to finish clearing the centre section of the site, and what they found there confirmed what they had suspected. There was a large circle, scorched fairly regularly to a depth of about a metre. The stone inside the circle was at the same level, and was unmarked. Marie calculated the circle's diameter to be approximately fifteen metres, and that it lay exactly at the centre of the stone slab. Apart from the carbonised ring, there were no other markings, and drillings done every five metres had yielded no other findings.

"Well there we are then. We have a mystery to solve," said Pierre. "It is unlikely that it was made by primitive man because the regularity of the perimeter could only have been achieved with the use of sophisticated geometrical knowledge or instrumentation."

"It looks like a helicopter landing pad to me," said Jo, interrupting Pierre's train of thought. "Are you sure the army's not been on this site?" Pierre laughed.

"Quite sure. They are miles away to the south. But I see your point Jo, although why the burns?"

Rather than spend any more time on the centre section, it was decided to open up a trench on the southern perimeter, in conjunction with Henri's work on the northern edge.

Marie's hunch that there must surely be some auxiliary constructions surrounding the slab seemed to make sense, particularly as they had so far found nothing near the inner circle. It wasn't long before they hit on something about three metres long. It was a heavy metal rod, and exposing it carefully, they found it was connected to a whole network of metal bars. Cutting equipment was needed before any of it could be brought out.

"Look at this!" exclaimed Pierre. "These are obviously made of iron, and yet there is no sign of corrosion anywhere."

"Then it's obviously modern. Some farmer has dumped his old machinery here," said Jo, dismissing the find.

"Let's not jump to conclusions just yet. Look at this piece here; it's attached at right angles to that bit, and yet there is no sign of a join or solder, and see how solid it is! I think we should continue here and get out as much as we can. How deep does it go, Marie?"

"It's difficult to tell, until we have dug down a bit more, Professor. It seems to cover quite a large area, look! They're pulling more out over there," she added, pointing to Naseem several yards away.

They were suddenly startled by shouting and, turning round, saw an old man running onto the site waving something in the air.

"Oh no! We don't want trespassers running all over the place," remarked Pierre. Marie ran over to meet the neighbouring farmer who had lent them his digger. The old man seemed excited about something and was clutching what looked like a long piece of bone.

"What is it, Mr Easton?" she asked, as she led him into the van, to be joined by Pierre and Jo.

"Here you are Miss, I found you somethin'. I all but run over it wi' me tractor. Good job I stopped weren't it?"

"Thank you," said Marie, taking the bone, which looked very like a shin bone and was obviously not from a cow or a sheep.

"Where did you find it?" asked Jo.

"It were in my field over there, an' there's more," replied the farmer, pointing vaguely out of the van, his broad grin exposing his toothless mouth.

"Yes, well thank you Mr er…" muttered Pierre.

"Mr Easton," interrupted Marie, smiling. "We'll certainly take a look at your field, won't we?" she asked turning to Pierre.

"I doubt it will be anything of interest to us, but we'd better go over there, if only to make the old man happy," remarked Pierre to Jo.

They followed the farmer over to his field where, sure enough, just in front of the tractor, they spotted several fragments of bone just breaking the surface. Mary went back to fetch a couple of helpers who soon uncovered a long, metal, coffin-like container. As they lifted it out it started to disintegrate revealing its contents. The almost perfect skeleton that lay before them was that of a man, well over six feet tall. Jo was peering closely at a small piece of shiny material he had scraped from an arm bone. As he held it up to the sunlight, it glistened like silver.

"Look at this!" he exclaimed. "There's more on the legs too. It looks as if he was clothed in some sort of metallic skin suit." Pierre wasn't listening. He was engrossed with the container. It was black and carried signs of decoration on one side.

"My goodness me, what an extraordinary location for a grave!" he remarked, straightening up to look around. The field and surrounding land were completely flat, and there was nothing to indicate an ancient burial site.

"I wonder if he was alone," mused Jo.

The whole team of volunteers had by now joined them, and were crowding round eagerly, while the old farmer, equally excited, hobbled around the group, probably hoping that he had discovered a hoard of Roman gold.

Before removing anything they were obliged to report the find, so the section of the field containing the skeleton was roped off and covered with a tarpaulin. Marie, with one of the helpers, accompanied Jo to the Marlborough Police Station to arrange for the safe removal of the remains to the local morgue. The permit to excavate the field would not be granted until the cause of the man's death had been determined, so some frustrating days were to follow before they could confirm his age.

Returning to the dig site, they found that the metal construction, by then almost completely uncovered, was lying on its side. It was a hollow tower, and appeared to have been built entirely of metal rods and cables.

"Doesn't it remind you of something in Paris?" remarked Marie to Pierre.

They soon calculated that it would have stood about forty metres high, and covered a ground area of five square metres. Several small pieces were sent off to Athens by courier for analysis before the bulk was removed to Marlborough to be re-assembled in the society's hangar.

Marie and her team were pretty exhausted after the day's heavy work and excitement, so Pierre suggested that they take a break for a couple of days, while he and Jo returned to London.

"I changed my mind about the helipad; it looks to me now more like a rocket launching site," said Jo as he drove off. Pierre laughed.

"Impossible! Where are the burn marks from the booster rockets? The centre of the circle is totally unmarked."

"I'm not so sure. What if something was launched without the use of fuels as we know them today?"

"You're not thinking of a photon drive propulsion system, by any chance, are you?" mocked Pierre, confident that Jo's knowledge of physics was equal to that of his own, in that the thrust from such a system could never produce enough velocity to escape the Earth's atmosphere. "Let's just wait until the tests are complete before we get carried away by absurdities, and anyway, we may find something positive next week." And having scuppered Jo's ideas, they drove silently back to London.

The following Monday morning, having left Pierre at the Brigstone site, Jo returned to Marlborough to assist the Police doctor at the autopsy of the 'Brigstone Man', as he would be called.

Marie and her team were already hard at work, excavating

several different spots around the exterior of the granite platform. By mid-afternoon, they had uncovered a number of large foundation stones, one group on the eastern side, and others on the west. Marie's hunch that there must be auxiliary buildings nearby appeared to be bearing fruit. The fact that several of the stones appeared to be connected to what looked like a conduit caused great excitement, and digging continued in earnest throughout the day. At four o'clock, an excited Marie took Pierre and Jo to see what she considered to be an important find.

Connected to the stone base of the metal tower was a conduit running right along the southern edge of the centre slab. Pierre was perplexed. Why on earth would there be water conduits running around a stone slab in the middle of nowhere? But being familiar with such conundrums, he insisted they continue with the work before jumping to any conclusions. Jo, on the other hand, had an idea.

The following day Marie received a telex from the Athens laboratory. The pieces of metal which had been sent over had been analysed. The metal bolt was an iron ore containing lodestone, and the bars from the tower held traces of carbon, titanium, uranium and mercury.

"What an extraordinary amalgam!" remarked Pierre.

"It must be what I suspected," added Jo, this time refraining from further conjecture, to Pierre's annoyance. Meanwhile work continued around the perimeter of the slab, and it soon became obvious that the stone conduit running from the base of the metal tower reached right around the slab. The whole team were amazed and, towards the end of the week, as their excitement grew, they realised that they were witness to a major find.

Over dinner in their hotel, Jo turned to Pierre, a mischievous glint in his eye.

"I've changed my mind about the rocket launching site."

"No! And what do you think it is now?" Pierre was trying not to laugh.

"I'm convinced it's an airfield," announced Jo, oblivious of Pierre's astonished expression. "Now look Pierre; we have what appears to be some sort of magnetic energy captor with channels running from it around the site. We have a huge landing pad, strong enough to withstand enormous loads, and we have surrounding auxiliary buildings. What else could it be? Remember the channels at Tihuanaco, which were assumed to be water conduits? Well, as I am sure you know, it is now believed that these could have shielded some form of power source."

"Great Heavens, of course, the channels!" exclaimed Pierre. "I hadn't thought of that. Well done, Jo. Now this really needs looking into. My goodness, what a day!"

Over coffee, the conversation turned to the discovery of the skeleton in the adjoining field.

"Now tell me Jo, what happened this morning? I want to know all about our mysterious man."

"There's not a great deal to report at the moment, but I can tell you that he died of a fractured cranium. The laboratory will run a number of tests to establish his age, but he's obviously ancient, and will surely not concern the Police. In fact, I estimate him to be between one thousand five hundred to two thousand years old. My problem with that, Pierre, is that he is *not* a Homo sapiens sapiens."

"Good God!" cried Pierre, as Jo continued.

"I am forming an opinion in my mind about his race, but I cannot yet tell you anything further about that at present, as it would appear to you to be too far-fetched, if not totally ridiculous. However he is, of course, male, and I did find traces of hair follicles on his jaw, which suggests that he probably wore a beard."

Pierre, who was by now in a state of considerable agitation, was hardly able to conceal his enthusiasm.

"My goodness Jo, what an extraordinary find! Now I really do think it's time that I told you about my Delos men." But Jo wasn't really listening as he again continued.

"The coffin like container interests me, Pierre. From the impact damage to it, I would say that it fell from a great height. Our man certainly wasn't buried in it. In fact, I would go so far as to say that he missed what I believe to be an airfield, and crash-landed." Pierre sat up startled, as Jo continued.

"They started to clean it up while I was there, and it appears to have been built of nickel carbon steel. They also found an inscription on one side of it which had me a bit baffled because it resembled the Aramaic lettering I've seen in Syria; but you'll never guess what else came to light!"

"Yes? Go on," urged Pierre.

"There was also a drawing, etched in silver, and it looks very similar to the picture of Mycenaean weapons that were carved on some of the stones at Stonehenge! Do you remember them?"

"Good Heavens! Of course I remember them. It was I who discovered them," cried Pierre.

"Well there's a very similar drawing on the side of our man's coffin."

"Now this is quite extraordinary! When will you be able to tell me more about him, Jo?"

"The Police doctor is sending her report in tomorrow, and they should release the remains, so I suggest we take him straight up to London to start dating tests. But the other thing that really fascinates me, Pierre, is the shiny skin suit that he seems to have been wearing."

"Yes, I saw you looking at that. What do you think it was?"

"It's quite a puzzle, Pierre. It seems to be almost a part of his body, and yet it isn't hominoid skin; it is metallic and appears to be stuck onto him, perhaps having been sprayed on in liquid form. A kind of flying suit, I imagine, and possibly acting as some kind of electro-magnetic conduction."

"My goodness, Jo, this is truly amazing!" Pierre was sitting upright in his chair, his excitement rising.

"Jo, I have something very important to tell you," he announced, breathing heavily.

"Oh?" Jo felt tired, and confident that the day's revelations had come to an end, he took off his spectacles, folded them away into his breast pocket, and buttoned up his jacket ready to retire to his room.

"I think a Cognac is called for here," said Pierre, beckoning for the waiter. "Now Jo, this won't take long, but there is something I must tell you.

"Do you remember my mentioning Delos when we picked up that small piece of iron?"

"Yes, of course. Is there some connection?"

"There would certainly seem to be so," replied Pierre, his dark eyes gleaming. "I am sure you must know about a mysterious find on Delos some ten years ago, Jo?"

"Yes, I seem to remember there was a rumour about something being hushed up in Greece. Was that yours, Pierre?"

"It was, together with George; and I think you will be very surprised when I tell you what it was."

"Well go on, Pierre," urged Jo, moving his tall body around in his chair.

"We were excavating a small temple on the hilly northern side of the island when we came across some bones. After digging down we discovered a coffin-like metal container holding a skeleton. It was a male, measuring nearly two metres tall, and his container bore an inscription and a drawing, etched in silver, exactly as you have described seeing on our man's coffin."

Jo's mouth fell open. "Good God, Pierre!"

"A little way away, we found a second male skeleton, of around the same height."

"Why on earth didn't you tell me this before? How could you have kept it from me, you old buzzard." Jo was almost shouting.

"Well I'm telling you now, my friend, and as you know, our find was censored," replied Pierre.

"But where are they now, your Delos men?" Jo demanded.

"They are in Athens, locked away in the Archaeological Museum, and no one is allowed near them."

"Then I must get over there right away!" cried Jo, almost leaping from his chair. "This is the most exciting news, Pierre, and it confirms what I have suspected for several days."

"Do you mean you know who they are?"

"If I am right, then we will be witness to one of the most important discoveries the world has seen, and the history of mankind will be re-written," announced Jo.

"My god, Jo!" exclaimed Pierre, his brown eyes shining like lanterns. "Then we must go, of course. I'll arrange it straight away!"

The following morning, as the two professors struggled over a heavy English breakfast, Pierre received a phone call from his wife in London. His daughter, Aurora, was insisting on joining them for the day, and would be arriving by train in a couple of hours. Pierre was delighted. He adored his daughter, whom he considered would succeed him as Lebanon's leading archaeologist. She was highly intelligent and was currently in Paris, preparing a thesis for her doctorate.

"What on earth will I tell her?" he asked Jo. "She's bound to sense something's up."

"You don't have to go into details, Pierre. After all, we are still waiting for test results."

"That may seem easy to you Jo, but you don't know Aurora. She knows me so well, she's sure to sense my enthusiasm." Jo laughed.

"Then you'll have to hide it. I'll drop you off at Brigstone, then I'll met her at the station."

"That's good of you, Jo."

"Now what about Athens?" asked Pierre. "We really should stay with Marie. Shall I arrange a meeting with the museum for the end of next week? That should give us enough time to finish off here. What do you think, Jo?"

"You are right, of course, although I'd like to get over there today, as I'm sure you know!"

"Of course, old friend," laughed Pierre, patting Jo on the back; "but the Delos two have been waiting for you for over ten years, so a few more days won't surely matter."

On arriving at the dig site, Pierre immediately sought out Marie, determined to talk to her before Aurora arrived.

"Marie, my dear, I have something to tell you, and as this is your dig, I feel it is your right to know, but you must understand that what you are about to hear is to be kept strictly confidential."

"Yes, I understand, of course, Professor," she replied. "Does it concern our find here, or the remains in the other field?"

"It concerns both, Marie. They are probably connected."

"Yes I guessed that much." Pierre sat down at the small table in the caravan, beckoning her to join him.

"Do you remember when you first attended my lectures, about four years ago, Marie?"

"Yes, of course. That was when I became so keen on your work."

"You may recall my telling of an excavation I directed on Delos in Greece about six years earlier."

"Was that the one you were so disappointed about because the remains were taken away to Athens?" she asked.

"That's right, Marie. When the Director of Antiquities heard about our dig, we were forbidden to continue and the remains were removed and locked away in the basement of the museum. I was furious!"

"I should think you were. But what has that got to do with us here, Professor?"

"Everything Marie. The two finds, that of Delos and those here in Wiltshire, would appear to be connected. Jo and I are in agreement about it."

"My goodness, Professor. How exciting!" exclaimed Marie. "Jo spotted it first, and surmised that what we had found was a type of airfield, and metal tower being some kind of magnetic power grid."

"But Professor, the stone constructions are several thousand years old!"

"Exactly." Marie jumped up, her hands on her hips to face him.

"Are you trying to tell me that ancient man had flying machines, Professor, or have we perhaps found a landing site for flying saucers?" She was trying not to laugh.

"If you put it that way Marie – yes."

"*Ma bsadde*!" muttered Marie, shaking her head in disbelief. "Now look Professor, I don't mean to be disrespectful, but you surely can't be serious? There must be some other explanation?"

"No, Marie, and I'll tell you why, then you'll understand."

Almost as soon as Pierre had finished outlining the similarities between the Delos man and the Brigstone find to an already incredulous Marie, he began to question whether or not he had been right to involve her, and became aware of a feeling of unease.

What if the English authorities knew something and felt threatened by the find, and tried to prevent them from further research, just as the Greeks had done at Delos? If what Jo had said the night before was true, and their find meant that history would be re-written, then it seemed possible that some official body might try to put a stop to their work. But Pierre's thoughts were interrupted by Marie, who was now frantically pulling books and papers from her briefcase, checking references and trying desperately to make sense of it all.

"You do understand, don't you my dear, that this information is highly confidential," stressed Pierre. "Apart from Jo and I, you are the only person who knows of our conclusions. Henri and Naseem must not be told and, of course, none of the local volunteers must know anything."

"Of course, Professor, I understand perfectly, and I am very grateful that you have taken me into your confidence; but, my goodness, I think I am in shock. I just can't believe that what you have told me can possibly be true. It's just too amazing!"

"Don't forget, Marie, that nothing is confirmed yet. Jo has to compare the Delos man, and the vehicle there with ours, and I shall go to Athens with him as soon as we have finished here."

"But how will you gain access to them in Athens, Professor?"

"That should be no problem now," he replied. "The previous Director of Antiquities retired quite recently, and his successor is an old friend of mine. I doubt if he knows anything about what is stored in the basement of the museum, and I am sure he will have been far too busy to go looking through ten-year-old records."

"So how long will it be before you have confirmation of the connection, Professor?" she asked.

"That depends on several factors, including the amount of deterioration of the remains. I just hope that they have been kept properly sealed. But when we have the results, you will be the first to know, Marie, that I promise you." But Marie was looking rather worried.

"There is just one problem, Professor. Last night in the hotel, I was approached by a reporter from the local newspaper."

"Oh dear. I suppose he wanted to know if we had found

anything?"

"Naturally; and he seemed pretty convinced that we had uncovered something important. Several people overheard him asking me, and there seemed quite a lot of interest among the people in the bar."

"What did you tell them, Marie?"

"Not very much. I just said that there was an ancient construction there, and that it was too early to say exactly what it was."

"Well done, my dear. But what about the skeleton? Did he seem to know about that?"

"He didn't mention it," she replied; "but I am sure the farmer is bound to have been talking about it, so it won't be long before the whole village knows about it."

"Oh dear," sighed Pierre. "I think we had better prepare a statement for the papers before any rumours start getting out of hand. We must contact this reporter as soon as possible. By the way, Marie, we are going to have a visitor today."

"Oh? Is it someone important?" she asked.

"It's Aurora. Jo has gone to the station to meet her."

"How lovely! I shall so enjoy seeing her again. I'd better get some work done before she arrives."

"That's all right, Marie, I'll look after her," said Pierre, as they stepped out into the sunlight.

By the end of the day Pierre was convinced that Aurora had accepted their version of the finds, and Jo drove her back to Marlborough to catch the train for London. That evening the two men prepared a press release for Marie to hand to the newspaper reporter and retired to bed, confident that news of the importance of the site would not get out.

Before leaving for the dig site the next morning, Pierre telephoned Athens and requested a meeting with the Director of Antiquities. Without specifying his reasons, he persuaded his friend to agree to provide a room at the museum the following week for Jo and himself to carry out some research. He then called his friend, George Apostolonis, the Greek archaeologist whose metallurgy laboratory was testing their metal samples, and asked him to meet them when they arrived. He and Jo spent the day on site, working with the team of students as they finished uncovering the remainder of the stone conduit. Jo was obviously hoping to come across at least one more giant in a flying boat, but no traces of remains came to light.

A couple of days later, they heard that the Coroner had released the remains of the Brigstone Man, and they were free to take him. Jo collected the Coroner's and Police Laboratory reports, and took him, together with his flying boat, up to London, where he had reserved a room at the Natural History Museum. Pierre stayed on at the dig with Marie until, by the end of the week, the whole area had been cleared and mapped, and Pierre was satisfied that they had enough information and could close the site.

The central granite slab was surrounded by stone conduits linking six stone tower-like buildings and, with the added mystery of the man in the flying boat, it seemed that Jo's conjecture that the site was some sort of airfield was the only possible explanation.

Pierre, however, preferred to await the result of their visit to Athens before allowing himself the luxury of re-writing history.

The permit to excavate Mr Easton's field, where they had found their Brigstone Man, had still not arrived but, as Pierre was anxious to leave for Athens with Jo, he decided that the work could be handled by Marie later, if she wished to return.

Chapter Five

The following evening, having seen his wife and daughter safely onto their plane for Beirut, Pierre joined Jo for their flight to Athens where George Apostolonis was waiting to greet them.

"Welcome my friend!" cried George, throwing an arm around Pierre's shoulder and planting a loud kiss on his cheek. "And you must be Joseph Jordan," he added, grabbing Jo's hand in a vice-like grip.

George was a stockily-built man, and surprisingly tall for a Greek. His piercing green eyes stared out from a leathery sand-beaten face and, taking in his safari jacket and suede boots, Jo reasoned that here was a strong, determined man, a bit of a rough diamond, and probably a force to be reckoned with. Disengaging his bruised hand, Jo was surprised to notice that, in sharp contrast to the Greek professor's calloused hands, his fingernails were well-manicured and polished!

After working their way through the usual scrum of rucksack tourists at the airport, George drove them in his battered 1950s Mercedes to a small hotel near the museum, where they checked in before continuing on to George's home. George and his wife had divorced years earlier, and he lived alone in a cluttered bachelor apartment at the university.

The initial introductions over, George turned to Pierre.

"Now my friend, what is all this about. What is the mystery?"

"As I told you on the telephone, it concerns the remains we found on Delos. Jo is here to carry out some tests on them."

"Yes, but why now, after all this time? You haven't found something similar, have you?"

"You've got it in one, George," remarked Jo, as Pierre

continued.

"We were working on an excavation in Wiltshire, not far from Stonehenge, when we came across a male skeleton lying in what appeared to be a metal coffin."

"Oh?" queried George.

"When Jo got a better look at him in the local mortuary, he deduced that he was approximately two thousand years old. He was almost two metres tall and probably wore a beard. He had died of a broken skull at the age of about forty-five."

"Yes yes, go on. This is getting interesting," urged George, sitting upright.

"The container he was lying in was built of nickel carbon steel, as you know from the samples we sent you, and we found drawings and hieroglyphics on one side in silver."

George jumped from his armchair.

"My God! This is extraordinary! What else can you tell me?"

Pierre took up the story.

"I had decided to excavate that particular site in Wiltshire after studying some aerial photographs we had previously taken. We were uncovering a group of stone constructions surrounding a large granite platform, when we found what appeared to be an electro-magnetic power grid."

"Those were the pieces you sent over," were they not?" asked George.

"That's right."

"So what has this to do with the skeleton you found?"

"This is precisely what we are so excited about, George, and the reason it is essential for Jo to compare our Delos two with the Brigstone Man," replied Pierre to his now totally baffled friend.

"It is Jo's opinion, and I am inclined to agree, that what we uncovered can be nothing other than an airfield."

"What? Are you mad?" cried George, his green eyes glaring at Jo.

"No George, I am not mad. This is the only possible conclusion, and I will tell you why."

"Yes, please do," demanded George. Pierre stood up, and opening his briefcase pulled out the photographs they had taken at

Brigstone Down.

"Here you are George. These will help you to understand what we are talking about," he said as he handed them to George.

"The granite platform you see at the centre of the site covers an area of approximately 324 square metres, and is uniformly two metres deep. It is therefore capable of withstanding enormous loads. On it is imprinted a fifteen metre wide calcinated circle: there are no further burn marks inside the circle.

"Yes, yes, go on," muttered George, peering at the photos.

"The traces of six constructions you see around the platform were probably buildings used to accommodate the people using the site," Jo continued. "The metal tower we uncovered was probably forty metres high, and covered a ground area of about four or five square metres. It was built mainly of iron and, as you know, contained elements of carbon, titanium, uranium and mercury."

"All right, so where is this leading?" George was sounding impatient.

"Do you see anything else around the granite slab in the photo, George?"

"Is that a stone channel running along the side?"

"Quite right," replied Jo. "Do you remember, in Bolivia, the channels at Tihuanaco?"

"Of course.The water conduits."

"The water conduits which, it is now believed, could have had some other purpose. In fact, it is thought they may have shielded a form of power source."

"Ah yes; I did read about that, of course," muttered George.

"The channels we found at the Brigstone site are, in fact, conduits that were connected to the metal tower, and they run right around the granite platform."

"Good God! You don't really believe they carried some form of power around the site, do you?" George was shouting.

"That is exactly what I believe," replied Jo.

"Now, to get back to our Brigstone Man: when I started to examine him, I found traces of a fine metallic material attached to his skin, and deduced that he had been wearing some sort of magnetic flying suit."

"Why?"

"Because the container he was lying in had fallen from a great height, and he had died from injuries to his head. Therefore it seemed obvious to me that the container was a small, individual flying boat, which acted as a landing capsule from a larger craft."

"All right, all right. In the unlikely event that he was flying, where is the connection with my two? What are you saying?" George was by now becoming alternately irritated and perplexed.

"Remember the hieroglyphics we found on the Delos coffin, George?" asked Pierre.

"Of course, I've often regretted not having them deciphered before it was too late."

"Our Brigstone Man's coffin had exactly the same drawing of a Mycenaean weapon etched on the side, and the hieroglyphics looked very much like ancient Aramaic."

"So that is why you think there is a connection between our finds?"

"Is that not enough to convince you?"

"Perhaps," muttered George. "I do agree it is certainly worth looking into, and when Joseph has examined our two men, then we should know whether or not a connection exists."

"There are several other factors which have led me to my conclusion," continued Jo. "But I cannot tell you anything further until I have completed the autopsy here. However, I will go as far as to say that I believe I can identify the racial origins of these men."

"Well, Good Heavens, can't you tell us now, or at least give us an idea?" asked George.

"I'm sorry, it's not possible. Pierre knows that I believe we may have our hands on something so important that the history of mankind will be re-written, so until I can verify my findings I can say no more." George grunted.

"So the sooner we get to our Delos men in the museum, the better. But talking about flying, Jo, does make me wonder about Delos. Although the island is small, it was an enormously important trading centre, and the bank of the ancient world. There are dozens of ancient warehouses where goods transported between the Levant and Western Mediterranean were stored. The puzzling thing is that there was never a feasible deep harbour, so unless the ancient traders built enormous cranes, or used some kind of levitation, there was no way of ferrying boat loads of merchandise ashore!"

"Quite," agreed Jo. "And the people that I am interested in had definite ties with Athens and Delos, but I'll tell you more about that later."

"Now this really is getting interesting," remarked George, by now obviously warming to the American anthropologist.

"Let us see what the morrow brings," said Pierre, as he and Jo rose to leave. "You will come with us, will you not, George?"

"I wouldn't miss it even if the Acropolis caught fire!" came the response.

The following morning the three men met at Athens' huge Archaeological Museum where they were received by Dr Phillip Stavopoulos, the Director of Antiquities.

"Pierre, how wonderful to see you again!" he said, clasping Pierre's hands. "And Dr Jordan, I presume?" he asked, turning towards Jo. "I am delighted to meet you. I have heard so much about your work in the Americas. So what can I do for you, my friend?" he asked George.

"You have some remains stored here that were excavated by Pierre and I some time ago, and now that Dr Jordan is free, we would very much like him to take a look at them."

"I see," said Stavopoulos, looking slightly puzzled. "They have been here for some time, have they not? Why the interest now? Don't you think it will be rather too late to find anything of use?"

"Not at all, Doctor," replied Jo. "I don't expect to salvage any DNA, but their measurements, if nothing else, could tell me a great deal about their origins."

"Well I can't see any reason to refuse you access to them, and I have reserved a room for you in the Renovations Department. Will you need any assistance?"

"Thank you, but no," replied Jo. "Pierre will assist me if necessary."

"You will, I am sure, remember that everything here is

protected under Greek Antiquities Law, and nothing must be removed from the museum," reminded Stavopoulos. "Please keep me informed of your findings, won't you George?"

"Of course, Phillip," replied George, with an embarrassing wink towards Pierre.

Pierre and Jo followed George down the well-worn stone steps leading down to the basement storage rooms, feeling relieved to have gained access so easily.

"I have a feeling that Stavopoulos knows about the ban," mused Jo.

"I agree. He certainly gave the impression that he knows why we are here, if only because he didn't ask us anything about what we want to look at," said Pierre. "The important thing is that he didn't stop us." George grunted.

"Let's just hope that doesn't spell trouble ahead."

"I know exactly where they will be," said George, striding ahead of them through the dimly-lit corridors. "There's a separate section for Delos."

"I hope the flying boat is with them," remarked Jo, as they turned a corner to be faced with a group of huge marble statues.

"What about the hieroglyphics? Won't we need some help with that?" asked Pierre.

"Not if it resembles the one on our man's coffin," replied Jo. "I am quite familiar with Aramaic, and we really should not involve anyone else."

Some ten minutes later, having lugged four heavy wooden packing cases into a side room, the three men set to work laying out the two skeletons and the coffin onto work tables. Jo and Pierre donned surgeons coats and masks in preparation for the autopsy, while George busied himself with the coffin.

The two skeletons were in good condition, and Jo had soon recorded all their measurements. They were disappointed to find no traces of metallic skin suits on either of the remains, but Jo did find traces of hair stubble on both of their jaws. By lunchtime they were ready for a break from the dusty, airless room.

Following a hasty pavement lunch outside a nearby restaurant, flavoured with diesel fumes, and deafened by the roar of frenetic passing traffic, they returned to the museum for Jo's more detailed examination of the remains.

That evening, over dinner at the hotel, Pierre and Jo discussed the day's findings. Jo seemed satisfied that, from what he had seen so far, the Delos two were of the same origin as the Brigstone Man. Their brain tissue was almost intact, their brains approximately the same size as modern man.

"How do you explain their superior intelligence, Jo?" asked Pierre. "Would not their brains have been much larger than ours?"

"Not necessarily. Our brains are probably as large as Homo Sapiens will grow," replied Jo. "The fact is, that at present, we only use about half of our brain capacity, which explains man's continuing development. With the Delos two I noticed that their right lobes were much larger than the left, and as it is the right side of the brain which houses creativeness, this could explain, in part, their abilities to find solutions which we are not yet capable of."

"Meaning, for instance, moving heavy weights, as in the building of monolithic structures, or producing rustless iron?"

"Of course," said Jo. "They may have developed the use of their whole brain."

"I see. That is rather humbling, is it not Jo? That puts us in our place in the universe!"

"Perhaps Pierre. But don't you find it exciting to realise just how far we could go, if we could only use our brains to their full potential?"

"I think we are doing pretty well so far, don't you Jo?" was Pierre's response, as they rose to retire to their rooms.

The following day Jo took some samples of brain tissue, and sliced off some pieces of bone for analysis before they turned their attention to the coffin. George had done a good job of cleaning it, and they could now clearly see the lettering. The drawing on the side proved to be that of a spear-carrying Mycenaean warrior. George took samples from both the interior and exterior of the coffin for his metallurgy laboratory and, before packing up, they photographed everything from every possible angle. Pierre used his Polaroid camera to record the hieroglyphics on the coffin for Jo to study in the hotel that evening.

Before leaving the museum, the three friends felt obliged to call in at the Director's office and, with their cases bulging with sneaked-out samples, they knocked on his door.

"Ah my friends!" cried Stavopoulos, as he ushered them in. "Did you find what you were looking for?"

"Thank you Phillip. It was quite satisfactory," replied Pierre.

"Is that all you are going to tell me?"

"Yes, I'm afraid that is all for the moment. We have taken measurements and photographs of the remains, and until we have studied them, there really is nothing we can tell you."

"Now that really is a pity, Pierre. I was certain that you were working on something important." Jo smiled.

"You could be right Doctor, but we have a lot of work to do before we can confirm our findings."

"Naturally you will be first to know the results, Phillip," offered George.

"Thank you, and I am glad to have been of help," said Stavopoulos, as the three men turned to leave.

"I really am grateful to you, Phillip," said Pierre. "You will not regret helping us, I can assure you. Do let us keep in touch."

"Of course my friend," replied Phillip, as he embraced him. "I have always had confidence in you, you know that."

That evening George invited Pierre and Jo to dine at a well-known Athens restaurant, where he had reserved a table in a quiet corner.

"I presume you will be leaving tomorrow?" he asked Pierre.

"That is what we had planned to do. I must get back to Beirut, but Jo may prefer to go on to Delos."

"That may not be necessary," interrupted Jo. "I should be able to tell you something, before you leave, Pierre, bearing in mind, of course, that the symbols may not tell us anything."

"But what about the men, Jo? There must be something you can tell us about them now. Are they of the same origin as our Brigstone Man?"

"Yes, I believe I can safely say that all three are of the same race, although I have not yet fully examined our man, and that is what I intend to do as soon as I get back to London."

"Well this is wonderful!" exclaimed George. "So your journey was not in vain."

"Most certainly not," replied Jo. Pierre was not looking happy.

"Come on now Jo; you still haven't told us who they are. I think we have waited long enough, don't you, George?"

"I will tell you what I have suspected ever since I first landed eyes on our Brigstone Man, Pierre. But please bear in mind that I have yet to examine him fully."

Having finished eating, Jo wiped his mouth with his napkin and turned towards Pierre.

"It is my belief that the skeleton we found in Wiltshire is of the same racial origin as the two we have looked at here, and that they are Hyperboreans." George leaped up, slamming a fist down onto the table to knock over a glass of wine, while Pierre stared in disbelief at Jo.

"Are you crazy, Joseph Jordan?" yelled George, oblivious of the astonished diners at nearby tables.

"Hyperboreans?" exclaimed Pierre. "You can't be serious, Jo!"

"There's no such race!" shouted George. "Hyperboreans are the stuff of legends, they never existed. I should know, I'm Greek!"

"Exactly," replied Jo calmly. "And as a Greek you are surely aware that most legends were based on factual events. Look at Greek history; you don't believe that was all legendary, do you?"

"Of course not," snapped George.

"Then look again, and you will see numerous similarities between so-called legends and the known writings of ancient historians."

"But Jo," interrupted Pierre, "I know, of course, about the so-called Hyperboreans, but what exactly has led you to such an astounding conclusion?"

"That would take a little time to explain, but I assure you that I would not have told you this if I were not fully confident. I will, however, try to explain the basis of my reasoning." George, by now, had calmed down and appeared willing to listen.

"I am sure that you know that the Hyperboreans were written about in almost every ancient culture, and I have often come across the name in the course of my work in South America. You do know, Pierre, that I have participated in several excavations in Peru and Bolivia, and have examined hundreds of remains there."

"Yes, of course, Jo," said Pierre, as Jo continued.

"The huge city of Tihuanaco in particular is concerned."

"Are you referring to the possibility of power-bearing conduits?" asked George.

"That's a part of it. But the interesting thing about Tihuanaco is that it is known to have been built by a people named as the 'Culture Bearers' some six thousand years ago. The name Tihuanaco translates as 'The Place of Those Who Were', which infers that the site was occupied long before the city was built. The Hyperboreans were described as the Culture Bearers in several ancient manuscripts, as well as in legends, and were often described as being very tall, white-skinned people with long white beards."

"Yes, I did know about the culture Bearers, of course," said Pierre. "I also know that the so-called Hyperboreans settled in Britain around one thousand, seven hundred BC from the Eastern Mediterranean, and that traces of them have been found at Stonehenge as well as in Greece and Italy. In fact some burial sites have been found around Stonehenge holding intact skeletons belonging to the integrated society of these people and the local beaker population."

"Great Heavens! I didn't know about that," cried George. Jo continued.

"Early Greek historians wrote that it was the Hyperboreans who taught them mathematics, and they were known also to have been astronomers. Hecateus wrote that they arrived from Anatolia, and Diodorus also wrote about them and their temple, which could only have been at Stonehenge!"

"All right, but what about the connection with Delos?" asked Pierre.

"Well here I'm afraid we do have to rely on the so-called legends," said Jo. "It is recorded that the British Hyperboreans sent offerings to Athens and Delos by courier, and many legends talk of them flying, although, as we know, there have always been stories of 'men' flying."

"All right Jo, we do know about most of this, and I agree that our men being tall and with beards is interesting, but what about the coffins, or flying boats as you call them?" asked George.

"It was the Mycenaean pictures that decided me. When I re-read the history of the Hyperboreans in Britain, I found that a second wave of immigrants who arrived from Greece about five hundred years later, had been held as prisoners by the Mycenaeans for some years. This would surely explain the drawings of Mycenaean weapons at Stonehenge, and on our man's flying boat. Now can you understand my conclusions?" asked Jo of his two still perplexed companions.

"Supposing we accept that all three men are Hyperboreans, Jo; we still have no explanation of the flying boats," said Pierre. "You mentioned that they were probably a type of landing capsule, and that they must have travelled long distances in a far larger craft, but the capsules must surely have been powered; they wouldn't have just drifted down to land, and we have no trace of any engine or power system on them!"

"Yes I agree that is a problem, and that is why I am so intrigued by the metallic skin suit on the Brigstone Man."

"But Jo, what about Delos?" interrupted George. "There is no sign of anything remotely resembling a landing place, there, and you have found no trace of skin suits on the skeletons there."

"That is strange, I agree," said Jo. "But there may be a simple explanation. Despite its size, we know that Delos was densely populated with all the trading and commerce it attracted, in addition to the dozens of temples and monasteries, but it is possible that somewhere there were open spaces where small craft would land – perhaps on flat roofs of buildings, or courtyards."

"I think we should call it a day now, otherwise you two will have no time to study the lettering," said George, interrupting their speculation as he beckoned the waiter to bring the bill.

"I quite agree," sighed Jo. "I for one am feeling rather tired, and there is no point in continuing to ponder on uncertainties. Pierre's flight leaves in the morning, but as I have one more day here, I will call you tomorrow George, if we have anything to tell you."

"I'll fax you when I have the results of the tests on the flying boats, Pierre," said George, giving his friend a rib-crushing hug, and clasping Jo's hand in his paralysing grip. Then, having said their farewells, Pierre and Jo set off on their walk back to their hotel.

The two friends had no trouble in deciphering the lettering on the flying boat from the photos they had taken, and by eleven thirty they knew that what they had was a name, probably that of the capsule's occupant. It read 'Apolanus'.

Feeling slightly disappointed, the two men retired for the night.

Early the next morning, following Pierre's departure for Beirut, Jo called George at his metallurgy laboratory to tell him about the name on the capsule. George, too, was disappointed that the lettering had not revealed any further information. He would call Jo later in the day, when he had had a chance to look at the samples he had taken. Jo had already decided to spend the day at Athens' huge central library to see what they had on the Hyperboreans, in particular any reference to Delos and perhaps even the name, 'Apolanus'.

It was late in the afternoon when Jo returned to his hotel to find a message waiting for him to call George.

"Jo!" roared George. "You must get over here straight away."

"What is it, George? Have you found something interesting?"

"I should say so! You know I took a piece of the lining from the capsule?"

"Did you?"

"I did, and guess what I found?"

"I've no idea."

"Listen Jo. There was a tiny piece of papyrus tucked into the lining, and on it was a picture of a woman's face."

"Good Lord!" exclaimed Jo.

"And that's not all," continued George. "Underneath the picture is some lettering, again Aramaic I think, and I need your help to read it."

"I say, that's wonderful! I'll come at once, of course George.

Just tell me how to get there."

Less than an hour later the two men were peering over a scrap of papyrus on George's workbench.

"This is wonderful!" exclaimed Jo, squinting through a tiny microscope. "It is definitely local reed, and certainly ancient. But I wonder who the woman could be?"

"Let's hope the lettering will tell us. Can you decipher it, Jo?"

"I'll have a good try, but it is very faded. The symbols appear to be the same as the name we found last night. Let's have a go at it, shall we?"

It was almost day by the time the two men sat back, satisfied that their reading of the lettering was correct. Jo knew for sure that his assumption about the importance of the excavation in England would make history, but now, with the discovery of the identity of the Delos Man, and all that it implied, he knew that the three of them faced a fearful burden of responsibility.

The lettering underneath the picture of a woman's face clearly translated as:

MARY OF NAZARETH, BELOVED OF APOLANUS
BLESSED OF ALL WOMEN

Pierre was in his lecture room at the university in Beirut the following day when he received a package from a DHL courier. Seeing that it was from George, he hurried to his office where he could open it privately. Tearing open the large envelope, he started to read Jo's hastily written account of the previous evening's findings, but it was not until a photograph of the papyrus fell out from between the pages, that he became entirely aware of the magnitude of the discovery.

"Good Grief!" he exclaimed out loud. "I knew it. I knew there was something about the Delos Men. I always had a feeling that there was something important there." Pierre's pulse was rushing and his heart beating so fast, that he reached into his pocket for his small box of blood pressure pills. I must stay calm, he thought, as he sat down and carefully read through the report a second time. Then he stood up and taking the envelope, carefully locked it in his desk drawer, thinking that he would find an easier place later.

Pierre desperately wanted to discuss the findings with George and Jo, but to use the telephone was out of the question and, as he had already been away from the university for too long, there was no possibility of returning to Athens. There was nothing else for it but to write a letter, outlining his opinion and detailing any questions, and there would be many.

On his return home that evening, one question became uppermost in Pierre's mind. Why had he and George been prevented from carrying out any research on the two skeletons ten years earlier? If George and Jo had only now found the papyrus in Apolanus's flying boat, how could the Greek authorities have known about it? There would surely not have been another one, and even if they had deciphered his name, could they, or perhaps someone else, have known he was Mary's lover? And which Mary was it? He and George were the region's most experienced archaeologists and, apart from the legend of a Roman soldier, they had never come across any other such story concerning the mother of Jesus in any of the countries where they had worked. He decided that there must have been some other reason, but was at a loss to know what it was. Pierre decided to add that to the list of questions he would put to George.

Pierre sat up late that night studying Jo's report, and writing a long five-page letter to George and Jo. The next morning he took a photocopy of the letter to send to Jo in London, and sent the two copies off by DHL courier.

As soon as Jo had checked into his hotel back in London, he hurried off to the Natural History Museum, where the Brigstone Man awaited him in the locked room he had reserved. Before giving his attention to the skeleton, he decided to carry out a thorough search of the flying boat. Some sample scrapings from the exterior had been sent to the Athens laboratory, but he had paid little attention to the interior. It took Jo most of the morning to clean the vessel before he was able to peel off several pieces of the metallic lining, but, apart from the fact that it obviously contained some kind of magnetic element, he couldn't help feeling disappointed that there was no hidden message, as they had found in Apolanus's craft in Athens.

Following a quick lunch, Jo turned his attention to the hieroglyphics on the side of the vessel. The picture of a Mycenaean weapon was clear enough, but the etched lettering had been damaged by the impact on landing, and what remained was barely legible.

Taking out his book on Aramaic, and comparing the notes he had previously made, he slowly began to recognise several letters. The first was a 'J', then there was a gap followed by an 'H', then another gap. Jo was pretty sure that it would have represented the man's name, as with the Delos Man, but he felt totally frustrated that he was unable to make out the rest of it.

"Damn!" he muttered. "If only I could get his name, I might be able to find some reference to him among the legends of British Hyperboreans."

That evening, in the hotel, he was handed the envelope delivered by courier, from Pierre in Beirut.

Jo arrived at the museum early the next morning, and donned his surgeons gear ready for work on the Brigstone Man. He had already measured him, and knew that he had died aged about forty-five when his craft had crashed. Looking at the remains of the brain tissue, he was able to confirm that, as with the Delos two, the right side of his brain was much larger than the left.

Then Jo began to scrape off the remainder of the metallic skin suit. There was quite a lot still attached to the upper ribs and, as he started to peel off a large piece, he noticed that there seemed to be something tucked underneath it. It was a small piece of papyrus, folded in two! He carried it across to his microscope and, carefully opening it up, set it down. Then, adjusting his spectacles, he peered down through the lens. On it, in clearly legible handwriting were seven lines of lettering which Jo again recognised as Aramaic.

Jo realised that his hands were shaking as he settled down to decipher the symbols in front of him, hardly daring to think what they may reveal, when he was startled by a loud knocking on the door.

"My God!" he muttered, suddenly aware of the lack of security he faced with the Brigstone Man and whatever he was about to reveal, apart from the possible repercussions if news of their Athens discovery got out! The knocking continued, but Jo had wisely taken the precaution of keeping the door locked.

"Are you there, Jo?" asked a familiar voice.

"Good Heavens, is that you, Peter?" asked Jo, feeling slightly relieved as he approached the locked door. "Can you just wait a moment, I am in the middle of something."

"Of course."

"Damn and blast it," muttered Jo, as he rushed over to the table to pull a cover over the skeleton. He grabbed the flying boat and chucked it back into its packing case with a loud bang. Then he carefully placed his microscope, carrying the papyrus, on a shelf in a cupboard and slammed the door shut. Turning the key in the lock, he greeted his friend, Dr Peter Wilson from the museum's American Indian Department.

"Jo, you old reprobate! Somebody told me you were here. What the hell are you up to?"

"Oh Pete, it's great to see you. I'm sorry I haven't got round to calling you, but I have just got back from Athens."

"What are you up to? Have you got something interesting there?" asked his friend, peering past Jo towards the table.

"Not really. I have been helping an old friend with an excavation, that's all."

"Well it's good that you are keeping busy, Jo. Are you free this evening? We could have dinner together."

"That would be good Pete, but not tonight. I must finish my work here, but how about lunch tomorrow, before I leave?"

With their arrangements made, Jo showed his friend safely out and re-locked the door. That was a near miss, he thought, as he recovered his microscope from the cupboard and sat down to return to the task of deciphering the lettering on the scrap of papyrus.

It was early evening by the time Jo had finished translating, checking and double-checking his interpretation of the ancient Aramaic script on the papyrus which lay before him. It seemed to him to be utterly inconceivable that what he had found could be anything other than some enormous, elaborately-planned hoax, and he felt totally dejected because that would render the whole excavation at Brigstone, and perhaps also at Delos, a complete non-event.

"It can't be true, it just can't be true," he muttered, feeling totally numb with shock. If only Pierre was here, he might come up with some sort of explanation. This is too big a dilemma for me to handle alone. Then, perhaps for the sixth time, Jo checked each individual symbol again, only to reach the same staggering conclusion.

Jo sat slumped at the workbench, his head in his hands, unable to think clearly. In his mind he saw the pages of the Bible fly open to the Book of Genesis, Chapter Six, the words floating before him:THERE WERE GIANTS IN THE EARTH IN THOSE DAYS, WHEN THE SONS OF GOD CAME INTO THE DAUGHTERS OF MEN, AND THEY BORE CHILDREN TO THEM... Then he saw himself as a child again, walking down the aisle of the local church carrying the simple wooden cross, and the once-angelic face of his Sunday School teacher now scowling down at him with an expression of sheer malice.

A loud crash startled him as his heavy palaeography reference book fell to the ground and, as he bent to retrieve it, the lights went out.

"Damn!" he yelled. He had lost track of the time, and the museum was closing. The lights flashed on and off as he quickly recovered the papyrus from his microscope then, carefully lifting it with a pair of tweezers, he placed it between two torn pieces of skin suit. Minutes later, with the precious find sandwiched safely between some fine specimen glass, secured with sticky tape, and carefully wrapped in a bulky newspaper in his briefcase, Jo left the museum.

Back in his hotel room, Jo went, immediately to the phone and asked the operator to call Pierre's home number in Beirut. It was after eleven o'clock when the phone rang at the flat in Lyon Street, and it rang for some time before Pierre's wife picked it up.

"Good evening Nadine, it's Joseph in London. I am sorry to disturb you at this hour, but I must speak to Pierre."

"Good Heavens Jo, whatever is the matter? You sound quite

upset," she replied.

"Yes, I'm afraid I am rather anxious. Is he there?"

"I am sorry Jo, Pierre is not back yet. He had to go to a dinner tonight. Is there anything I can do?"

"Oh dear," sighed Jo. "Would you just tell him that something very important has come up, and it is vital that we meet. I intend to get a flight over tomorrow, and will come straight to your home, if that will not be inconvenient for you, Nadine."

"No, indeed not Jo. Of course you must come, but whatever can it be that has so upset you? Could you not discuss it with Pierre on the telephone?"

"I'm afraid that is quite out of the question, but I do thank you for your concern. There is one more thing, Nadine: would you mind asking Pierre to call George Apostolonis as soon as he gets back? He should be there too. Please tell Pierre that it concerns something particularly traumatic."

"Oh Jo, I hope you are not in trouble?"

"Of course not. But it is something that must be kept absolutely confidential."

"I understand," said Nadine. "Pierre may be rather late tonight, but I will leave a note for him, so he may call you back later, if that is all right?"

"Certainly it is," replied Jo. "Well good night Nadine; I do hope I didn't waken you."

"Good night Jo, and I shall look forward to seeing you tomorrow."

Early the next morning, Jo quickly photographed the precious piece of papyrus then carefully re-packed it and left the hotel. He took a taxi to the Chase Manhattan Bank in Piccadilly where he deposited the package in the bank's vault. Then, having safely negotiated the security scanners at Heathrow with his loaded camera, he caught the eleven o'clock flight to Beirut.

Chapter Six

When Sally returned from work on Monday evening, John had a message for her from the hospital. The Almoner had rung, asking her if she would collect Dr Jordan's effects.

"Oh please! I only saw him for half an hour. How can they assume that I will be responsible for him? I don't want to know, and anyway, I'm tired. I'm going to have a bath." And closing the bathroom door behind her, she left John to prepare the evening meal.

Remembering that she had had a heavy day, John avoided the subject over dinner, but later whilst sipping coffee, he asked, "Have you not thought any more about Dr Jordan, Sal? I mean, don't you think you should try to find out a little more about him?"

"Look John, it was you who said it was nonsense, and that I should forget all about it, and that's just what I am trying to do. In any case, I've had my hands full today with the presentation, which went very well by the way: I think we've got the account."

"That's great, Sal. Well done." Sally dropped to the floor to rest her head against his legs.

"I'm sorry John, I didn't mean to be churlish, but I was so tired, I feel better now that I've eaten, but I really can't think about that man just yet. It's just so confusing. There he was lying in hospital, saying he was my father, about whom I know absolutely nothing, then he tells me I'm the only person he can trust with some terrible secret; and to top it all, he goes and dies! I mean, for Heaven's sake, what the hell am I supposed to do now?" John pulled her up onto his lap, stroking her hair back from her face.

"What you must do now, Sweetie, is just relax and try not to worry about it. The hospital will have to wait. You're tired and need a good night's sleep, then, if you feel like talking about it in the morning, we'll see what should be done."

The following day was quite an anti-climax in Sally's office, and she enjoyed a quiet, relaxing morning. Julie brought her a sandwich in for lunch but, as they sat talking, she was suddenly startled by a vision flashing through her head. A pair of metallic blue eyes stared into hers, and a voice was urging her to be careful.

"Oh God!" she exclaimed, jumping to her feet.

"Whatever is it, Sally?" asked Julie.

"Oh it's nothing, just someone walking over my grave," she replied, trying to hide her unease. "Is there any more coffee?"

While Julie was out of the office Sally made a decision. She would solve the mystery of Dr Jordan once and for all! She would collect his things from the hospital, and hopefully then find out a bit more about him. She would not tell John what she was doing. She didn't really know why, but she just felt that it should be her secret. She would solve the puzzle alone. She picked up the phone and called the hospital.

The following Saturday morning Sally returned to the hospital and found her way to the Almoner's office. Having offered his condolences on the loss of her father, the Almoner handed her a carrier bag containing Dr Jordan's clothes and personal effects.

"The Police have been through them, and said you may take them now."

"The Police? Why on earth the Police?" she asked.

Well, as you know, my dear, your father was the victim of a hit and run driver, and if the autopsy shows that his heart attack was as a result of the accident, his death may be treated as manslaughter."

"Oh, Good Heavens, whatever next!" cried Sally. "And anyway, he wasn't my father. I never saw him before the other day!"

"I'm sorry Miss Wincott, we can only act on the facts as given to us. Dr Jordan insisted that you were his daughter, and that we contact you urgently."

"Yes, I do understand that. You did what you had to do. I'm sorry I'm not very appreciative," said Sally, as she pulled open the carrier bag.

"There doesn't seem to be much personal stuff here? Were there no papers?"

"It's all there, I assure you," he replied. "Dr Jordan's things were locked in a cupboard when he was moved to Intensive Care, but now that you mention it, there was some disarray around his bed when they found him."

"Disarray? What sort of disarray?"

"I don't really know. You'd need to speak to the night nurse who was on duty. I think his clothes were scattered about, and there were other things on the floor."

"But that's terrible!" exclaimed Sally. "Something may have been stolen. Did he have any money on him?"

"I really can't say. You'll have to check through his things, and if you think there is something missing, let me know," he said, as he rose to dismiss her. "I'm afraid we won't be able to release the body until after the autopsy."

"Great Heavens!" cried Sally. "I can't possibly be responsible for that! He's a complete stranger to me."

"Try not to worry about it, my dear," he replied. "I suggest you go through his things and see if you can find some reference to his family or friends. There must be somebody who should be informed of his death."

"But what if there isn't anyone? I'm certainly not going to bury him!"

"Then in that case, Miss Wincott, he will be interred in the local common grave, unless, of course, you agree to his body being donated for medical research."

"Now that is a good idea," said Sally. "As he's a doctor, he would approve of that." And feeling one problem was solved, she returned home with the paper carrier bag containing Dr Jordan's belongings.

By the time Sally got back home, John had left for the airport. Sally decided that after she had finished her normal weekend chores, she would spend the rest of the break trying to resolve the mystery of Dr Jordan. By seven thirty she had eaten a quick dinner and was just settling down to make a start on the carrier bag when the phone rang.

"Damn!" she muttered as she lifted the receiver to be greeted by a child's voice.

"Hello, is Daddy there please?"

"No, I'm sorry, he's just left. Is that you, David?" she asked, recognising the voice of John's ten-year-old son.

"Yes… er, hello Sally. I want to speak to Daddy." His voice was wavering. "Where is he? Will he be back soon?" Sally thought she heard a sob.

"Whatever's the matter, David? Are you all right?" she asked, concerned at the sounds of distress reaching her.

"I want Daddy," he wailed.

"But Darling, he's left for the airport, and he won't be back for a couple of days. Is there anything I can do?"

"No! I just want Daddy!" the wailing continued. Oh Lord! thought Sally. How on earth do I cope with this?

"What is it David? Just tell me. What is the matter?"

"I can't stay here," he sobbed. "I hate her. I hate her!" he yelled into the phone.

"Who, Darling? Who do you hate?"

"Her… *I hate her*!" Sally stood up and walked over to the window. If only John was here. He'd know what to do, she thought, before sitting down to try again.

"Look David, it's no use shouting like that. Just tell me who you hate and why. Is it Liz? Has she done something bad?"

"No. 'Cors it's not Lizzie; it's Mummy. I *hate* her!" he yelled again.

"Why do you hate Mummy? What has she done?"

"Oh, everything. She hates me. She hates Daddy, and she's horrible, and I'm *not* staying here. I want to come and live with you and Daddy, *please* Sally."

Hell! She swore inwardly. This is all I need, and with John away.

"Now you know that's not possible David. I am out at work all day, and Daddy is often away and, anyway, we're miles from your school."

"I don't care about school," he cried. "I just want to live with you and Daddy."

"Look David, I don't know what's happened, but I'm sure Mummy doesn't hate you. Would you like me to speak to her?" tried Sally gamely.

"No, I would not," was the response.

"Please stop shouting at me, David," she said as sternly as she could. "How would you like to spend the day with me tomorrow? We could go to Windsor Safari Park, if you like. They've just opened a dolphin pool there."

"Oh, yes Sally, can I?" he asked eagerly.

"I can't promise, I'll have to ask your mother first, but if she agrees, I'll pick you up at ten o'clock."

"Super!" he yelled, the sobbing suddenly past.

"All right David. I'll ring your mother now, and I promise not to tell her what you said."

"Oh thank you Sally. See you tomorrow… bye," and he hung up.

"Damn and blast it," muttered Sally. "There goes my Dr Jordan research."

After her long day with the unhappy ten-year-old, and a near scene on the return to his mother, when he wouldn't get out of the car, Sally felt shattered. A good night's sleep was what she needed. Dr Jordan's carrier bag would have to wait until the next day.

Sally woke up and sat bolt upright. Turning to look at the bedside clock she saw that it was three o'clock.

"The note! Where's the scrap of paper he gave me?" she cried, scrambling out of bed. "I don't know what I did with it," and pulling on her slippers she stumbled into the living room. She grabbed her handbag from the table by the door and tipped the contents out. Oh Lord, it's not there! What on earth did I do with it? Then, feeling down into the tiny zipped rear pocket, she found it. Breathing a sigh of relief Sally sat down clutching the screwed up scrap. She switched on the lamp by her desk and smoothed it out.

On it was written 'H/b' followed by three rows of numbers, nothing else. She turned it over but the reverse was blank. It must surely be the numbers of a safe combination lock or a bank deposit box, she thought, but where? There must be a clue somewhere.

Perhaps if she could find out where he lived? Then, jumping up, she retrieved the carrier bag from the hall cupboard.

Kneeling on the floor, Sally tipped the contents out onto the carpet. There was a tweed jacket and twill trousers, a tightly-folded Burberry raincoat, a pair of expensive looking brown loafers and a cashmere sweater. He must have been quite well off, she thought as she reached the bottom of the bag to pull out a small plastic bag containing his personal effects.

The first thing she noticed was his passport. It stated that he was an American citizen, born in Portsmouth, New Hampshire in 1913, and that he was an anthropologist. Sally was surprised, having presumed that he was English. Turning the pages she saw that he had been in England the year before, and had also visited Greece and the Lebanon several times, as well as Egypt, Peru and Bolivia previously.

Her eyes fell on his gold watch. It was a Baume and Mercier on a brown crocodile strap and, turning it over, noticed an inscription on the back: 'To Jo from all your friends at the Little Apple'. Wondering what that could mean, she picked up his wallet. Inside were four hundred pound Thomas Cook traveller's cheques, five one hundred dollar bills, fifty pounds in notes and an American Express card. A separate section held a faded photograph of a woman and a number of visiting cards. Pulling them out Sally started to read them. There were six of his own professional visiting cards: 'Professor Joseph Jordan PhD, Department of Anthropology, University of Minnesota, Minneapolis'. Two others were from Professor Pierre Soulaya, Department of Archaeology at the American University in Beirut, Lebanon, and one from Professor George Apostolonis of Athens University. That's not much to go on, thought Sally, unless the woman in the photo is his wife. She must be in Minneapolis. She could call the university to ask for their home address. Then, returning to the remainder of the contents, she retrieved a Pan American flight ticket, a typed itinerary from a Minneapolis travel agency, and a confirmation slip from the Hotel Russell. There was no diary, no letters or papers, and no bunch of keys. That's not right. There must be something missing, thought Sally. Perhaps in his hotel room. Of course! He must have had a briefcase at least, and some luggage. She decided to go there the next day, after work.

Feeling slightly disappointed, but confident that she would find something at the hotel the next day, she put Dr Jordan's things away safely into her desk drawer. As she pushed his clothes back into the carrier bag, something dropped to the floor. It was the key to his hotel room attached to a metal tag, and marked 'Room No 150'. Sally put it into her handbag before returning to bed. That should make getting into his room a lot easier.

When Sally rolled out of bed at seven thirty the next morning, she felt exhausted. She had woken from a disturbing dream and felt thoroughly shaken. Drinking her coffee, she wasn't sure if she had dreamed it or if she was just remembering what had actually happened at the hospital. She felt haunted by the dying man and, whether in her dreams, or her memory, she could not shake off the vision of his steel-blue eyes.

Remembering what the Almoner had told her, and that his clothes were scattered about the room when they had found him dead, it all suddenly began to make sense and a feeling of unease crept over her.

"My God!" she exclaimed, addressing Felix, "What if he wasn't mad, and what he told me was true?" But wait a minute, why is the note so important? Surely he could have memorised the numbers. Why write them down and then give the note to me if it was so risky? There must be something more to it than numbers. She thought of invisible ink, but then had a different idea. Of course! The scrap of paper must hold a tiny microchip, perhaps hidden in one of the numbers. But no… this is silly. I must be imagining things. I must get to work. Under the shower Sally determined to put the whole business out of her mind. She had a group meeting that morning and, after quickly dressing and feeding Felix, she grabbed her briefcase and left the flat.

Sally was just turning the key in the lock when she noticed two men standing in the corridor.

"Miss Jordan? Miss Sally Jordan?" asked the taller one, stepping forward.

"What? No, sorry. There's no Miss Jordan here," she replied as she walked towards the lift.

"Just a minute, Miss," said the second man, almost blocking her way. "Miss Sally Wincott, isn't it?" A chill shuddered down Sally's spine as she considered making a dash for the service stairs.

"Look," she said nervously pushing the lift button three times. "I don't know what you want but I'm late for work. I must go."

"It's quite all right, Miss Wincott, we won't keep you," said the tall man. "We are police officers. I am Detective Inspector McGregor and this is Detective Sergeant Jones from the Bankside CID. Could we just have a quick word with you?"

"Oh, you gave me quite a fright!" said Sally, turning to face them. "But I'm sorry, I really can't stop now. I have to be at a meeting in half an hour. If it's about the hit and run, can't it wait until this evening?"

"I'm afraid it's rather more important than that," replied the inspector.

"Oh?"

"Yes Miss, we're investigating a case of murder," added the sergeant.

"What? A murder?" she exclaimed. The inspector moved closer.

"I am sorry, Miss Wincott, but Dr Jordan's death was no accident. He was murdered in the hospital." Sally stared wide-eyed at the two policemen, her heart thumping.

"Oh my God!"

Struggling to recover her composure, Sally turned back, and pulling her keys from her bag, opened the door to her flat.

"Then I suppose you'd better come in," she said. "But first, may I see you identification please?" The two officers held up their badges.

Having seated the two men, Sally picked up the phone to ask Julie to stand in for her at the meeting, promising to be in later.

"Why do you think Dr Jordan was murdered Inspector?" she asked.

"Because the autopsy showed that he was poisoned."

"Oh please, no!" she murmured, her hand going to her mouth.

"Are you all right, Miss Wincott?" asked the sergeant, noticing her agitation.

"Did you say poisoned, are you sure?" she was almost whispering.

"Quite sure. Somebody got into the intensive care ward and shot something into his drip."

"Oh God!" murmured Sally. The sergeant took out his notebook.

"I am sorry, Miss Wincott, but we would like you to tell us what you know about Dr Jordan. Do you know what he was doing in London?"

"We understand that he was a stranger to you, but we need to know what he said to you when you met him," added McGregor. "This man was obviously killed for a reason and, rather than being a mere coincidence, it now seems likely that the hit and run was a botched first attempt."

Pulling herself up straight in her chair, Sally then recounted how she had been called to the hospital to see someone who was insisting he was her father, carefully leaving out any reference to the scrap of paper he had given her, or his strange warning. When she had finished, McGregor stood up.

"Mmm… well, that's not much to go on, is it? Are you sure there is nothing else you can tell us?"

"Absolutely," lied Sally, "except perhaps this," and she handed him the small photograph Dr Jordan had given her.

"I think it's him with my mother."

"Do you know who took it, and where it was?" asked McGregor.

"I don't know. Perhaps it was just after the war in France, where they met."

"May we keep it? It may give us a lead."

"I suppose so, but I must have it back, please. It's the only picture I've seen of my mother."

"Of course. Well Jones, I think we've taken up enough of Miss Wincott's time," said McGregor.

"If you can think of anything else, please let us know," added Jones, handing Sally a card.

As they reached the door, the inspector turned back. "I understand you have taken possession of Dr Jordan's effects, Miss Wincott?"

"Yes. The hospital said I should take them. I didn't have much choice. But, as I told you, he was a complete stranger to me, and I can't be responsible for his burial."

"That's all right, Miss Wincott," said the sergeant. "He'll be kept on ice until we've finished our enquiries. Good morning." Sally gasped, a shiver running through her.

"Hell!" swore Sally as she closed the door behind them. I'd forgotten they'd been through his stuff. They must have seen the hotel confirmation which means that I had better get over there quick! Let's hope they've only just started their enquiries this morning. Then, following a brief call to the office to say that she needed the rest of the day, she dashed outside and caught a taxi.

Sally's cab seemed to take forever to get to the hotel. It was the morning rush hour and the driver took an indirect route through a myriad of one-way streets. Having paid him off, she dashed up the steps to the foyer and made straight for the lifts. Coming to a sudden halt, something told her that it would be wiser to take the stairs in case the police were already there.

Once up on the first floor, she carefully peered up and down the corridor. There didn't seem to be anyone around and, taking the key from her bag, she followed the room numbers along until she came to Room 150. She was just turning the key in the lock when she heard the lift door opening. Quickly looking around for somewhere to hide, she noticed a door marked 'Private' and, pushing it open, went into a dark linen cupboard.

A middle-aged couple walked past and went into a room further down. After hesitating for a moment, Sally peeked through a crack in the door and, seeing that there was no one else, ventured out again. She returned to Room 150, unlocked the door and went in.

The room looked empty. There was no sign of occupation and no luggage. The bed was made up and the bathroom was spotless, with clean towels and new wrapped soap bars. Sally quickly opened the wardrobe, but it was empty. She checked the drawers and bedside cupboard, but there was nothing apart from a Bible. There was no sign that Dr Jordan, or anyone else had been in the room.

Damn! Where's his luggage? It must be somewhere. She felt totally let down. The police couldn't have been there already surely? Now she would have to ask at reception, and working out what she could say, she returned to the foyer leaving the key in the door.

"Good morning Madam!" greeted the smartly dressed girl behind the counter.

"Good morning!" replied Sally, trying to look as though she had just come in.

"I'd like to see Dr Jordan, please. I believe he's in Room one fifty." The girl tapped into the register.

"Oh… I won't keep you a moment, Madam," she said, turning to disappear into the back office. Sally's heart was beating fast. Perhaps the police had been already. The receptionist returned with a senior looking man in a dark suit.

"Dr Jordan has left the hotel," he announced, looking Sally up and down. "May I ask what is your business with him?"

"I'm his daughter, and we arranged to meet here," she replied brightly.

"I'm very sorry, Miss Jordan, but there must be some misunderstanding. Dr Jordan left some days ago without paying his bill." Sally tried to look suitably surprised, and before she could think what to say, he was beckoning her through to his rear office.

"I'm Trevor O'Neill, the General Manager. May I have a few words with you?"

Declining his outstretched hand. Sally sat down in an armchair by the manager's desk.

"I have to say it came as quite a surprise when your father took off like that. He's been a regular guest of ours for some years," he said.

"I know," lied Sally. "Can you tell me when he arrived? You see, I had lost touch with him for some time."

"Dr Jordan checked in two weeks ago and seemed his normal self until, that is, last Sunday when he went out early and didn't come back."

"Did he not tell anyone where he was going?" Sally hoped she was giving the impression of a concerned daughter.

"No, he didn't, but there is something else, Miss Jordan." O'Neill was leaning forward over his desk.

"Oh?" queried Sally.

"When the maid went in to clean his room that morning, it had been completely ransacked."

"What?" Sally was gripping the arms of her chair, her eyes wide with fright as he continued.

"I'm afraid so. The whole place had been turned over. Your father's clothes were strewn all over the floor; the bed was stripped, and the mattress slashed and left leaning against the wall. The curtains were torn, the pictures smashed and the drawers pulled out!"

"Oh my God!" cried Sally.

"Are you sure this was after he had left?" she asked.

"Certain. The night porter saw him go out at seven o'clock and swore that no one came in before eight thirty, when he went off duty. After that, the maids were about and the foyer fully staffed. In the circumstances, Miss Jordan, I'm afraid I must ask to see your identification."

Sally felt scared. She wished she could just stand up and walk out without her legs shaking, but she had to keep her wits about her. Mustering up her most charming manner, she replied, "That is a slight problem, Mr O'Neill, you see, my name is Wincott, not Jordan. I was adopted and Dr Jordan was… I mean is my natural father."

"I see," said O'Neill, glancing at the driving licence and library ticket which Sally handed to him. "That makes it difficult, but I'll take your word for it."

"Thank you," she said. "I suppose you did call the police?"

"Oh, yes. They came straight away. They checked the room and interviewed the morning staff, but as no one suspicious was seen, they left, so I'm afraid that's all I can tell you."

Sally stood shakily to her feet. "Thank you Mr O'Neill. You will let me know if you hear anything further from my father, won't you? I'll leave you my phone number."

"Of course. I hope the police will be able to help you," said O'Neill, as he stood up to show her out just as the receptionist knocked on the door.

"There's two gentlemen asking for you Mr O'Neill. They are from the police."

Sally froze. This is it. I bet it's Inspector McGregor, she thought and, backing away from the door, she positioned herself behind O'Neill, declining his gesture that she should precede him.

Trevor O'Neill walked out of the office behind the receptionist to greet the visitors. Turning her head away, Sally carefully slipped out behind him, then, dropping to her knees, she crawled as fast as she could to the far end of the reception area. Straining to hear the conversation. She recognised Sergeant Jones' nasal voice. She stood up, crouching as low as possible, and carefully opened the hatch at the end of the counter.

A group of noisy tourists were waiting a little further down and, taking advantage of their cover, she walked quickly round the corner towards the rear of the hotel where she found a fire exit. Please God let it be open, she prayed, as she struggled to push the heavy iron bar. She was shaking all over when the door suddenly flew open and she almost fell out into a side street. It was pouring with rain but she didn't care. She sat down on a rubbish skip and burst out laughing. I must be mad! How stupid. That manager's bound to tell inspector McGregor that I was there. Why on earth did I run away? Surely I'm entitled to try to find my father? But no, wait a minute. The inspector will tell O'Neill that Dr Jordan was murdered last Sunday, and I would obviously have been told by now. So why did I tell O'Neill that I had gone to meet him if I knew he was dead? If he lets on to McGregor that I was lying, I will be suspect number one! Oh God! I can't cope with this. It's getting too complicated. I will have to tell John.

Sally stood up, feeling slightly better. She took a mirror from her bag and ran her comb through her wet hair before setting off to find a taxi. Of course there were none and by the time she arrived home by tube, it was getting on for lunchtime.

Felix was overjoyed to see his mistress home so early. It made a welcome change from his usual routine of watching the pigeons on the windowsill, prising open the kitchen cupboard door, or digging new holes in the carpet whilst trying to recover his ping pong ball from under the sofa. He wound himself around her ankles, biting affectionately and yowling for food.

"I'm very busy Felix," she said, bending down to stroke him. "Go back to your chair, there's a good boy." But Felix wasn't having it. He jumped up onto her shoulder and bit her ear, meowing loudly. I must make those phone calls, thought Sally, pushing him down. I wonder what time it is in Minneapolis now? And walking over to her desk to find the visiting cards, she fell over Felix, who had placed himself in a strategic position between her feet.

"Eeeowww…" he yelled, and bit her again.

"Damn you Felix!" she shouted, giving him a swipe, then, deciding it would be prudent to surrender, she marched into the kitchen to open a tin of Whiskers.

Chapter Seven

Sally opened the wallet and took out the cards. She wanted to call the university if Minneapolis first to try to find Dr Jordan's home address, but it would still be early morning there. Beirut would be about four hours ahead, which would make it late afternoon in the Middle East.

She found the direct dialling code for Beirut in her phone book and dialled the number of the American university.

"*Mer haba*!" came the reply.

"*S'il vous plait, parlez vous Français*?" she asked in her school French.

"*Oui Madame.*"

"*Je voudrais parler avec Professor Soulaya de le Department de Archéologie*," said Sally.

"*Ne Quittez pas.Je vous passe.*"

"*Na-am*?" replied a young voice.

"*Pardonnez-moi Monsieur*, but do you speak English?" tried Sally.

"Yes I do. How may I help you?"

"I would like to speak to Professor Soulaya."

"I am sorry, he is not here. May I take a message?"

"No, I really need to speak with him. Do you know where I may call him now?"

"He may be at home. You could try there. Do you have his number?"

"Yes I do, thank you. I'll try him there," said Sally. This is going to be more difficult than I thought. What if he only speaks Arabic?

The phone at Professor Soulaya's home was answered by a

woman.

"*Pardonnez-moi, Madame*, but do you speak English?" asked Sally.

"Yes I do. How may I help you?" asked the pleasant sounding lady.

"I am calling from London, Madame, and I need to speak to Professor Soulaya. It concerns a friend of his, Dr Jordan from Minneapolis."

"Oh, Joseph! How is he? May I take a message? My husband is not here, but I am expecting him back at any time."

"Thank you, but I really should speak with him. It is rather important. May I call back in an hour? My name is Sally Wincott."

"Of course Miss Wincott. I am sure he will be here before then. I will ask him to expect you call."

"Thank you, Madame," said Sally, and hung up.

Oh Lord! I suppose I'd better try Athens now, thought Sally, and I don't know a word of Greek either. This time, she dialled the home number of Professor Apostolonis.

"*Ehmbross – ne*?" The gruff voice sounded like an elderly man.

"Hello! Do you speak English?" asked Sally.

"Yes, yes," came the reply.

"I would like to speak to Professor Apostolonis, please," she said slowly.

"I am Apostolonis."

"Ah, Professor," greeted Sally, relieved. "You don't know me, but I am calling from London; it's about Dr Jordan from Minneapolis."

"How is Jo?"

"I'm afraid I have some bad news, Professor."

"Oh? Jo is not ill, I hope?"

"No. It's worse than that, Professor. I am sorry, but Dr Jordan died last Sunday." Sally heard a sharp intake of breath at the other end of the line, then a few seconds of silence. "Are you all right, Professor?"

"Of course. It was a shock to hear that over the telephone. But tell me, who are you?"

“My name is Sally Wincott, and I am Dr Jordan’s daughter,” said Sally.

“What? I didn’t know that Jo had a daughter,” exclaimed Apostolonis.

“I don’t think anyone did. I met him for the first time last week, when he was in hospital following a heart attack.”

“Good Heavens!” muttered the Greek. “So poor old Jo died of a heart attack. That’s terrible.”

Now for it, I’ll have to tell him, thought Sally.

“I’m afraid it wasn’t quite like that, Professor. The police are saying that he was murdered.”

“Oh my God! No! No! It can’t be!” Sally could hear laboured breathing and sensed that he was seriously shocked.

“Are you sure you are all right, Professor?” she asked again, feeling that perhaps she had been too blunt. Then his voice came back firmly.

“Are you quite sure, Sally? How was he killed, do you know?”

“The police said that somebody got to him in the hospital, he was poisoned.”

“My God!” he yelled. “Do you know why he was in London? Did he have any papers with him?”

“I really don’t know anything more, Professor. I only met him once for half an hour, and he was not at all well. I’m sorry, I can’t tell you anything more.”

“Sally… I may call you Sally, may I not?” There was a frightening urgency in the Greek’s voice. “I am coming over. I will book a flight for tomorrow. Will you meet me at the airport? It is very important.”

Oh, Lord, thought Sally.

“I’d like to help Professor, but I really have to work tomorrow.”

“Sally, I can’t tell you how important this is, but it is vital that I talk with you tomorrow.” The Greek professor sounded deadly serious. “Give me your phone number, and I will call you when I arrive. We will arrange a meeting then.” Aware of the urgency in his voice, Sally began to feel really concerned.

“All right Professor, if you call me tomorrow, I will meet you as soon as I can."

This is getting to be quite frightening. What on earth is worrying Professor Apostolonis? Could he be involved in whatever Dr Jordan was killed for? Sally's heart began to pound. She scooped up the now sleeping cat, holding him close. I'm not going to answer my door to anyone. Oh, John, come back, I'm scared.

Standing in the kitchen, waiting for the kettle to boil for a calming cup of tea, Sally called her office.

"Julie, I have quite a big problem to sort out, and it may take some time, but I'll be in tomorrow to explain. Meantime, if anyone unknown calls, would you just say that I am away. Don't in any circumstances say where I am, or even if I am in London."

"All right Sally, don't worry. I won't tell anyone you are at home, but it does sound mysterious. Are you sure you are all right? You're not in some sort of trouble, are you?" Julie was concerned. She and Sally had become firm friends. Sally laughed nervously.

"You could say that 'trouble' is the understatement of the year! But don't worry, I'm fine. I'll be in early tomorrow and we'll have a talk."

Sally carried her mug of tea into the living room, suddenly remembering that she hadn't eaten anything all morning. She grabbed a banana from the fruit bowl and collapsed onto the sofa, pushing the outstretched Felix into a corner. Sipping her tea she started to think through all that had happened since the phone call urging her to go to the hospital.

"My God!" she cried, suddenly springing up. "Of course! How could I have been so stupid. It's the note!" How could I have missed it? Whoever murdered Joseph was obviously looking for something, first in his hotel room, and then at the hospital. Perhaps he was killed after they had found whatever it was, or, perhaps they didn't find it *because he no longer had what they were looking for*! Joseph told me that my life could be in danger if anyone knew what he had given me, and what he gave me was the note with numbers on it!

Sally stood up shaking all over. She walked across the room feeling as if she had been dealt a sharp blow on the head. Catching sight of herself in the mirror her face looked drained of blood and almost grey.

"What am I to do?" she sobbed feeling, for the first time in her life, like a helpless, defenceless woman. She glanced out of the window. There were several cars parked in the side street below, but no people about. She bolted the window then went quickly to the door, double locked it and put the chain on. Then she picked up the phone to call Bill, the porter on the ground floor. No one was to know she was there, or indeed where she was, she told him. He was to say she was away and didn't know when she would be back.

Sally's practical side was taking over, but she knew she needed help. Should she call Inspector McGregor, and if so, what could she say? She couldn't tell him what Joseph had said, or mention the note. The note! Where on earth could she hide it? She started to panic again. No, calm down, she told herself. Let's just get hold of Professor Soulaya and see how he reacts to the news of Joseph's murder. If he is as distressed as the Greek professor, then it may be that the three of them were involved in something together.

Sally looked at the clock. It was time to call Beirut again. She dialled the number and got what she thought must be an engaged tone.

"Oh please be there," she sighed. A long five minutes later, she tried again.

"*Na-am – Allo*!" came the reply.

"Professor Soulaya?" she asked.

"Yes, speaking. You are Miss Wincott in London?"

"Yes. Good evening Professor," replied Sally. "I am sorry to call you like this, but I'm afraid I have some bad news. It concerns Dr Jordan."

"What is it? Is Jo ill?"

"Dr Jordan is dead, Professor."

"Dead? Oh no! What happened?" Soulaya sounded shaken.

Here we go again, thought Sally.

"It is rather complicated, Professor. Dr Jordan was involved in a road accident, then had a heart attack, but the police are treating his death as murder," said Sally, going the whole hog. A stunned silence followed.

"No... *no no*!" came the anguished cry from Beirut. "Not murdered. No it can't be true!"

"I'm afraid it is, Professor," said Sally, wondering how she might glean some clue from the shocked archaeologist.

"Are you absolutely sure about this, Miss Wincott?" he asked, now sounding calmer.

"Yes, Professor. The police came to see me yesterday. They told me that he was poisoned in the hospital."

"But Miss Wincott, who are you? I don't know who you are."

"I am Dr Jordan's daughter. At least that's what he told me."

"But Jo didn't have any children."

"I am his illegitimate daughter, and I only met him for the first time on the day he died."

"Great Heavens! How was he when you saw him? Did he talk to you? What did he tell you?" Sally was aware of the urgency in his voice. Perhaps now he might give her a clue.

"I was only there for a short time, and he wasn't at all well, but he did seem rather agitated about something."

"Agitated? Did he not tell you why?"

"Not exactly Professor. It was very strange, but he did warn me to be careful." Sally heard a sharp intake of breath.

"My dear girl, you must tell me everything. It is vital that I know what Jo said to you."

This is it, thought Sally. The three of them must have been involved in something important.

"I'm sorry Professor, I can't really tell you anything. But can you tell me if you were working on something with him and Professor Apostolonis in Athens?"

There was another stunned silence at the other end of the line.

"I can't answer that, Miss Wincott. But let me just say that our fields of interest have often coincided, however, it is obvious that we do now have a problem on our hands. Does Professor Apostolonis know about Jo's death?"

"Yes Professor. I spoke to him a short time ago." Sally was beginning to feel that she might not be alone after all.

"I'm coming to London!" announced Soulaya. "Give me your phone number, Sally, and I will call you when I arrive. And please, my dear, do be careful. Don't talk to anyone about this, do you understand?"

"I understand perfectly, Professor," she replied thinking, if he only knew how scared she was!

Sally felt almost relieved as she hung up. Now we're getting somewhere. The three of them must have dug up something so important that someone else is determined to find it. They've killed my father because of it, and now two archaeologists are flying to London to find out what he told me! They don't know that he gave me the note; should I tell them? How will I know if they really were working with him? Joseph said that I must tell no one. I will have to wait and see what they say. I daren't take any risks.

Sally stood up feeling slightly more positive. She knew she had to find a safe place to hide the note. Joseph said that no one must know who I am, but several people at the hospital do, and they know where I live because they phoned me here. So I must hide it somewhere else, but where? I can't take it to the office, because they could easily find out where I work, and anyway, I couldn't put Julie at risk. I must think of somewhere with no obvious connection with me. Somewhere where I can get at it quickly in an emergency. But where? Then, remembering that she still had to call Minneapolis, she went into the kitchen to prepare a quick supper.

Sally walked across the living room to her desk and found the card with the number of Joseph's university. Then, afraid that the living room lights might show through the curtains, she lit the small lamp on her desk and dialled the number.

"University of Minnesota," replied the operator.

Thank goodness the Americans speak English, she thought. "I'd like to speak to someone in the Department of Anthropology, please." A woman came on the line.

"Professor McCloud's office. How may I help you?"

"I hope you can," said Sally. "I need to get in touch with Dr Jordan's wife. It is rather urgent."

"Did you say Dr Jordan's wife?"

"Yes. I am hoping that you have their home telephone number."

"I'm afraid there must be some mistake," came the reply. "Dr Jordan's wife died three years ago."

"Oh! I'm sorry, I didn't know." Sally swore inwardly.

"Would you mind telling me who you are?" asked the woman.

"I am Dr Jordan's daughter, and I'm calling from London. I need to speak to someone close to him. Do you know if he had any family?"

"Just one moment please, I'll put you through to Professor McCloud."

Sally wondered if they had been contacted by the English police.

"Professor McCloud," announced a young sounding male voice. "I understand you are Joseph's daughter? I wasn't aware he had a daughter."

"I didn't know I was his daughter, until he told me, Professor. I was born in England, just after the war," said Sally, by now rather fed up with having to explain her illegitimacy.

"Good Heavens! But what can I do for you, Miss Jordan? Your father is in London, is he not?"

"Well yes and no," she replied. "I'm afraid I have some bad news."

"Oh? Has something happened to Jo?" he asked.

"Joseph died in hospital last week," announced Sally, "and I was hoping to contact his family."

There was a stunned silence from the other end of the line.

"That's terrible news! What a shock. He only recently left us, and was just beginning to enjoy his retirement."

"Have the police been in touch with you, Professor?" asked Sally.

"No, they haven't. Why? Was there some sort of an accident?" he sounded genuinely upset.

"The police are treating Joseph's death as a murder," she announced.

"Murder! Jo was murdered? Oh, my God, that's awful. Look Miss Jordan, Jo didn't have any family. There was only Jean, his wife, and she died three years ago. His work was his family. He did have a good friend at the American University in Beirut!"

"Yes, I know. I have already been in touch with him, Professor. Do you know, by any chance, what they were working on together?" Please let it be yes, she prayed.

"I didn't know he was working on anything. But I believe he met the Professor in England last year. Perhaps it was in connection with the book he was writing."

"Yes, perhaps," demurred Sally, disappointed. "So you are sure you have no idea if he was involved in something important, Professor?"

"Absolutely. If he were, I am sure he would have confided in me."

"Thank you, Professor. I will write to you when all this is cleared up."

"Yes, please do, Miss Jordan, and if there is anything we can to do help, please do not hesitate to call me."

"Thank you, I will," she said and hung up.

"Well Felix," said Sally, turning to the cat lying curled up beside her. "That didn't tell us much, did it?" Now back to the problem of the note. I must find somewhere to hide it. But Sally lay awake through another almost sleepless night, with her father's note under her pillow, boring its way into her thoughts.

Sally leapt out of bed at dawn, her head suddenly clear.

"I've got it!" she cried. "I know exactly where I'll put it."

She felt a lot better that morning, confident that once she had got rid of Joseph's note, and met the two archaeologists, she could somehow extricate herself from the whole predicament. After all, Joseph's warning that her life could be in danger might have been the exaggerated imagination of a dying man.

Sally opened the living room curtains and carefully pulled up the sash window to look down on the street below. There seemed to be no one about, and quietly locking the door behind her, she padded down the four flights of service stairs and left the building by the side entrance. She walked quickly round the corner to her car. She would have felt better taking the tube to work that morning, but she knew she couldn't leave it parked near her flat if she was supposed to be away.

Julie greeted Sally at the agency as though she had returned from holiday, throwing her arms around her and bombarding her with questions. After a short meeting with the creative team, the two friends settled down behind the closed door of Sally's office.

"Tell me all, Sal," pleaded Julie, as she handed her a cup of coffee. Then Sally told her about the phone summons to the hospital to meet a dying man who insisted he was the father she had never known.

"Shite!" exclaimed Julie. "And did he die?"

"Yes he did; and now I've got the problem of arranging his funeral and contacting his family." Sally would not tell Julie any more. There was no way she would involve her in all that had happened. She would have to take some time off and might have to go away. Having been assured that her work would be safe in Julie's hands, and that the group's senior account director would oversee her big new account, Sally called in to see the Personnel Director before leaving the agency to drive to the city.

Sally's adoptive father had worked for a large accountancy group in the City of London, and his solicitor's practice was nearby. Half an hour later, Sally climbed the dusty stairs to the third floor offices of McCrockett Smithers and Browne in Throgmorton Street.

"Sally, what a surprise! How lovely to see you again," exclaimed the now elderly Mr Smithers. "How are you my dear?"

"Hello Mr Smithers. You are looking very well," she replied as she was ushered into his office.

"Do sit down. What can I do for you, Sally?" he asked.

"This is rather embarrassing. As you know, Mr Smithers, I do have my own solicitor, but I need to ask a service of you," said Sally.

"Of course, my dear. I will help in any way I can," he replied. Then Sally told him that she had met her natural father who had since died.

"He entrusted me with something of great value, and I need to deposit it somewhere secure."

"Of course, my dear. That will be no problem at all, so long as it's not too bulky." He was struggling to hide his surprise.

"No, it's not bulky. It's this," said Sally, and opening her handbag she handed him a small envelope containing Joseph's note. The old man opened a drawer in his desk and pulled out a large brown envelope and placed Sally's note in it.

"I'll put this straight into my personal safe," he said, as he wrote Sally's name and the date on it. "It will be quite safe here."

"I'm sure it will. Thank you, Mr Smithers. I feel so much better now that I know it is in safe hands, but, if anything should happen to me Mr Smithers, you must burn it immediately. Please note that down; it is very important."

"Good Heavens Sally!" exclaimed the solicitor, his eyes popping out over the top of his rimless spectacles. "Whatever can it be?"

"I'm afraid I can't tell you that, but if it becomes necessary, it *must* be destroyed by burning." The old man broke into a spasm of coughing, startling Sally who thought he was about to choke.

"Well, dear me! I sincerely hope there's no terrifying deadly virus in the envelope," he said, trying valiantly to make a joke. Sally smiled at his unease.

"It's only a piece of paper, Mr Smithers. Just think of it as a valuable Russian share certificate, or something." She daren't tell him it might contain a microchip.

"There is one more thing, Mr Smithers," said Sally, changing the subject. "Do you have a spare set of keys for the house?"

"Of course, Sally. Would you like them?"

"Yes please. I seem to have mislaid mine, and I'd like to go down there and have a look around." Sally had inherited her parents' house in a small Hampshire village and, as she had not wished to live there it had been rented out ever since their death. She had thought that morning that it would be an ideal place to hide out, if it ever became necessary for her to leave London for a while.

"You do know that the last tenants have left, Sally? I did write to you about it," said Smithers.

"Yes of course. I'd like to see what sort of condition they've left it in, before I decide whether or not to continue to let it." Then, after collecting the key, and some lighter general conversation, the meeting ended and Sally returned to her car.

Before driving off, Sally went to a nearby phone box and dialled her home number to pick up messages on her answerphone. Professor Apostolonis in Athens had rung, asking her to meet him in the ground floor bar at the Hilton Hotel at five o'clock that evening.

One down and one to go, thought Sally. Great!

Chapter Eight

Sally arrived at the Hilton at five fifteen. She recognised Professor Apostolonis immediately in the dimly lit cocktail lounge. He was seated at a small unobtrusive table, and could only have been a Greek, she thought. He wore a white rose in his buttonhole, just as he had described in his message. He looked up as she approached.

"Professor Apostolonis?" she enquired.

"You must be Sally," he replied, standing to greet her. "I must say I never imagined I would be meeting a daughter of Jo's, and in such terrible circumstances." Sally sat down.

"It's all very strange, and I don't quite know what to tell you, Professor. Did you know Joseph well?"

"Well enough, although we had worked together only once."

"When was that, Professor? It must have been fairly recently, because I found your card in his wallet." The barman placed a glass of beer on the table and stood looking expectantly towards Sally.

"May I offer you a drink, Sally?" The Greek professor was ignoring her question.

"I'll have a glass of Chardonnay, thank you."

"Now Sally," he said, leaning towards her; "tell me about your meeting with Jo. I need to know everything."

"There's really not an awful lot to tell you, Professor. I was only with him for half an hour."

"But what did he say to you? Surely you can remember?" Sally shifted in her seat. She didn't like the Greek's manner. He sounded almost aggressive. She hesitated, wondering what she could tell him without mentioning the note.

"He didn't say much at all. He was barely conscious. He talked about my mother and said how like her I was, and he gave me a photo."

"A photo!" exclaimed Apostolonis. "Where is it? Have you got it with you?"

"No. I gave it to the police."

"The police? Why ever did you do that?" He was almost shouting, his green eyes glaring into Sally's.

"They thought it may help with their enquiries. Is there a problem with that?" she retorted. "After all, they would want to contact Joseph's friends, past and present, would they not?"

"Yes, yes, I know all that," muttered Apostolonis impatiently. "But I don't understand why you gave it to them. Didn't you want to keep it?"

"Of course, Professor. They'll return it to me later."

"My God, I hope so! What else did he say? Did he say nothing about his work?"

"No, and anyway I understand that he had retired. But you still haven't told me when it was that you worked with him, Professor."

"It was a while ago, Sally." He was still dodging the question. "Now are you sure you can't tell me anything more? What else did he say to you?"

"Only how happy he was to have met me and… oh yes… he did say that I was to be careful."

"What? Is that all? Didn't he say why?" Apostolonis was almost shouting again, and Sally felt her hackles rising.

I must keep calm, she told herself. I still don't know if I can trust him.

"He was very weak. I tried to understand what he was saying, but he was falling asleep, so I had to leave." Apostolonis sighed heavily.

"Are you sure that was all? Didn't he give you anything else, apart from the photograph?" he again insisted.

"No Professor, he did not," lied Sally.

"Then you must get the photograph back immediately," he snapped, staring straight at her.

Sally sat up in her chair, her face flushed.

"Look Professor. There is something that I must know. Were

you working on something recently with Joseph and Professor Soulaya from Beirut?"

Apostolonis looked startled.

"Why do you ask that, Sally?"

"Because I spoke to Professor Soulaya after I called you, and he asked me if I had contacted you. He sounded extremely worried about something." The Greek put his beer glass down shaking his head.

"You have rather jumped the gun, Sally. Professor Soulaya will be joining us at any moment. We had intended to talk to you when we were both here."

"Well thank you very much Professor. Now perhaps I might find out what's going on and why I have to be careful!" Sally was beginning to dislike and distrust the Greek archaeologist.

The strained atmosphere was broken by the barman who returned with a dish of nuts.

"Let's have another drink while we're waiting, shall we?" suggested Apostolonis, as he ordered the same again. "Ah, here he is!" he exclaimed, standing to greet a plump, dark-haired man who approached them, smiling broadly.

Thank God for that, thought Sally, relieved. Now perhaps we'll get somewhere.

Sally liked Pierre Soulaya immediately. There was something about the small man with liquid brown eyes that made her feel totally at ease. He also had a sense of humour that kept bubbling to the surface, in sharp contrast to the Greek's dramatic urgency.

"Well, here we are, George," said Pierre, as he grasped Apostolonis's hand and planted a kiss on his cheek. "What a terrible shock, and what a situation we now find ourselves in."

"I'm so glad you could get away, Pierre," replied George, placing an arm around Pierre's shoulder, before remembering to introduce Sally.

"I'm very pleased to meet you," said Sally, as the Lebanese archaeologist sat down beside her. "Thank you both for being here, but perhaps you will now explain your reasons for coming to London at such short notice. The news of Joseph's murder is obviously causing you great anxiety." The two men glanced at each other, surprised at Sally's assertiveness. She wasn't going to be fobbed off any longer. If any more lives were in danger, there was no time to be lost in polite conversation.

Pierre took Sally's hand in his. "Sally I am delighted to meet you. I knew straight away from our telephone conversation that we were going to be friends. I can see that you have your father's perspicuity, but let's just take this problem one step at a time. You told me that the police are investigating Jo's murder. Is that right?"

"Yes of course," replied Sally.

"Do you know how far they have progressed?"

"No, I've only seen them once, when they came to tell me that he had been poisoned."

"And do you know if they took anything of his away with them?"

"I'm afraid I have no idea, but the Almoner at the hospital told me that they had looked through his things."

"What things, Sally?" interrupted Apostolonis.

"Just his clothes and whatever he had with him when he was admitted. There wasn't very much."

"What about his briefcase? Didn't he have it with him?" asked Pierre.

"Well that's just it. I haven't seen a briefcase, or any luggage," said Sally. "When I went to his hotel to collect his belongings, the room was empty."

"Oh, no!" cried Apostolonis. "You didn't tell me that!"

"You didn't ask me," said Sally.

The barman had returned to the table. Pierre ordered a beer before turning again to Sally.

"There is something more that I haven't yet told you about," she said, looking directly at Apostolonis. "When I spoke to the hotel manager, he told me that Joseph's room had been almost totally wrecked. This was last Sunday, after Joseph had left. By the time I got there yesterday, it had been completely restored and cleaned. There was nothing to show that Joseph had ever been there, so I have no idea if there was a briefcase, or indeed, what happened to his luggage. Somebody was obviously looking for something, and I wish to God I knew what it was!" There now,

I've said it. Now let's see what they come up with. The two men were looking at each other, their faces a picture of consternation.

"But Sally," said Pierre, shifting in his seat. "Surely the hotel would have taken Joseph's luggage, would they not?"

"No, they didn't. the manager said that when the chambermaid called him to the room, there was of sign of anything belonging to him."

"Are you sure he was speaking the truth?" Apostolonis wanted to know.

"Of course. Why would he lie?" The two men exchanged glances.

"Damn Jo's memory!" muttered Pierre, some moments later. "Now look what a fix he's got us into!"

"What do you mean?" asked Sally.

"Your father had a problem, Sally. I believe I was the only person who knew about it."

"Knew about what?" asked Apostolonis.

"He had been diagnosed as suffering from the onset of Alzheimer's, and he was terrified," announced Pierre. "I noticed a marked deterioration in his memory when we met last month, and that was when he told me. Numbers were the biggest problem; he couldn't even remember his own phone number, and he had to write everything down. His pockets were stuffed with bits of paper."

"Good God, Pierre! Why didn't you tell me? Now it's too late!" cried Apostolonis. Sally was equally surprised. So that was why Joseph had given her the note! He had had to write down the numbers because he couldn't remember them.

Pierre turned to Apostolonis, who was visibly shaken, beads of sweat glistening on is bushy eyebrows.

"I take it that Sally had told you about her meeting with Jo?"

"She has, although I'm not sure that she had told me everything." Sally glared at the Greek before interrupting.

"As I said, there is very little to tell."

"But she did tell me that Jo gave her a photograph."

"A photograph?" exclaimed Pierre.

"Yes, a picture of himself with Sally's mother."

"So where is the photograph now?"

"That's just the problem. She's given it to the police," snapped Apostolonis.

"The police! Whatever for?"

"I had to give it to them," said Sally. "They are investigating Joseph's murder, remember? And anyway they've promised to return it when they've finished. It's the only photo I've seen of my mother."

"All right, my dear. But are you sure it was only a photograph?" asked Pierre. "What was it in? Was it in a frame, was it in an envelope or wrapped up? How did he give it to you?"

"It was in a small frame," she replied.

"Good God! You didn't tell me that!" cried Apostolonis.

"You didn't ask me," was Sally's response yet again.

"But did you take the photograph out of the frame, my dear?" asked Pierre.

"Yes I did, before I handed it to the police, and I assure you that there was nothing else in the frame, and nothing written on the back of the photo."

"There was nothing written on it at all: are you sure?" insisted Apostolonis.

"Yes, I'm certain, unless something was written in invisible ink!"

"And where is the frame now, Sally?" asked Pierre.

"It's at home in my flat. There's nothing extraordinary about it. It's just a cheap little frame made of wood."

"And are you certain, Sally, that he did not give you anything else?"

"Absolutely certain," she lied. "I've already told Professor Apostolonis, and I've really nothing else to tell you. Now, I really have to leave. John, my boyfriend will be wondering where I am. He must have been home for hours by now."

Pierre smiled. "Will you just give me your address, Sally?"

"You have my phone number, Professor," she replied.

"Yes, but I'd like to have your address as well in case there is a problem."

"All right," agreed Sally, as she turned away from the Greek;

but could I just have a quick word with you, Professor Soulaya."

"Oh… I'm sorry, I'll leave if you prefer," muttered a flustered Apostolonis, making as if to rise from his chair.

"It will only take a minute," said Sally, as Pierre followed her across the room.

"What is it, my dear?"

"There is something else, Professor, and I need to talk to someone, but I honestly don't have a lot of confidence in Professor Apostolonis. I really need to know a little more about your relationship with Joseph before I can tell you anything further."

"I quite understand," said Pierre. "May I telephone you tomorrow, Sally, and we'll arrange to meet somewhere and have a talk."

"Yes, thank you Professor, but it does seem obvious to me that the three of you were working on something important, and you and Professor Apostolonis seem to be very worried about it. I need to know what it is before I can feel confident, before I can give you any more information, although I don't have very much, I assure you."

"I see. It is a very tricky situation Sally, especially since poor Jo was murdered. We all have to be on our guard, you too probably. Does anyone know you went to see Jo in hospital, for instance?"

"Well yes, John my boyfriend knows, and the people in the hospital knew, of course."

"But did they know who you were?"

"Yes, they had to because they telephoned me to ask me to go."

"So they knew that your name is Sally Wincott, and not Sally Jordan?"

"That's right. And they probably have my address as well."

"Yes well this is not very good news," said Pierre, obviously concerned. Sally handed him her business card.

"I have to go into the office tomorrow, but if you call me in the morning, we will arrange to meet."

"Yes my dear, but please be careful, and don't say anything more about this to your boyfriend."

"Oh, John is absolutely trustworthy, but I did tell him what happened at the hospital," she said.

"Oh, dear, that could have been a mistake."

"Well I won't tell him anything more, or that I've met you."

"That's good, Sally. Now go straight home and keep your wits about you, and tomorrow we'll decide the best action to take. Don't worry about Professor Apostolonis. He can be a bit brusque at times, but I assure you there is nothing dishonest about him. He is an old friend of mine; we have worked together over a number of years, and I can assure you that he is absolutely trustworthy."

"Well that's a relief. I just felt that he didn't trust me, and probably because of that, I didn't like him very much. I just didn't."

"Don't worry about it, my dear. We'll have a good talk tomorrow. Now, how are you going home tonight Sally?"

"Oh, that's all right. I've got my car here."

"Well just be careful, won't you? And don't talk to anyone about our meeting."

"I won't Professor, and thank you. I shall look forward to talking with you again tomorrow. Good night."

Sally drove straight back to her office and using her staff pass card, drove down into the underground car park where she left her car for the night.

In the taxi on the way home she thought again about Professor Soulaya's warning: it was the second time she had been warned to be careful, and she began to feel scared again. It was beginning to sound really quite dangerous. What if her father's killers found her address? Perhaps she should go away. She determined that when she had found out more the next day, she would tell the Lebanese archaeologist about Joseph's note.

Sally was thinking clearly now and starting to worry about John. How on earth could she prevent him from becoming involved, after what she had already told him. The house would be the ideal place to hide out, but she had never told him that it was hers, and if that came to light now he would feel that she had been less than honest with him. Then she remembered that her agency were opening a new office in New York.

"That's it!" she cried aloud. "I'll tell John that I have to go away on business for a couple of weeks." John would be leaving again in a few days, and she could tell him that she preferred to take Felix to the kennels. Then she would take the cat down to the house and John needn't know any more. The police would surely have caught Joseph's killers before he got back, wouldn't they?

"John will have to look after himself," she muttered, feeling already guilty. "I can't warn him because if I do, he'll know that I'm holding something back, not that I know what it is, and anyway, I just can't involve him." The taxi driver was now peering at her through his rear mirror, wondering what this pretty young woman was muttering about. She looked quite sane, but then you never know who you might have in the back of your cab these days.

Sally leant forward and asked the driver to drop her off a few blocks away from her flat then, having paid him off, she started to walk back home.

It was a quiet evening and the road seemed deserted. She was about halfway back when she heard footsteps walking behind her. Oh, no! she thought. Please don't let it be somebody after me already… please! She walked a little quicker, steeling herself not to panic, but the heavy footsteps were still there. In fact they seemed to be coming closer. Sally's heart was pounding.

"Don't panic, don't panic," she muttered then, remembering what a friend had once told her, she ducked behind a parked car and crossed quickly to the other side of the road. That's it, she thought. I'll just keep crossing over and back again, then at least I'll know if he is following me. But there was no doubt about it; someone was following her.

Sally decided to change direction, away from her flat, striding quickly around a nearby building site and down a busier street. Several minutes later, feeling pretty sure that she had shaken him off, she turned back down another road towards her block. She was just approaching the main entrance when she heard the steps behind her again.

"Hell!" she muttered. "What do I do now?" Without really thinking, she bent down and took off her high-heeled shoes then sprinted barefoot round the corner to the side entrance where Bill the porter would be on duty.

"Hello Bill!" she greeted him breathlessly.

"Good evening Miss Wincott," he replied, glancing up from his racing pages. "Is everything all right?"

"I hope so Bill, but please, just remember that you haven't seen me… right?"

"Yes, I remember Miss," he replied.

"If anyone comes in behind me, just… you know… you haven't seen me, *Please Bill*!" she pleaded. Then, instead of taking the lift, she dashed round the corner and was just starting up the service stairs when she heard Bill's voice.

"Good evening Mr Brown."

"Good evening Bill," came the reply. "Was that Miss Wincott ahead of me?"

"Oh no sir. Miss Wincott's away on business."

"Oh? That's strange. I could have sworn it was her. Well good night, Bill."

Sally breathed a sigh of relief as she heard the lift doors open.

"Thank God for that," she muttered. "It was only that awful man three floors up."

John was in the kitchen when Sally limped in holding her shoes.

"Hello Darling!" she cried brightly, dropping her coat to the floor to fling her arms around him. "It's good to be back home."

Over dinner that evening, Sally told John about her worries over David, and his distressed phone call.

"I'm sorry, Darling, but you'll have to go up to see Jill. There is obviously something very wrong there."

"All right, I'll see her if I must, but that's all I need now after a tiresome tour."

"What's happened, John? Have you had problems too?"

"We had a bit of a scare on the flight back, Sal. I thought we had a hijacker on board and were about to get blown up."

"Oh, no! Whatever happened?"

"Just a false alarm, as usual," he said. "Some idiot in Tourist Class drinking champagne. But it is quite unnerving."

“Yes, it must be,” agreed Sally, as remembering Pierre’s warning, she realised that John might be in danger too, although from a very different source.

Sally woke up and turned to look at the bedside clock. It was two o’clock and John was fast asleep. Afraid of waking him, she lay still with everything going round her head again, trying to work out what she had to do the next day. She had told him about her supposed working trip to New York, but how was she going to get her stuff out of the flat if he was there? Taking Felix to the kennels was easy, and packing clothes was no problem, but she wanted to take her answerphone and fax machine down to the house. She would just have to make sure that he was out of the flat by the afternoon.

John stumbled, sleepy-eyed, into the kitchen the next morning as Sally was downing a cup of coffee before dashing off to work.

“I’ve been thinking Sal, I think I’ll make a surprise visit to Jill this afternoon, then I’ll call in at David’s school and have a talk with him.”

“Good idea, Darling,” said Sally.

“I’m afraid I’ll be off again tonight, for four days this time, Sal.” Sally felt a rush of relief at the news that John would be safely away, at least for the next few days. If whoever had killed Joseph were to break into the flat, at least John and Felix would be safe.

“Oh, Darling, I’m sorry, but that works out well with me being away, don’t you think? I must be off now, but I’ll call and let you know what flight we’re on, but I think it will be tomorrow, so I’ll take Felix this afternoon.”

“That’s fine Sal, but I’ll miss you,” he said.

“And me too, Darling, and do take care,” she replied as she kissed him farewell.

Chapter Nine

True to his word, Professor Soulaya rang Sally the next morning to arrange to meet for lunch. As the waiter handed her the menu in the small restaurant, Sally felt sure that, at last, she would find out exactly what was going on.

"I'll start at the beginning of the story, Sally," said the Professor, as the waiter headed off with their order.

"A couple of years ago I did an aerial survey of land north of Stonehenge."

"Oh yes?"

"The pictures showed traces of an ancient construction. Now the reason I am interested in Wiltshire, is because I have done quite a lot of work on the hieroglyphics at Stonehenge, on the Egyptian pyramids, and on some of the other megalithic structures in South America and elsewhere."

"Didn't they find some at Stonehenge that were similar to those on the pyramids, Professor?" asked Sally.

"That's right; and the reason I am interested in this Sally is that I am trying to find a connection between the building of these huge structures, because as we now know, they were probably built a lot earlier than was previously thought. Perhaps even before the great floods."

"Gosh!" exclaimed Sally.

"And these buildings," Pierre continued, "must have been built by intelligent people, because, there is no way that enormous structures like that could have been erected by man-power alone."

"No, I see," said Sally, now becoming intrigued.

"So the people who built these megalithic structures were obviously extremely intelligent. They had knowledge perhaps beyond our understanding, and used techniques that we are not yet aware of."

"That's exciting, Professor," said Sally.

"Now about ten years ago on Delos, in Greece," Pierre continued.

"Oh, Delos? I went there once on holiday," interrupted Sally.

"Well on Delos we dug up a couple of skeletons, and they have been hidden away in Athens ever since. Their discovery was totally hushed up, and I'll tell you about that later, Sally. But to get back to Jo..."

"Yes. How did he get involved?"

"Jo was about to retire from his university post last year, and he wasn't looking forward to it one bit. I had told him that I planned to return to England to open up a dig in Wiltshire, and he decided that he would like to join me. We went down to Wiltshire to join my team from the university, led by Marie, a very capable post-graduate student of mine, who had already made a start on mapping out the site. It resembled an airfield, but it was obviously several thousand years old."

"Good Lord!" muttered Sally, puzzled.

"We didn't realise immediately quite how important it was, but of course, after all the tests were completed, we knew we had got our hands on something quite spectacular."

"How exciting! So what happened then?"

"But it was what we found in a field adjoining the dig site that was even more extraordinary," said Pierre.

"Oh, do go on," urged Sally impatiently.

"Under the wheels of a tractor lay the skeleton of a man in a coffin-like container, and this skeleton was very similar to the two we had dug up on Delos."

"Good Heavens!" cried Sally. "Do you mean the two you found ten years earlier?"

"Exactly," replied Pierre. "It was a man, almost two metres tall, lying in what we originally thought was a burial coffin, but on it were the same hieroglyphics and the same drawing that we had seen on the Delos skeleton's container, and also at Stonehenge.

Sally's eyes were now shining with anticipation. "But that

must mean that there was a connection between these people, and Delos is half a world away from Stonehenge Professor. How could that be, unless they were flying?"

"That's exactly what it seems like, Sally," he replied. "You can imagine how thrilled Jo was. It really is extremely exciting, but I'm afraid there is a lot more to it than that, and this is the reason why it all has to be totally hushed up."

After they finished their meal, Pierre ordered some strong Turkish coffee.

"Now Sally, before going into any more details about our find, I'd like you to tell me what it is that is worrying you. Was it something that Jo said to you when you saw him?"

"Yes it was, and I'm ready to tell you now."

"That's good," he replied, relieved.

"As I told you and Professor Apostolonis, Joseph was barely conscious when I got to the hospital. In fact I thought he was asleep. I was just wondering what on earth I could say to him, when his eyes opened and he stared straight at me. Then he started to talk, but it was difficult to hear what he said with all the tubes and stuff coming out of his nose and mouth. He mentioned my mother's name and said he'd been looking for me, and then he produced a crumpled up piece of paper from under his pillow and pressed it into my hand." Pierre sat up.

"A piece of paper?"

"I thought it was a piece of rubbish, but when I smoothed it out on my lap I saw that there were two letters written on it, like initials, 'H' something and…"

"HB," prompted Pierre.

"That's right. 'H stroke B', and then three rows of numbers."

"Three row of numbers. Now I wonder what that could be," mused Pierre, as Sally continued.

"Then he suddenly seemed to wake up and looked at me really earnestly. He said that I had to be careful, and that the numbers held the key to a secret that would change the history of the world, and if anyone knew who I was, or what he had given me, then my life could be in danger!"

"Oh, Good Heavens!" exclaimed Pierre. "Poor old Jo really

has wrecked all our plans and put us in a terrible fix. I blame myself; I should have seen it coming."

"I was flabbergasted. I could hardly stop myself from laughing," said Sally. "I mean he was a complete stranger to me, and I thought he must be mad. I felt embarrassed. I wanted to run away."

"I quite understand. It must have been quite an unnerving situation to find yourself in," said Pierre.

"He seemed to calm down after that, and I promised to be careful. It was then that he gave me the photograph, but he didn't say much about it, or that it was particularly important. It was just a picture that he wanted me to have."

"Well that's a relief. We don't have to worry now about the police holding it, do we?"

"No, but I don't see why you are so worried about the police, Professor. After all, they are bound to be looking into Joseph's murder, aren't they?"

"Of course, my dear," agreed Pierre. "But because of the significance of our discovery, it is absolutely essential that no one in official circles knows what we found. The government and the church would be determined to hush it up, and unfortunately, as we now know, there has obviously been a leak somewhere, and someone is ready to kill to prevent it from being made public."

"Oh Lord!" exclaimed Sally. "That's really frightening. So does that mean that there is a religious connection, and that no one else must know about your discovery, including the police?"

"That's it exactly, Sally," said Pierre.

"This is getting too complicated for me. It's difficult to grasp all the implications and I'm getting really frightened now."

"I understand, my dear, and I don't think it would be advisable to tell you any more about it because I feel that Jo has already put you into enough danger."

"That's very kind of you, Professor, but it's not very nice being left in the dark, and whether or not Joseph was my father, he did entrust me with the note, which I think gives me the right to know what it's all about. I may be in danger anyway if anyone knows I went to see him. If whoever killed him was looking for something that they didn't find on him, they are going to think that I've got it, whether I know what it is or not, so you might as well tell me the rest."

Pierre was looking more than a little concerned.

"Yes Sally, I see your point. We'll think about that later. I'll have another talk with George. Try not to worry too much, my dear. There are the three of us in this, and we'll do all that we can to help you, I assure you."

"The most important thing now, Sally, is the note that Jo gave you. You said it had three rows of numbers on it?"

"Yes."

"Can you remember what they were?"

"Oh no, I'm sorry. I didn't memorise them. I just wanted to put it somewhere safe."

"So what have you done with the note? It's not in your flat, is it?"

"No. That's all right, Professor. I've found a very good place to hide it, and it's in safe hands. I've deposited it in the City of London with an old friend of my father's, and nobody could possibly know where it is."

"Well that's a relief," said Pierre.

"I've given instructions that it is to be handed over to no one but me and, if anything happens to me, then it is to be destroyed. I told them to burn it because I thought it must contain a microchip or something."

"Good Heavens Sally! Why ever did you think that?"

"Because why would Joseph carry a piece of paper around with him if it was so dangerous, then give it to me, his daughter, putting me at risk, when he could have memorised the numbers. So I decided it must contain something more, perhaps in a microchip hidden in one of the numbers." Pierre laughed.

"Oh I see. So that was why you seemed so relieved when I told you about Jo's Alzheimer's!"

"Yes of course. He had to write the numbers down because he couldn't remember them. But it was a terrible risk, wasn't it?"

"Yes it was, but I'm afraid that poor old Jo was becoming very much the absent-minded professor, Sally."

"Oh, dear. I am sorry."

"Jo was a very good friend of mine, Sally. I had known him for over twenty years, and we always got on well together. Our wives too were good friends."

"So it must have been a terrible shock for you when I told you on the telephone. I wish it could have been another way."

"Yes it was a shock," he demurred. "We were together just a month ago, when he came over to Beirut."

"Oh, did he? Was that in connection with your find?"

"I'm not sure. He did seem unusually secretive Sally. Ah... that's given me an idea. That must be it! Did you think those numbers might be those of a bank safe deposit box?"

"Yes I did wonder that, or perhaps a left luggage locker somewhere."

"That's it, of course," exclaimed Pierre. "The bank! That must be where he's hidden the papers. I know Jo wasn't working on anything new when he came to Beirut, and he had opened a bank account there some years ago, when we were working there. Now, if I think carefully, I might be able to remember which bank it was. It may have been the Chase Manhattan. No, it was near the MEA office in Bab Edriss, I'm sure. Yes, it must have been the British Bank of the Middle East, that's it! I think we may be getting somewhere, Sally."

"Thank goodness for that," she remarked. "But Professor, if Joseph deposited some papers there, wouldn't it be better to leave them there? If you take them out, what will you do with them if they are so dangerous?"

"We'll worry about that if and when we come to it, my dear," he replied.

Their lunch almost ended, Sally turned to Pierre.

"There is one more thing that's been niggling at the back of my mind, Professor, and that's Joseph's luggage. What happened to it? When I went to the hotel the manager told me that Joseph had arrived the week before, so he must have had some clothes and at least a briefcase; so where are they? The manager said there was nothing of Joseph's in the room. So that means whoever broke into his room must have taken all his things."

"Yes Sally, I hadn't thought of that."

"But how could they have got out of the hotel without anyone noticing? Surely no one could walk out of a hotel carrying luggage without going to the reception desk to pay the bill, or hand the key in?"

"That's a good point, Sally. This is why I am wondering about the hotel manager. Someone on the staff could have stolen his things, I suppose, or perhaps someone there was paid by the people who ransacked his room."

"Oh, dear!" sighed Sally, remembering her embarrassment in the hotel manager's office. "After the manager had told me about Joseph's room being wrecked, he asked me for some identification. He wanted to ensure that I was who I claimed to be. Why had I turned up saying that I was the daughter of someone who had disappeared without paying his bill and whose room had been wrecked? So I showed him my driving licence, and I had to tell him my name was not Jordan, and explain that I'd been adopted and that my name was Wincott. So now somebody else knows my name!"

"Oh, dear, oh, deary me," sighed Pierre.

"There you see? Now I am getting in deeper and deeper, aren't I? So don't you think you should tell me everything now, because if the hotel manager is involved, then they are going to be after me anyway!"

"Now calm down Sally. It's not as bad as all that. It may not have been anything to do with the hotel. Perhaps the police took his things."

"Yes but the police too said that there was nothing of Joseph's in the room," she cried.

"Look Sally, whether or not the police have got Jo's things, it doesn't really matter does it, because we know that there was nothing important there."

"Do we?"

"Of course, because Jo handed you the note, Sally. So let's stop worrying about that for the moment, shall we?"

Pierre signalled for the waiter to bring the bill.

"The most important thing now, Sally, is your safety. I think we should get you away from London."

"I've already thought of that, Professor," she replied. "I'm very lucky in that I inherited my parents' house in Hampshire and, as I work in London, I didn't want to live there. The last tenants left recently, so I got hold of the key yesterday, and I think I will hide out there for a while."

"That sounds ideal, Sally, but what about your boyfriend? What does he think about it?"

"He doesn't know, Professor, and I'm not going to tell him. I have taken your advice, and I am not going to involve him. When I got home last night I avoided the subject of Joseph totally, and luckily he had other problems to sort out, so that was good. While John is out tomorrow, I shall pop back home to pick up some clothes and other things, and I shall move into the house in Hampshire." Pierre stared at her astounded.

"But you can't just disappear, my dear! You'll have to tell him something." Sally laughed.

"Oh, that's all arranged. I've told John that I have to go to New York for a couple of weeks, and it's worked out well because my company has just opened an office there."

"Well done, Sally. But you will keep in touch, and let me know where you are?"

"Of course, Professor. I'll give you my phone number, so there will be no problem. But how long will you and Professor Apostolonis be staying in London?"

"I'm not sure, Sally, but we will have to go down to Wiltshire to talk to the people who were helping us on the dig last year. None of them were told exactly what we had discovered, and we must ensure that no one has found out, so it could take some time."

"Yes, of course. I hope they are all still around," said Sally.

"So do I," agreed Pierre.

"You will be able to come and see me, won't you?" asked Sally. "It won't be much fun holed up on my own in the house. Perhaps you could both drive down for dinner when you have finished?"

"I don't think that would be advisable," said Pierre. "We could be followed from Brigstone, and I think we should avoid being seen with you as much as possible."

"Oh, Lord! I'm beginning to feel like some sort of secret agent or something."

"Surely not, my dear. We're not about to start carrying arms, or anything like that! You don't have a gun, do you Sally?"

"Good Heavens no! Nobody in England has a gun; except farmers or criminals, of course. Thank goodness we are still quite a law-abiding nation."

"I wish we were," said Pierre. "It is getting a bit tricky again in the Lebanon."

"So I've heard, but I'd still love to go there. I've heard so much about Beirut. It sounds fascinating."

"Perhaps we'll take you there one day, when all this is over, Sally."

Sally turned to Pierre as they left the restaurant. "Thank you so much for meeting me for lunch, Professor. I really do appreciate your concern, and I do feel much better now, and really quite excited about what you have told me, but I do wish you would tell me the rest."

"That is enough of the 'Professor', Sally," he replied. "Please do call me Pierre. I will tell George about our meeting and then we'll decide if it would be wise for you to know any more, although, as I said, I feel that Jo has already placed you in a dangerous enough situation. George and I will be going down to Wiltshire in the morning, so I'll call you this evening, Sally."

As they stepped out into the street, Pierre grasped Sally's hands in his and kissed her on both cheeks. "Goodbye, my dear, and do take care of yourself."

"Goodbye, Pierre," she replied, returning his embrace.

As soon as Pierre's taxi had turned the corner, Sally went back into the restaurant and went down the stairs to the telephone box to call her flat. Her answerphone clicked on with her own bright greeting. Good! That means that John has gone and I can go back there quickly to collect my things.

"Sure enough when Sally arrived home, John had gone, leaving her a note propped up by the telephone.

Sal, Darling, have gone to see Jill. Will be leaving tonight – back in three days.
Don't forget to call me. Will miss you.

Love John.

PS: an Inspector McGregor called.
Said he wanted to talk to you about Dr Jordan. Told him you had already left for NY.
So glad you have forgotten all about that little episode!
XXXJ

"There Felix, that was a lucky escape, wasn't it? said Sally, as the cat wrapped himself around her ankles purring loudly. Thank goodness John has no idea about my involvement, she thought, breathing a sigh of relief.

Felix, of course, was again overjoyed to see her in the middle of the day, but not quite so happy when she took down his travel case from the top of the wardrobe and tried to get him in it! This he did not like at all. Pretending that she had changed her mind, Sally packed a few clothes in a weekend bag, unplugged the fax machine and answerphone, and filled her cold box with a few food supplies from the fridge.

Then, having left everything ready to go by the door, she fetched a towel from the bathroom, threw it over Felix and grabbing him firmly, pushed him yowling and struggling into his travel case. Bill, the porter downstairs, had a taxi waiting for her and thirty minutes later, she was unloading the still-howling Felix with her things, into her car in the office car park.

Chapter Ten

Sally crossed the river and left London on the A3 as the evening rush hour was starting to build up. Before turning onto the A31, she stopped at a supermarket outside Guildford to pick up enough supplies for a couple of weeks. By then the traffic had thinned out and, half an hour later, she turned off onto the road leading to the Meon Valley.

The house was situated on the outskirts of a small friendly village, and Sally's spirits lifted as she drove down the main street, its picturesque, bow-fronted shop windows fronted with wooden barrels planted with trailing plants. At the end of the street stood the village pub, its gardens backing onto a green governed by a cricket pitch, while all around stood a group of 18th century thatched cottages, their gardens stocked with Larkspur, Delphiniums and old English roses.

"Well Felix, what do you think of this?" she asked the dribbling cat, who by then had resigned himself to his fate and given up trying to be sick.

Sally parked the car in a lane at the side of the house and opened the envelope containing the old key to the front door. She pushed the key into the rusty keyhole and tried to turn it, but it wouldn't budge.

"Oh Lord!" she exclaimed, as Felix in his carry case started to howl. She dropped her handbag to the ground and, taking the key in both hands, tried again, this time turning it in the opposite direction. It worked, and the door flew open. Stepping into the hallway, she felt around for the main electric switch and pulled the handle. The house leaped into life as all the lights came on. Breathing a sigh of relief, Sally let Felix out of his box, turned on the water and made for the kitchen.

An hour later, Sally had settled Felix and made up a bed in her parents' old bedroom. She didn't feel hungry but felt she deserved a drink; then, with a frozen meal turning in the microwave, she flopped onto the chintzy sofa in the living room with a large glass of wine.

The silence that night after London was quite eerie, and she felt strangely alone, but a quick call to Pierre soon reassured her. Later, tucked up in the comfortable old bed, she fell into a deep sleep.

Sally awoke to the call of ring-tailed doves, the sun streaming through the bedroom window. She had slept for nearly ten hours. She jumped out of bed and pulled open the curtains to look down through the branches of an overgrown tree at the lane below. Breathing in the fresh, clean air through the window, she realised how lucky she was, and how sad that she couldn't live there. Then she padded downstairs to feed Felix.

The first thing she had to do, Sally decided, was to go to see the estate agent who looked after the house. It was only a short walk to the premises of Smith, Jones and Crump in the High Street. They had managed the letting of the house ever since she had inherited it, but she had never met them.

A young, bespectacled man was seated in the office when Sally walked in and asked to speak to one of the partners.

"I'm afraid Mr Crump is out with a client," he told her.

"Well what about Mr Jones or Mr Smith?" she enquired.

"Oh, there isn't a Mr Jones or a Mr Smith," he replied.

Here we go, thought Sally, reminding herself that this was not the West End. "Can you tell me when Mr Crump will be back?"

"He should be back before lunch. Perhaps I can help you?" he offered. "Are you looking for a property?"

"No. I am Miss Wincott, the proprietor of Lark Cottage in Bridle Lane, and I would like to speak to him." The boy blushed.

"Oh, I'm sorry, I didn't know."

"That's all right," said Sally. "Would you just tell him that I am staying in the house for a while, and will telephone him later?"

"Yes, of course," he agreed.

"There is just one more thing," said Sally as she turned to leave. "No one else is to know that I am here. Do you understand? It is vital that no one knows I am in the house. I must rely on your absolute discretion."

"All right, Miss Wincott," he replied, looking more than a little puzzled.

"Thank you. Please don't forget, will you? It really is terribly important." And with that she left the office.

The telephone was ringing as Sally let herself back into the house.

"Good morning, Sally! How are you? Did you sleep well?" It was Professor Apostolonis calling from his hotel.

"Good morning, Professor," she replied. "Yes, I'm fine. Well installed and enjoying the clean country air down here. Are you going down to Wiltshire today, Professor?"

"Yes, we are Sally. Pierre and I are happy that you have taken yourself out of London. You must stay there as long as you can."

"I will. But please do keep in touch with me, won't you?"

"Of course, Sally. We will call you this evening, but in the meantime, please do be careful. You haven't told anyone in London where you are, have you?"

"No, of course not, Professor. I hope you can find all the people you need to see in Wiltshire."

"So do I. Now I must be off, Sally. Pierre will be waiting for me."

"Goodbye, Professor, and good luck."

"Goodbye, Sally," he replied and hung up.

Sally decided that she must have been mistaken about him at their meeting. He sounded really kind today. Perhaps she should not always rely on her first impressions being correct.

It was a bright, sunny day, and Sally decided that as she was going to be stuck there for a while, she might as well busy herself with a little tidying up. The house had been empty for over a month and most of the furniture was covered with dust sheets. She knew that the estate agent had employed a local woman to keep the house clean, but there was little sign that anything had been done for weeks.

Having arranged the kitchen to her taste, Sally slowly worked her way through the rest of the house. Memories of her parents and her happy childhood came flooding back at the sight of a familiar armchair where her father had sat, a favourite picture on the staircase, and the cracked antique mirror in the bathroom. By the time she had examined and touched everything familiar that remained in her old bedroom, she realised that she was starving hungry.

Returning to the living room after a quick lunch, she picked up her phone and tapped in the code to pick up messages from her home number. John had rung and said he had presumed she must have gone to take Felix to the cattery. Relieved that she hadn't had to lie to him, she realised that she was feeling quite guilty. At the start of their relationship they had agreed the importance of being absolutely honest with each other. John had felt betrayed and badly hurt by Jill's affair with a mutual friend, and Sally was determined to prove that their partnership was based on true friendship and absolute trust. Surely it must be preferable to protect him from any danger this Joseph business might bring, than worrying about whether or not she was being totally honest? But she couldn't entirely convince herself.

Feeling a lot better after her meal, Sally decided to have a look in the attic upstairs. She remembered that some old trunks and boxes had been left up there when they had prepared the house for letting, and she was anxious to see what souvenirs remained.

It wasn't long before she came across an old metal chest marked 'Private Papers'. The lock was rusty, but Sally managed to force it open quite easily. It was less than half full and, scooping up the contents in her arms, she returned to the living room to examine them.

An official-looking brown envelope caught her eyes, and on it was written 'Sally's Adoption'. Her heart leaped, of course! Now perhaps she could find out if Joseph really was her father. And carefully extracting the yellowing papers form the envelope she sat down to read them.

There was a legal-looking document headed with the crest of Hampshire County Court, confirming the date on which the adoption had been legalised. It stated that her name was Sally Gibbs, and that she was adopted by James and Peggy Wincott. A letter from an adoption agency in London, sent to her parents, stated that they had a pretty blonde baby girl available which they thought would be suitable.

It said that the baby's mother had died in hospital after giving birth and that there was no other family. There were several other letters from the agency, and from her parents concerning the proposed adoption, but nowhere was there any mention of her natural father.

Well, at least I know my original name now, thought Sally, feeling slightly disappointed. But surely now that means that I can find my birth certificate? That, at least, might show the name of my father. Sally began to feel more confident, and determined that with her true identity confirmed, she would search through all Joseph's papers until she had got to the bottom of the mystery, even if it meant going to Minneapolis.

But Sally needed proof that she was Joseph's daughter, so how could she find her birth certificate if she was stuck in Hampshire? Then she thought of Julie. She had already told her about her meeting with Joseph, so it would be quite natural for her to want to see her birth certificate.

Sally called her office.

"Where are you?" asked Julie.

"I'm calling from Minneapolis," lied Sally, and I need a favour Julie. When you're not busy, would you mind going down to St Catherine's House? I need a copy of my birth certificate for my father's lawyer."

"Yes, I could do it tomorrow."

"That's great, Julie."

"Shall I fax it to you, Sally?" asked Julie, as she noted down Sally's date of birth and her mother's name. Sally's mind went blank.

"Damn!" How was she going to get hold of the certificate without Julie knowing where she really was?

"What?"

"I'll let you know where to send it," said Sally, giving herself time to think.

That evening Sally took Felix out into the overgrown garden at the rear of the house, and spent a relaxing evening playing cat and mouse and digging up weeds. It was after ten before she remembered that she hadn't called John, and, feeling like a naughty child, she called the flat. He ticked her off sharply for not having called on her arrival in New York! She had tried, she said, but had been unable to get through. Things were going well in the new office, she assured him, and promised to keep in touch.

The next few days passed quickly as Sally busied herself in the house, having disposed of the services of the cleaning lady.

The afternoons were spent exploring the countryside around the village, and enjoying long, exhilarating walks through the local woods. Pierre called her from Marlborough to tell her that he and George had contacted all but two of the students who had helped on the Brigstone dig.

It was almost a week later when George phoned from London to tell her that he had to return to Athens, and would like to see her before leaving. They arranged to meet for lunch at a restaurant in Winchester. During the drive over there, Sally wondered why he wanted to see her. Could it be that he and Pierre had decided to tell her the rest of the story at last?

Chapter Eleven

Sally arrived at the restaurant full of anticipation, to find George studiously studying the menu displayed in the entrance foyer.

"Sally, it's good to see you! How have you been, my dear?" And taking her arm, he led her into the restaurant. His concern seemed genuine, and Sally felt immediately at ease with him.

"It is so good of you to come down to see me, Professor," she said. "I was beginning to feel as though I had stepped into somebody else's life. Do you have any news? Has something happened?"

Sally had chosen a restaurant serving traditional English food, and, while waiting for their starter, George's face took on a troubled expression.

"Pierre is very upset, and may have to return home sooner than he had hoped."

"Oh dear, why? Is there a problem over there?"

"Perhaps not. He may be worrying unnecessarily, but all the same it could be serious."

"What is it, George?" asked Sally.

"It's Marie, his student at the university. She seems to have disappeared."

"Is that the girl who was in charge of the dig over here?"

"That's right. She hasn't been home for two nights, and nobody knows where she is."

"And does she know all about your find?"

"Of course she does, she had to. So now, of course, Pierre is afraid that something may have happened to her."

"Oh, no!" exclaimed Sally. "But Joseph was killed in London and Marie is in Beirut. Surely those people couldn't have found her, could they?"

"Who knows?" muttered George. "If they have made the connection between our Delos men and the Wiltshire find, they probably know who was involved. Pierre and I knew we were in danger after Jo was killed, but I'm afraid we gave little thought to Marie."

"So what can you do?"

"There is not a lot we can do, Sally. But Pierre is in touch with her family, and her father has informed the police. The problem now is that if they in turn make the connection between Pierre's work in England and Jo's murder, they may contact Interpol and involve London, and that will put us into an impossible situation."

"Do you mean that you will be obliged to tell them what you have found? Oh, Lord! But what about poor Marie, George. Can't you do anything?"

"Pierre is going back to organise a search with her university friends and students."

"But aren't her family going to wonder what is going on? She must have told them about the Brigstone find."

"She wouldn't have done that, Sally. She knew that it had to be kept absolutely confidential between the four of us."

"This beef is delicious, Sally," said George as he speared a whole Yorkshire pudding with his fork. Sally laughed.

"I'm glad you like it," she said. "But to get back to your mystery find, George: Pierre told me that somebody had found out about the importance of your find. So who do you think could be responsible for the leak? How can you be sure that Marie didn't tell someone in Beirut?"

"Oh, no Sally. Pierre and I are convinced that Marie would never have passed on such dissenting information, knowing full well what the consequences could be."

"Then perhaps it was one of the two local helpers that you haven't yet found?"

"That his highly unlikely Sally. It was after Pierre had closed the dig that Jo and I confirmed what we had found. However we did trace one of the missing students to London University, so we shall speak to her. The other was a French theological student at a

Dominican monastery."

"Oh, dear, so how will you see them if you are both leaving?"

"Don't worry, my dear; one of us will come back."

Taking them for a couple of foreign tourists, the waiter broke into their conversation reeling off a long list of traditional, sticky English puddings, causing them both much amusement.

"Do the English eat puddings every day?" George enquired.

"Not every day; just on Sundays," joked Sally. Then, having watched him guzzle up a large dish of steamed sultana pudding topped with creamy, yellow custard, she decided it was time to ask the question that had been burning at the back of her mind.

"Now that we are here, George, I hope you are going to tell me what all the mystery is about. Pierre did tell me about your find on Delos and a connection with the Brigstone dig, but, apart from that, I don't really know how you became involved."

"I became involved, Sally, because Pierre was using my laboratory to test the metals found in Wiltshire, and when Jo came over to Athens to compare the three skeletons, we were able to confirm the connection between the two finds. It was not until then that we knew that we held the knowledge of something so shocking that, whatever happened, it could never be revealed."

"So if your Delos two and the Brigstone Man were connected, who were they, and where did the come from?" asked Sally.

"As far as Pierre and I were concerned, it was a complete mystery. They appeared to be of some totally unknown ethnic origin, and we had no idea how they had got there."

"But George, why the big secret?" insisted Sally. "Was it something terrifying?"

"No Sally, not terrifying, but utterly inconceivable. You see, my dear, the problem lies in Jo's discovery of the identity of two of the skeletons."

"Good Lord! So they had names, these people?"

"Yes Sally, and that is precisely why I am unable to tell you anything more. Pierre and I are in absolute agreement about that."

"Oh, no, George! Why ever not?"

"Because it is that knowledge which, if made public, would overturn two thousand years of history and threaten religious beliefs. There now, I hope I have made the position quite clear to you Sally."

"Yes, I suppose so," she said. "But I still think I have the right to know. After all my father was killed because of it, and now perhaps poor Marie is in danger too." Sally was not giving in.

"Please do not insist, my dear. We do know what is best," replied George, firmly.

"But George," said Sally, as the waiter brought their coffee, "if you were all four so determined to keep the finds secret, why was Joseph killed, and why do you think we are all in danger now? It hardly makes sense. Is it something to do with Joseph?"

"Yes, I'll try to explain that, Sally," he said. "It concerns our religious and ethnical beliefs. You see, as a Greek I was brought up in the Greek Orthodox Church and, despite being a scientist, I am a believer, although not a practising Christian. Pierre, on the other hand, is a Maronite Christian, and obviously a religious man; while Jo was raised as a non-conformist Protestant, but became agnostic. Despite our different backgrounds, however, when we realised the importance of our find, we were in complete agreement that it could never be made public. It was only recently that Pierre warned me that he was so concerned about Jo.

"During his visit to Beirut, Jo had seemed troubled and secretive about something. They had a conversation one evening that had so worried Pierre, that he called me at three o'clock in the morning. Jo had become obsessed with what he considered to be his moral responsibility, and Pierre was afraid that he had changed his mind. To Jo the only thing that mattered in life was the truth. He believed that we, as scientists and seekers of truth, had a moral obligation to be totally open in our work, and that it was our duty to disclose whatever was discovered, despite the consequences or the cost to ourselves."

"I see. So do you think it was his illness that was affecting his reasoning?"

"Without a doubt Sally, and if only Pierre had told me about it then, we may have been able to prevent things from going the way they have."

"Oh, dear. I'm so sorry George."

"You certainly can't be held responsible for Jo's irrational behaviour, my dear," said George, kindly.

"I know, but I did take the note." George sat up.

"Ah… the note! Yes, Pierre did tell me about that, of course, and I am happy that you have put it somewhere safe, Sally. Pierre thinks that Jo may have hidden the papers about our research in his bank in Beirut, and that he gave you the numbers of his strong box in order that you carry out his wishes to publish our findings."

"I agree that is what seems possible," said Sally. "But rest assured that I have no intention of doing so, even though you still haven't told me the whole story. Anyway, I still have no proof that Joseph was my father, and without that I will have no access to his estate or his bank strong box, or whatever it is."

"Of course," agreed George.

"I did find my adoption papers in the house yesterday, George, so I do now know that my birth was registered in my mother's name, so I hope that my birth certificate will show the name of my father. If it doesn't, or if it was someone else, then that will be that, and whatever Joseph had hidden will lie rotting in some bank vault for ever which, come to think of it, could be the best solution, don't you think?"

"You could be right, Sally," said George, expressing a wry grin.

"Of course we don't really know if the numbers on the note were for a bank strong box, do we?" continued Sally. "They might just as well refer to something else."

"That doesn't seem very likely."

"No, but what about the initials?"

"What initials?" he asked.

"The initials on the note. Didn't Pierre tell you?"

"He didn't say anything about initials, Sally. What were they?"

"H B or H stroke B. before three rows of numbers."

"Of course! H B for Hyperboreans!" exclaimed George.

"Hyper-what? Whatever is that?" she asked.

"Hyperboreans. Have you never read about them?"

"No. Never heard of them. Who are they?" asked Sally.

"The Hyperboreans were a legendary race of highly intelligent people, pockets of whom were thought to have survived the floods of pre-history. The name Hyperborean signifies someone from a land where the north wind blows, which, according to some ancient historians, means Britain."

"Gosh! How fascinating."

"When Jo announced that the Delos two and the Brigstone Man were Hyperboreans, I thought he must be mad, but, after checking through all the latest information, I was able to concur with all that he and Pierre told me.

"Almost every ancient culture mentions the Hyperboreans, and early Greek historians wrote that it was the Hyperboreans who taught them mathematics. Nearly all the legends described them as being very tall and white-skinned, often with long white beards.

"They may also have been mentioned in the Bible as 'The Mighty Men of Old', and in South America, they may have been known as 'The Culture Bearers'. The huge City of Tihuanaco in Bolivia was built by The Culture Bearers, six or seven thousand years ago."

"Yes, I read something about that," said Sally. "What an incredible place. But I thought we were supposed to be cave men then!"

"Well we may have been, but the people who built that certainly were not!"

"But what have these people got to do with our Brigstone Man, George?"

"I'm coming to that," replied George, now thoroughly enjoying himself, as he signalled for more coffee.

"The Hyperboreans first arrived in Britain around one thousand seven hundred BC from Anatolia. At that time, the people living in the area of Stonehenge were known as the 'Beaker Folk', and they were already building a single stone circle there. There had been forms of construction on the site for several thousand years previously, Sally, and it is know that a wooden rotunda was destroyed by a tidal wave three thousand one hundred years before Christ, following the impact of a huge meteorite. Both sides of the Atlantic were demolished by the floods, and there were probably very few survivors left in Britain at that time."

"Good Heavens, George. This is a really new history lesson for me!" exclaimed Sally.

"The further you go back in history, Sally, the more exciting it becomes. That's the reason I became an archaeologist. But to get back to the Hyperboreans and Stonehenge, Sally; it is known that they integrated well with the Beaker Folk, who eventually died out. It was the influence of the immigrants that added lintels and megalithic arrangements to the site, until it became a new kind of temple, devoted to astronomy and the study of the movements of the Sun and Moon. The Greek historian, Diodorus, often mentioned the Hyperboreans and their great, round temple, and described their island, whose position and climate sounded very like Britain. Stonehenge was then the only round temple in the northern hemisphere devoted to astronomy."

"So are you saying, George, that Stonehenge was built by the Hyperboreans, and that our Brigstone Man was one of them?" asked Sally.

"Well, yes and no, Sally. But let me continue.

"A second wave of Hyperboreans arrived in Britain from Greece about five hundred years later. They had been held as slaves by the Mycenaeans for some years. This must surely be the explanation for the Mycenaean influence in the drawings found at Stonehenge, and also on our flying boats, Sally."

"Of course, but what about the flying boats, George? You don't really believed they could fly in those tiny coffin-like contraptions, do you?"

"Well, no; it would seem absurd to me, as a scientist, if it were not for the apparent airfield we uncovered, and the evidence of the drawings on the flying boats, and the magnetic clothing. However, they would surely have travelled in some larger vehicle, and their container would have been a type of landing craft. So we cannot now discount the legends which tell of the Hyperboreans flying."

"Really?"

"One Greek legend, Sally, tells of a Hyperborean who rode on 'Apollo's Arrow' to Athens and Delos, and we know that the British Hyperboreans regularly sent offerings to Delos by 'courier'. Even ancient Egyptian Literature spoke of 'Gods' who flew in the sky in machines!"

"But, George," interrupted Sally, "I know you are an archaeologist, but these Hyperboreans sound like people from outer space!" George chuckled at Sally's astonished expression.

"All I can tell you, Sally, is that although they look like humans, they are not Homo Sapiens."

"So are they extra-terrestrials, George?" she whispered, hardly able to hide her excitement, as her left hand went up to cover her mouth, her eyes fearfully scanning the nearby diners.

"Sally, my dear, that is right outside my sphere of cognition, but you, of course, are at liberty to believe what you like."

George finally settled back in his chair as Sally struggled to take in all that he had told her.

"So there you have it, my dear. A science-fiction writer's dream, and a scientist's nightmare."

"But George, it's not a nightmare. I think it's fantastic. Absolutely marvellous, and to think that, thanks to Joseph, you and Pierre could prove that all the legends and ET stories are true! How can you possibly keep it secret? I understand now why Joseph must have wanted it to be known."

"No, no, Sally, steady on. It's not the discovery of the flying Hyperboreans that we have to keep secret, it's the identity of two of them that can never be told."

Chapter Twelve

Back at the house, Sally picked up the phone to call her office.

"Sally! Thank goodness you've called. Are you still in Minneapolis?" Julie sounded harassed.

"More or less," lied Sally. "What's up? You sound upset."

"Everything's fine here, Sally, but something has happened in your flat, and I didn't know what I should do."

"Oh, no! Is it John? Has something happened to him?"

"No, I don't think so, but the police came here looking for you. An Inspector McGregor. I told him you were in New York, and he asked me to contact you urgently because someone has broken into your flat."

"Hell!" exclaimed Sally. "That's just what I was afraid of."

"What?"

"Sorry, Julie," said Sally, trying to sound calm. "It was just that I was a bit afraid of leaving the flat empty, because there have been a lot of burglaries in the area lately. But what about John? Is he back, do you know?" Sally felt suddenly afraid.

"I don't know. But shouldn't someone get in touch with your insurers?"

"Yes of course, you are right, Julie, and I'm sorry to have to ask you, but as you know the flat, do you think you could cope with it until John gets back? You will find the policy in my personal files at the office."

"All right, Sal, I'll do my best. But what about the police? What am I to say to that inspector?"

"Just say you'll let him know when I'm expected back. You can liaise with John, if you like. He should be back at any time now. I'm so sorry to have to burden you with this, Julie."

"Don't worry. Call me tonight, and I'll let you know if there are any problems, and by the way, Sal, I've got your birth certificate. If you need it in America, I'll fax you a copy." Sally's heart missed a beat.

"That's great Julie! I'm dying to know about my father. Could you just look at it and tell me if it gives his name?" she asked.

"Hold on a minute, I'll just get it," replied Julie.

Sally could barely breathe as she waited to hear Julie's voice again on the other end of the line. What if it didn't give Joseph's name? But it did, and she knew immediately what she wanted to do.

"Could you put a copy in the post to my solicitor, and keep a copy for my file, Julie?" she asked. "And thank you so much. You have done me a big favour." And promising to buy her friend a super lunch when she got back, she hung up.

Sally sat down on the sofa and tried to collect her thoughts. So much had happened that day that she felt quite distracted. Her initial excitement over what George had told her was now replaced by the fear she had managed to control since leaving London. What on earth had happened at the flat, and where was John? Was he all right? She must call the flat; he would surely be there by now. But what time would it be in New York? She looked at her watch. It was five minutes past five, so it would be mid-morning there. She picked up the phone and tapped in her number.

"Sal, Darling!" he cried. "I've been trying to call you. Where the hell have you been?"

Oh Lord! Now he's bound to find out that I'm not in New York, she thought.

"I thought you'd forgotten me. How's it going over there?" asked John.

"I'm sorry, John. It has been pretty hectic, and we've had trouble with the phones. But tell me, what's happened at the flat? Are you all right?"

"I'm fine, Sal. I got back this morning and the break-in was yesterday."

"Thank God you are all right," said Sally. "Julie told me what happened, and I was worried."

"They've made one hell of a mess, but don't worry Sal, I'll sort it out."

"You are wonderful, Darling. I don't know what I'd do without you, I need you John. You don't know how much."

"Steady on, Sal. You'll be back soon, won't you? I've got a break coming up, so we'll have a long weekend away somewhere romantic, shall we?"

"Oh, yes please, Darling. That would be wonderful."

"There is just one slight problem, Sal," said John, now sounding rather solemn.

"Yes?"

"It's the police. They've been here all morning poking about and asking questions. I think you may be holding something back from me, Sally."

Oh, Hell! It must have been Inspector McGregor again. What on earth has he told John? She wondered. "Why? What do they want?" she asked.

"The inspector thinks the break-in may have some connection with that man in hospital. He told me that he had been murdered Sal. Did you know about that?" Sally felt her face flushing. Now what would she say? She would have to tell him something.

"Yes, John, I did know but I didn't want to worry you. It was after you left. Two policemen came to see me."

"But Sally why on earth didn't you call me? This is beginning to look quite serious after what you told me about him. If the flat's been broken into, you could be in danger, don't you see?" Sally's hand started to shake as she clutched the phone.

"Don't be cross with me, John," she pleaded. "I was only concerned for you. I know that you have enough worries to contend with, and I didn't want to involve you."

"That's ridiculous, Sally, because I am involved, and God knows what might have happened if I had been there."

"I know, John, that's why I have been worried about you," she replied.

"Well, thank you, and a lot of good that would have done if I'd been assaulted!"

Sally didn't know what to say. She knew that she should have warned John, and yet she remained convinced that she should not involve him.

"Well, Sally, all I can say is, thank God you are in New York, because if you had been here, you could have been killed! Perhaps now you will tell me what's going on?" Sally's courage returned.

"I'm really sorry, John, but there really is nothing to tell. How could I have known that someone would break into the flat?"

"That's not good enough, Sally. You are not being honest with me, and I am angry and terribly disappointed. I suggest that you arrange to get back here as soon as possible, and we'll talk it through together. In the meantime, you had better get in touch with the inspector. I don't want him on my back all week. Just let me know what flight you'll be on, and I'll meet you at the airport." And before Sally could object he had hung up.

Sally replaced the receiver and burst into tears. John had every right to be angry with her, but she had never experienced it before, and it hurt. She felt she had betrayed his confidence, and she couldn't see how she could make amends. Felix crawled up onto her lap and licked her face. He couldn't bear to see Sally cry.

It was almost dark when Sally woke up on the sofa. She unwound the sleeping cat from her arms and went into the kitchen to make a cup of tea. She needed to talk to someone and, remembering that Pierre was returning to Beirut, decided to call him to ask his advice.

Pierre was not in a very receptive mood to help Sally with her problems. He had been on the phone to Beirut all afternoon, trying to reassure Marie's distraught family.

He too felt guilty. If Marie had been kidnapped, it could mean that someone knew that he had taken her into his confidence. On the other hand, it could have been some Muslim extremists who had taken her as an easy ransom victim. Everyone in Beirut knew that Marie's father was a wealthy man.

"George told me about Marie, Pierre," said Sally. "I am sorry. Do you really think her disappearance has some connection with your Hyperborean find? Couldn't she have just gone away for a few days?"

"No Sally, I am terribly afraid that something has happened to her, and I am going back tomorrow to see what I can do to help. She is such a responsible girl, she would never just go off without telling someone, and she is devoted to her family who, of course, are terribly worried."

"I'm sure she'll turn up, Pierre. You never know, she may be back home before you get there."

"Thank you Sally, but I doubt it," he said. "Now tell me, Sally, how are you getting on down there? You haven't had any problems, have you?"

"Not until today," she told him.

"Oh, my dear, what has happened?"

"My flat has been broken into and ransacked, and now John, my boyfriend, is convinced that I am hiding something from him, and he is furious."

"Thank goodness you were away, Sally. But what about John? Was he involved?"

"No. Luckily he came back the following day, but the police were there and have told him that Jo was murdered and that I am in danger! So of course, John is absolutely furious with me, and to make matters worse, he thinks that I am in New York, so I just don't know what to do. I really think that I will have to tell him something, Pierre."

"Oh, dear me, poor Sally. What a mess we have got you into. But you are right, of course. You will have to give him some explanation. Could you not just say that you thought the police would have caught Jo's murderer long before he got back, or something like that?"

"Yes, I'll try."

"If John loves you, once he gets over his anger, he will understand your motives for not wanting to involve him. I think you could safely tell him that Jo had made a very important discovery, and that there are people who want to know what it was; but you must stress, Sally, that it is to be kept strictly confidential. He must not mention it to the police, or anyone else. Do you think you can do that?"

"Yes, of course, Pierre," she agreed.

Sally then told Pierre about her birth certificate.

"My natural father was Joseph William Jordan," she announced.

"That's wonderful! I always knew it. You are very like Jo, Sally, in many small ways. But I suppose this means that when you have access to his estate, and will be wanting to go to Beirut to see what he has left there?"

"Exactly," she replied.

"Well I wouldn't be in too much of a hurry if I were you, Sally," he warned. "In any case you will have to see Jo's lawyer, won't you?"

"I know. But don't worry Pierre, if I do decide to go, I will let you know, I promise."

"I too have some better news, Sally. We managed to find one of the missing students who helped us on the dig."

"And did he convince you that he knew nothing of the results?"

"It was a girl at London University and, although she was very interested, I am convinced that the leak could not have come from her."

"So that leaves just one more?" asked Sally.

Yes, the French boy, but he seems to have left the college where he was studying, so he remains a bit of a problem. But we will trace him, even if he has returned to France."

"Oh, dear, and he sounds a possible candidate, don't you think?"

"Perhaps, but let us hope not," he replied.

"Are you leaving tomorrow, Pierre?"

"Yes my dear. I really must see what I can do to help Marie's family, and anyway, I have to get back to the university."

"I shall miss you, Pierre, and with George leaving too, I shall feel really alone with this business hanging over my head."

"Try not to worry, Sally. I am sure that once you have had a talk with John, he will give you all the support you need."

"I hope so, but I am afraid that he is just too angry and disappointed with me at the moment to understand anything."

"We will keep in touch with you, Sally," said Pierre. "But please don't forget that if you have any problems at all, you must call me or George immediately."

"Thank you so much Pierre. I really do appreciate all your help. You have been a real uncle to me, and I will never forget your kindness."

"Goodbye, Sally," said Pierre. "You just look after yourself, and we'll meet again soon." And with that, he hung up.

Sally sat down on the sofa and started to weep uncontrollably. She had never felt so alone and afraid. She wanted to call John, but she knew that he would still be angry. She would call him in the morning, by which time she hoped he would be ready to listen. It would be feasible to tell him that Jo had made a discovery so important that somebody was determined to prevent it from being made public, but she was certain that he would never believe there were pre-historic men who could fly! It was a pity that she had told him about the note because he would want to know what she had done with it, and she wasn't going to tell him. She couldn't see a problem in telling him that she had contacted Pierre and George after finding their cards in Jo's wallet, but if he didn't believe that she didn't know the whole truth about what they had found, it was too bad.

A wave of sobbing startled Felix, who was curled up on her lap. How on earth could she explain her decision to leave London without either warning him, or telling him where she was going? There was no answer to that, other than that she panicked on hearing that Jo had been murdered. But what about the house? He would be even more angry that she had never told him about that!

Sally's mind was in a whirl. She just couldn't work out any rational explanation for her behaviour that would be acceptable to John. Whatever she said was bound to make things worse between them. She couldn't eat anything and, continually topping up her glass from the bottle of wine she had opened, did nothing to stem the flow of tears which came and went all evening. Eventually she tried writing down all the possible explanations on a piece of paper, dividing them into acceptables and impossibles, but that only confused her even more and she tore it up in a rage. By the time Sally crawled upstairs to bed at one o'clock, her mind was a complete blank and she fell into an exhausted sleep.

Sally awoke with a headache the next morning.

"I'm going to ring John now, and if he doesn't like it, I don't care," she announced to Felix, as she chopped up a small piece of liver for his breakfast. "If he can't understand that I was trying to protect him and never meant to hurt him, that's just too bad. I'll manage without him." And she clonked into the living room armed with a strong mug of coffee.

The phone rang in the flat for some time before John picked it up.

"Hello John, it's me," said Sally.

"Sally! I'm sorry, I couldn't get to the phone. I had shaving foam all over my face."

"Listen John; please don't be cross with me, but I must talk to you. I can't come to London just yet."

"Fair enough, Sally. I'm sorry I was so angry with you yesterday, but you do owe me an explanation."

"I know I do, John, but it's not something I can talk about on the phone."

"Well, when are you coming back, Sally? I want to know what's going on."

"Of course you do, Darling, and I'm going to tell you, but please be patient and try to understand what I am going to say to you now." Then, crossing her fingers, she took a deep breath.

"I am not in New York, John, in fact I haven't been there at all."

"What?" yelled John down the phone. "Then where the hell are you?"

"I am in Hampshire, and I want you to come down here for a few days so that I can explain everything to you."

"Are you mad? Why the hell should I go down to Hampshire? I've only just got back."

"I can't come back to the flat yet, can't you see? It's too dangerous. You know that. The inspector told you that whoever broke in was looking for something, and it may be the note Jo gave me, remember?"

"All right, but I'm here now, Sally, and they've already been here. They are hardly likely to come back."

"But they killed my father, and they didn't find anything on him," cried Sally.

"That man was not your father, Sally!" John sounded angry again.

"Yes he was."

"Oh, come on, Sally, now you really are talking nonsense."

"I am not talking nonsense, John, and please stop shouting at me. My birth certificate confirms that he was my father."

"Ah… so now you've found your birth certificate," he mocked. "And how did you do that if you are in Hampshire or God knows where?" Sally sighed.

"Because I found my adoption papers in the house, John. That's how."

"In the house? What house?"

"In my parents' house, of course," she said.

But your parents' house was sold, wasn't it?"

"No, it was never sold. It was let."

"Excuse me for appearing to be a bit dim," shouted John, "but how did you find your adoption papers in the house if it was let?"

"Because, John, it is my house, and that is where I am staying," said Sally.

"What?" he yelled again. "Your house? What the hell are you telling me now, Sally?"

"I'm telling you, John, that I am staying in my house in Hampshire," said Sally as loudly and firmly as she could. "And that I would like you to join me here for a few days so that I can have a chance to talk to you calmly about my father and his discovery."

"Not bloody likely!" yelled John, now furious. "Do you think I am some sort of an idiot, Sally? Not only did you omit to tell me that that man in hospital was murdered, but you took yourself off out of London, pretending that you were in New York; and to top it all you now announce that you own a house in Hampshire! Well that's it, Sally. I've had enough of this nonsense. I don't want to hear any more about it." Now it was Sally's turn to lose her temper.

"If you think it's nonsense," she shouted, "why do you think my father was murdered, and my flat ransacked? Just tell me that?"

"I don't know, and quite frankly I don't care. All I know is that you have lied to me Sally, and that I will not tolerate," replied John in his airline captain's voice.

"Fine," snapped Sally. "If you won't even give me a chance to explain, you have obviously never had any confidence in me. I don't want to argue with you, John, but as you are determined to mistrust me, I see no reason to continue trying to reason with you. Goodbye!" and she slammed down the phone.

Sally was shaking with anger. How could John speak to her like that? The arrogant pig! How dare he say she was talking nonsense. She couldn't believe that it had happened. Of course, he would be annoyed that she had kept her involvement in Jo's find a secret, but to refuse to even listen to her reasons was intolerable. Then his fury over the house! She had never intended to keep that from him. She had just never thought about it, had almost forgotten that it was hers.

"Well Felix," she said as she scooped the cat up into her arms and marched into the kitchen.

"They say you never really know someone until you live with them, but I'd say it's more that you never know them until they lose their temper, wouldn't you Felix?

"Damn John! Damn, damn, damn all chauvinistic bloody men!" she yelled, as she grabbed a large wok pan and threw it against the wall. The crash sent Felix flying across the room and straight out of the window. Sally sank to the floor and burst into tears.

"Now I've lost Felix," she sobbed. "He'll get lost and I'll never see him again!"

Sally crawled out of bed and looked at the clock. It was half past three. She sat at her dressing table and peered at her blotchy face in the mirror. She had cried herself to sleep and her eyes were puffed and swollen. What a stupid fool I was to get so upset. Pierre was right. If John loves me he will get over his anger and forgive me, and if he doesn't, then tough luck. I'll be better off without him. The sun was shining and she needed some fresh air, so after a quick shower, she set off for a long walk. On her return an hour later, she found Felix sitting perched on top of the gatepost.

Chapter Thirteen

Sally wanted to talk to someone. She picked up the phone and called Julie.

"Is everything all right?"

"Fine. It's very quiet here; there's not much happening. But is John back Sally? I've been ringing your number, and there's no reply."

"Oh, Lord! Yes, John is back, and we had a terrible row. If you do get hold of him can you do me a big favour, Julie?"

"Of course."

"Please don't tell him that I am in Minneapolis, or he will go completely spare."

"Why ever not?" asked Julie, giggling.

"Because I am not in America, Julie. I'm down in Hampshire, and I told him that I was going to New York."

"Yes, I know you did, Sally. But what on earth are you doing in Hampshire?"

"I am sorry Julie, but it is too complicated to explain on the phone, but I did tell you that I had to find my father's family."

"Yes, you said they were in Minneapolis."

"That's right, but the fact is that I had to leave London because I am in danger, Julie."

"Why? How can you be in danger, Sally?"

"My father didn't just die in hospital, Julie. He was murdered."

"Oh, God! Was he the American professor found dead in hospital that was all over the news?"

"That's right."

"But what's happened? Can't the police help? That inspector who came here keeps calling, and I don't think he believes me anymore."

"Oh Julie, I'm so sorry. I really didn't want to involve you. I had to tell John where I was, and he was furious and refuses to come down here."

"Are you sure you shouldn't talk to the police, Sally?"

"Absolutely. They must never find out why my father was murdered, or that I am in any way involved."

The following day Sally had a visit from Mr Crump, the estate agent, who wanted to know how long she would be staying in the cottage and if she wished him to find another tenant. He was a fusty old fuddy-duddy, and seemed quite put out that he hadn't been advised of her stay. He was even more surprised when she told him that she preferred not to re-let the cottage for the time being, thus cancelling out his management fee. Sally apologised for not having kept in touch, although she felt no sympathy. He had put in three lousy tenants, causing problems and expensive work for the solicitors. She was in her business mode that morning, and nobody was going to upset her anymore.

Sally had just shown Mr Crump out when the phone rang, causing an unwelcome jolt. She was sure it must be John, and she didn't want ./to speak to him, at least not yet.

"Hello!" she answered carefully. It was Julie. "Thank goodness. I thought it was John. Is everything all right, Julie? You sound upset."

"I'm not sure," replied Julie. "I had a bit of a scare this morning, after what you told me yesterday."

"Oh, no! What happened?"

"I popped out for a coffee, and when I came back there were two strange men wandering round the office."

"Good grief! Who were they?"

"I don't know, that was what worried me, Sally. I asked them what they wanted and they said they wanted to see you. I assumed they must be more policemen, but when I asked to see some identification, they laughed."

"Shite!" exclaimed Sally. "What did you do? Did you tell them you are my secretary?"

"Well yes, of course."

"Shite!" swore Sally again. "What did they look like, Julie?"

"They were both dark, quite swarthy, and smartly-dressed in business suits. I thought they looked at bit Mafioso, and the one who spoke had an accent, like Italian."

"Oh, no! But how did they get past reception, Julie?"

"I suppose they just walked straight in. There's a 'temp' on reception this week, so she probably thought they worked here." Sally felt suddenly dizzy.

"Now listen, Julie, I want you to go straight to Personnel and tell them you need to take the rest of the week off. I'll call and arrange everything. You must leave as quickly as possible. Do you understand?"

"But Sally, what about work? I can't just go off and leave everything," objected Julie.

"Yes you can; you must. But before you go, would you take all my papers of out my personal file and put them in the cupboard downstairs?"

"Of course, Sally. I'll do it straight away, but I really can't see why you are so worried."

"I am deadly serious, Julie. This is no joke, I promise. You must be away within the hour. Promise me you'll go?"

"All right, I promise," said Julie with a sigh.

"Thank you, and don't worry. You just go straight home and I'll call you tonight."

"All right, Sally, I'll do what you ask, but I do wish I knew what all this is about."

"So do I, believe me. But just remember that my father was murdered, so forget about work, and let's keep ourselves in one piece. Take care, and we'll talk later." And she hung up.

All of Sally's resolutions for a calm, level-headed day went out of the window. She felt really concerned for Julie, and downright scared for herself. There was now no longer any doubt in her mind that she was in real danger. Whoever it was that killed Jo must have assumed that he had given her something. They had smashed up her flat and traced her to her office, and now, because of their connection with her, both John and Julie were in danger too.

Sally needed help, but who could she turn to? Surely now she should call Inspector McGregor? There was no way she could risk anything happening to either John or Julie. Both Pierre and George had insisted that the police must never know about their Brigstone find, but as she still had no idea what the big secret was, she could surely ask for their help. The police were already investigating Jo's murder, and knew that someone was looking for something, so why not say that she thought that Jo must have found something valuable? There may be other lives at risk whatever they thought of her story.

Sally was almost ready to call the inspector when the phone rang again. This time it was George calling from Athens. As soon as she had finished recounting the day's events to him, she sensed that he was on the defensive.

"What are you going to do now, Sally?" he asked.

"I'm going to call the police. I simply cannot risk anything happening to John and Julie. I don't have any choice, George."

"Sally, I beg you, don't do that. Don't you remember what I told you? If news of our discovery gets out it could mean absolute chaos, and probably war! I thought you had understood the religious implications!"

"How can you expect me to understand when you refuse to tell me exactly what it was that you found, George?" Sally's frustration was turning to anger.

"We thought you at least understood that we were trying to protect you, Sally."

"But you can't protect me, or anyone else George," she shouted. "You are in Athens and Pierre is in Beirut, looking for Marie, and I'm here with my flat broken into and Mafioso-type men wandering around my office. What do you expect me to do? Just lie down and wait for them?" Then she outlined what she planned to say to Inspector McGregor.

George listened patiently.

"That sounds all right, Sally, but surely you realise that once the police get on to the story of the dig in Wiltshire, they won't leave it at that. They will be down there, interviewing anybody who knows anything about it, and it won't be long before they hear about our Brigstone Man. No Sally, I'm afraid it is out of the question. You simply cannot involve the police."

"Then I'll talk to Pierre," insisted Sally. "I am not going to leave Julie or John without some sort of protection, and that is final!"

"Well Sally, I am very sorry that you refuse to heed my warning, but at least promise me that you won't do anything before you have spoken to Pierre."

"Fair enough, George," agreed Sally. "But I'm afraid that my mind is made up."

Sally wandered out into the garden. She really didn't know what to do. She was reluctant to call Pierre again, knowing that after his sudden visit to England, he would not only be busy at the university, but also occupied with the search for Marie. If only John had agreed to come down, she would at least have another viewpoint. She desperately wanted to talk to him, but was still afraid to call. She couldn't face another row.

This is ridiculous, she told herself, as she walked about pulling out weeds. I've got to talk to him about the insurance, and I'm not going to let him upset me again. I must warn him. He can't stay in the flat. He'll just have to come down here.

Sally marched back into the house and picked up the phone. She was hoping that he would still be out so that she could just leave a message. The phone rang once before his greeting clicked on.

Thank God! Thought Sally. She took a deep breath, determined to sound confident. "Hello John; it's me," she said into the machine. "John I'm really worried about you and Julie. Some strange, foreign-looking men have been to my office looking for me, so I have arranged for Julie to stay at home for the rest of the week. I just can't risk anything happening to her if they break in and smash up my office, like they did the flat, and you really mustn't stay there, John. Please try to understand. However angry you are with me, you must come down here. I am so worried about you. Call me as soon as you get back and I'll tell you how to get here. I need you so terribly, Darling, and I do love you; you know that." Then she hung up as tears started to roll down her face.

Sally went into the kitchen to feed Felix.

"If he doesn't call tonight, I'll know that he's still angry with me, so we will just have to manage without him, won't we, Felix?" she said to the cat. There was a good film on the television that evening and, by the time it was over, it was past eleven o'clock, and John hadn't rung back.

"Damn you, John!" she muttered. "If you ring now, you can leave a message." And she went to bed.

When Sally awoke the next morning, John still hadn't phoned. She went downstairs and called her insurance company. Then she called Pierre's office number at the university, but she was told that he had not yet arrived. Hoping that he would still be at home, she called his number. Nadine Soulaya picked up the phone immediately.

"*Na-am*?"

"*Bon jour Madame*," said Sally. "*Puis je parle avec Professor Soulaya, s'il vous plait*?"

"*Il n'est pas la. Qui êtes vous*?" Nadine sounded harassed, even angry.

"It's Sally Wincott, calling from England, Madame," answered Sally, breaking into English.

"Oh, Miss Wincott, Jo's daughter! I am so sorry, I was expecting another call. I can't talk to you now, Sally. We have a problem here, and I must keep the line free."

"I'm sorry, Madame," said Sally, "but is Pierre not there?"

"Pierre is not here," said Nadine, "and I don't know where he is. He didn't come home last night, and I am terribly worried."

"Oh no!" cried Sally. "You don't think that something has happened to him, do you?"

"I don't know what to think, my dear. Pierre has never done anything like this before. It is just not like him, but with Marie's disappearance, I am quite terrified, and I have called the police."

"I am sure he will turn up. He is probably out looking for Marie with her friends, don't you think?"

"No. I have called them all, and her parents too, and nobody has seen him since yesterday. Now I really must hang up, Sally, in case somebody calls."

"Of course. I understand," said Sally. "Goodbye, Madame, and

I will be thinking of you."

"Goodbye, Sally, and thank you for your concern."

Sally put the phone down. She felt a knot forming in her stomach and her head started to pound. Oh, please don't say that something has happened to Pierre, she thought despairingly. Not to sweet, kind Pierre. It can't be true! What on earth should she do now? She wanted to crawl into a hole and hibernate. Why did her father have to pick on her with his secret?

"Oh, God!" she yelled.

Sally made herself a mug of strong, black coffee and topped it up with whisky.

"This is a great way to start the day," she muttered, as she sank down onto the sofa.

"George!" she cried suddenly. "I bet he doesn't know. I'll have to warn him," she told Felix who sat crouched next to her, his head cocked to one side. She picked up the phone and dialled his number at the university, but he wasn't there. Then she tried the metallurgy laboratory, but he had just left. Finally Sally called her flat again.

"Be there, John, please," she muttered, but the answerphone came on. He was still out. "What the hell do I do now?" She wanted to scream; she felt so useless and frustrated. "It's at times like this that people go mad, letting out farm minks or something. I think I'll just get drunk!"

Minutes later, and in a calmer frame of mind, Sally picked up her notepad and wrote out a message.

> URGENT: For the immediate attention of Professor Apostolonis.
>
> Dear George, tried to call Pierre but his wife told me he didn't go home last night. She thinks something may have happened to him and has called the police. Do call her, she is terribly worried.
>
> Please take care of yourself.
>
> Sally

Then she faxed it to the university.

Sally spent the rest of the day in a haze, wandering about the house, unable to concentrate on anything. She washed all the old bed linen, mowed the lawn and painted the garden fence. By four o'clock George hadn't phoned and neither had John, and she started to believe that it was all over between them. She went inside to make a cup of tea and switched on the television, determined to block out her fears about Pierre.

Sally awoke with a start, the telephone ringing in her ears. She jumped up in the dark, knocking the phone to the floor.

"Sally, are you there?" It was John. She scrambled to pick up the phone, her hands were shaking.

"Hello! Yes I'm here, John. I fell asleep."

"Are you all right?" he asked. "I've only just got back from seeing David."

"Oh, good. How was he?"

"David's all right, but it's you I'm worried about, Sal."

"Well that's very kind of you, John," she said with more than a hint of sarcasm in her voice.

"All right, Sal. I know I was a bit rough on you, but surely you can understand my anger?"

"Perhaps I do, John; and that is precisely why I asked you to come down here so that I could explain everything to you, but if you prefer to stay in the flat and be the next person to disappear, then be it on your own head."

"What do you mean, the next person to disappear?" he demanded.

"For Heaven' sake John, stop asking questions on the phone! Why can't you just come here as I ask? I can't tell you anything like this. It's all far too complicated."

"But what's all this about people disappearing, Sally? Just tell me that." Sally sighed heavily into the phone.

"Look, John," she said forcefully, "Joseph Jordan, my father, was murdered in London by someone who was looking for something, right? Then my flat was ransacked, and two foreign men came looking for me in my office; and now, one of his archaeological colleagues and his assistant are both missing in

Beirut. Now, are you coming down here or not?"

"All right, Sally, you've made your point. I'll drive down tomorrow if you promise to tell me everything that's been going on. But I still don't understand why you haven't called the police inspector. Sally. He's left another message here. Surely this is a matter for the police?"

"No, John the police are not to be told anything. Promise me you won't tell them where I am, please? I'll explain everything when I see you."

"All right, Sal, calm down. I'll see you tomorrow. Just tell me how to get there." John sounded almost his kind, fatherly self again.

Sally explained the route to John, and arranged to wait for him in the market square at Petersfield.

"That's fine, Sal; and by the way…"

"Yes?"

"Where's Felix?"

"He's with me, of course."

"Ah, another lie."

"For God's sake, don't start again, John!"

"See you tomorrow, Darling," he said, and hung up.

Chapter Fourteen

Sally and John were eating dinner the following evening when the phone rang.

"Leave it Sal. Let's at least have this evening together without any more upsets. If it is any of your archaeology friends I don't think I can take any more about giant hyperwatsists, or whatever it was they dug up."

"Well, how do you think I feel, John? I've been scared silly, trying to make sense of it for weeks!"

"If you'd been honest with me from the start, Sally, I may have been able to put a stop to all this nonsense. I would have told your so-called friends to sort out their own problems."

"But, John, you know damn well that, like it or not, I was involved from the moment Jo gave me the note."

"That's just where you went wrong, Sally. As soon as you heard that he had been murdered, you should have handed it to the police, but what did you do? You went and hid it!" Sally sighed.

"Please stop arguing about it now, John. I did what I thought was right, and, after all, he was my father. There's no point in going on about it. I've told you everything I know and I just wish you would try to understand and give me some support."

"All right, Sal, I'm sorry. You are right. What's done is done. Let's try to forget about it, shall we? At least for tonight."

As Sally switched off the lights in the living room later, she noticed the signal flashing on her answerphone. Someone had left a message. She felt tired, and following John's advice, she followed him upstairs to bed.

It was almost eleven o'clock when Sally awoke with John's arms wrapped around her. She stretched languidly, reliving their blissful night together, then, realising how near she had come to losing him, she vowed that she would never withhold anything from him again. She climbed carefully out of bed and padded downstairs to feed Felix and make some coffee.

The phone was ringing when Sally and John returned from their walk an hour and a half later.

"Now will you let me answer it, John? It may be Julie," asked Sally, a hint of sarcasm in her voice.

"Of course," he replied with a grin, as Sally rushed into the living room and grabbed the receiver.

"Sally! Where have you been? I have been trying to reach you since yesterday. Are you all right?" It was George calling from Athens.

"Oh George, I'm sorry, but did you get my Fax?" she asked.

"Yes I did, Sally, and I called Nadine Soulaya straight away."

"How is she? Is Pierre back?"

"Listen Sally…" George's voice was almost breaking. "I have some very bad news."

"Oh, no!"

"I'm afraid so." Sally slumped down onto the settee, her heart pounding as George continued. "There's been a terrible accident. He was found yesterday, out on the Junieh road. His car was completely burnt out."

"Oh, please no!" yelled Sally, breaking into anguished sobs.

"What the hell?" shouted John, as he rushed into the room. "Whatever it is, Sal?" he cried, grabbing the phone from her hand.

"Hello! Who are you?" he shouted.

"It's Professor Apostolonis in Athens," replied George. "You must be John. Thank Heavens you are there with Sally."

"I quite agree," snapped John. "Now tell me Professor, what has happened to upset Sally so?" Sally grabbed John's arm.

"It's Pierre. They've killed him," she sobbed.

"Yes, I'm afraid that Pierre is dead," said George. "The police found him yesterday, but they are treating his death as an accident."

"Is this your friend in Beirut who was working with Sally's father?" asked John.

"That's right. I take it Sally has told you everything."

"She has, and not before time."

"Sally was trying to protect you, John. We advised her not to involve you."

"So what would you advise her to do now, Professor."

"She must just keep her head down and stay where she is until this has blown over," was George's reply.

"And how do you suggest it will 'blow over', Professor?" mocked John. "Are we to wait until both you and the girl, Marie, are killed too?" There was no reply from the other end of the line.

"For God's sake, John!" shouted Sally. "How can you talk to George like that when his friend has been killed and his own life is in danger?" And she yanked the receiver from his hand.

"George, I'm so sorry. It's just such a terrible shock. I can't take it in. May I call you back later?"

"Of course, my dear," agreed George quietly.

"I'm really afraid for you, George. You will take care of yourself, won't you?" pleaded Sally.

"Don't worry about me, Sally. You two just look after yourselves, and we'll have a talk tomorrow. Goodbye, my dear," said George, and hung up.

Sally turned on John.

"How could you speak to George like that, John! He must be beside himself with grief, and fear too probably. How can you be so heartless?"

"All right, Sally, I was a bit over the top. I'm sorry, but I am still feeling angry over this whole affair, and to see you getting so upset just made me see red."

"George, as well as Pierre, has been a good friend to me these last few weeks, John. I don't know what I would have done without them so, if you can't at least be civil, I prefer that you don't speak to him again. I don't know what's got into you John. Where's that understanding, cool, calm airline captain whom I fell in love with?"

"He's still here, Sally," he replied, sheepishly. "I apologise. Can we just forget that little incident now?"

"Well, I can't forget that lovely, kind Pierre is dead," sobbed

Sally, breaking down completely. "What on earth are we going to do now? I'm so frightened, John."

Sally's whole body shook with sobbing as John held her tightly against his broad chest. He could find no words to comfort her, for he realised that he felt almost as useless and frustrated as she did. Thirty minute later, John went upstairs to the bathroom to fetch a cold face flannel to bathe Sally's swollen eyes.

"Buck up Sal, I'm going to make you a nice strong cup of tea, then I think we must try to work out exactly what we are going to do."

"Yes, John," she said.

It was past two o'clock when John picked up Sally's large lined notepad.

"Right, first things first. I have got to contact your insurance people."

"And I simply must call my office. I hope Julie's all right," said Sally.

"Fine. Then I'm going to call the police."

"Oh, no, John! You mustn't do that!" cried Sally.

"Look Sal, this is quite ridiculous. You know yourself that you are in danger. That is why you came down here, and you are even worried about Julie because she works with you."

"But I promised George and Pierre that I wouldn't say anything to the police, and George warned me that if anyone ever found out what they had dug up, it could mean chaos, or even war!"

"That's just too far-fetched, Sally. Come on, be reasonable. The police are already investigating your father's death, and have decided that whoever killed him was looking for something, right? Now with the break-in at the flat, it seems obvious that the killers think that you must have it."

"Yes, you're right, John. But what if they start asking questions?"

"Then you'll just have to convince them that you don't know what it's all about, and you don't do you? Just ask the inspector for some protection. I'm going to call McGregor now, Sally. You just tell him you came down here because you were frightened, and remember, no mention of archaeologists. If he asks you if you have contacted your father's family, just tell him you called his university and they told you his wife was dead."

"All right, John. Go ahead. I'm ready," she agreed.

Inspector McGregor was out when John got through to the police station, and as he was transferred to Sergeant Jones, he handed the receiver to Sally.

"Ugh, I don't like that sergeant."

"Never mind. Just say what I told you, Sal. I'll leave it to you." And giving her an encouraging hug he went out into the garden.

"Jones," replied the nasal voice on the other end of the line.

"Good morning, Sergeant. It's Sally Wincott speaking. I gather that the inspector is not available?"

"Ah, Miss Wincott! We've been trying to contact you. Have you been away?"

"Yes, in New York," lied Sally.

"Inspector McGregor is out, but we need to talk to you urgently, Miss Wincott. Would four-thirty be convenient? We could come to your office."

"No Sergeant, please don't do that. I am not at work today, in fact, I am not in London."

"Oh? Well where are you, Miss Wincott, if you don't mind me asking?" Sally's hackles started to rise at the sneering nasal tone of the policeman's voice.

"That is exactly why I am calling, Sergeant, and I think it would be better if I spoke to the inspector. What time are you expecting him back?"

"That's difficult to say, Miss. It may be later this evening. Perhaps you would prefer to come to us in the morning. Would ten o'clock suit you?"

"No, it wouldn't Sergeant. I am not in London, and I have no intention of returning just yet."

Jones tried again. "Look Miss; I don't know where you are, but wherever it is, we need to talk to you. Do you understand that?"

"Yes, I understand perfectly Sergeant Jones. Please tell Inspector McGregor that I will telephone him at eight o'clock this evening." Then she hung up.

"That bloody sergeant!" she shouted, as John came through the door.

"What's happened?"

"Nothing. The inspector wasn't there, and that b – awful sergeant gets up my nose!"

"For God's sake Sally, you can't go upsetting the police! Now they are going to suspect that you are involved."

"Oh, just leave me alone John. I'll deal with it myself."

Sally went up to her bedroom to call her office. She asked the personnel director to ensure that the receptionists note down the description of any strangers entering the building, and to contact the Bankside Police Station, who were investigating her father's murder. She would explain everything on her return.

"I'm going out to do some shopping," she called to John, who was reading in the garden. I'll be back in an hour," and before he could object, she drove off in her car.

Sally went to Petersfield where she wandered in and out of the shops, feeling tired and rather lost. She went into an 'olde worlde' tea shop and ordered a cream tea. It was crowded, and as she waited for her order, she felt herself nodding off, the voices of chatting ladies around her fading into the distance. 'Goodbye, Sally. You just look after yourself and we'll meet again soon.' Startled she realised that it was Pierre's voice saying goodbye to her just days earlier. Her eyes misted over as she struggled to hold back the tears.

"Is everything all right, Madam?" asked the young waitress, placing a teapot on the table. "Can I get you anything?" Sally sat up, forcing a smile.

"Thank you, but I'm fine really," she mumbled, embarrassed.

Sally sat in her car weeping softly. "Pierre," she muttered as she thought back to their meetings. He had explained everything so well and he was so understanding, and all she had done was to unload her silly problems about John.

"Please forgive me, Pierre, I'll never forget you," she sobbed. Fighting to compose herself, she took out her compact and dabbed her puffy eyes, then she drove off to the covered market to stock up on provisions before returning to the house.

John was standing in the kitchen, covered in flour, when Sally walked in.

"Good Lord! What are you doing, Darling?" she asked.

"Oh, so you are talking to me again, are you?"

"Yes, of course I am. I'm sorry, John. I know you are trying to help, and I do appreciate it, but it's all just too much; and now hearing about Pierre… I just can't think straight anymore."

"I do understand, Sal. Come here, silly, and give me a kiss." And he grabbed her with his floury hands, knocking the pastry board onto the floor.

"Look out! It's all over us," she yelled.

"Hell!" he exclaimed, as the two of them fell to their knees in the flour, helpless with laughter.

It was dark by the time Sally and John returned to the living room.

"What are we going to eat tonight, Darling?" she asked.

"I was trying to make an onion tart, until you interrupted me," laughed John.

"Well, we'd better think of something else then, hadn't we? How about lamb chops?"

"Fine." John had switched the television on when Sally picked up the phone in the kitchen to call the Bankside Police Station.

As they relaxed after dinner, finishing off a second bottle of wine, Sally told John that she had spoken to Inspector McGregor, and that he had insisted on coming to the house to see her the next day.

"Well done Sal. Now, do you feel like trying to sort out what should be done?"

"All right John, so long as you don't do the heavy father bit with me. You know I hate being told what to do."

"I do! And I appreciate that you are a capable and independent girl, and used to coping with problems on your own, but you must admit that there are times when you should accept the help and advice of others."

"I know," she agreed. "But, if you would just forgive me for not telling you about it earlier, then we can discuss the problem calmly."

"Of course, Sally. Let's start again, shall we?"

An hour later, having gone over Sally's story for what seemed to her the hundredth time, John had an idea.

"Where was Joseph when he made the discovery that no one must know about?" he asked.

"I'm not sure. It was the identity of two of the Hyperboreans that Pierre and George insisted had to be kept secret, and I think that one of them was one of the Delos skeletons they had found ten years earlier."

"Which means that the other must have been the Wiltshire man. So where did Joseph carry out his examination of him, your Brigstone Man? It must have been in England, surely?"

"I suppose so."

"Do you know if Joseph had a bank account in England, Sally?"

"I've no idea, but if he did…"

"Exactly. He may have hidden something in London, Sally."

"Hang on a minute, John," Sally interrupted. "What was it that he found that enabled them to name the two skeletons?"

"Yes, Sal. That's what we should be looking for. If the Brigstone Man was one of the named skeletons, and if it was in England that Joseph carried out the autopsy, that must mean that it was then that he made the big discovery!"

"Of course," agreed Sally.

"Then we'd better find it!" announced John.

"And destroy it straight away," added Sally.

"Why?"

"Because it is something so shocking that it will rewrite history, and its religious substance could cause a terrible war!"

"But you don't know that, Sally," argued John.

"Perhaps not, but what I do know is that I have absolute confidence in Pierre and George, and they were deadly serious when they told me that."

"But Sally, didn't Joseph pass the note on to you because he wanted you to publish news of the find?"

"Yes John, perhaps he did, or perhaps he didn't; and this is the dilemma that I have been struggling with ever since that day."

Chapter Fifteen

The next morning John was up early, leaving Sally sleeping on in bed. By the time she had got up he had gone out, leaving a note propped up by the coffee percolator.

Sal: As I have only two more days' leave, have decided to go down to Marlborough. The skeleton must have been taken there so am going to see what I can find out.

It wouldn't be safe for you to go, so hope you understand.

See you later.

Love John

"Damn you, John!" she cried. "He's taking over again." Then, thinking that perhaps it was not such a bad idea, she settled down to making a few phone calls.

George was in his office when she got through to Athens. The Lebanese police had recorded Pierre's death as an accident, despite Nadine's protestations and, although he was going to Beirut, George knew there was nothing he could do to convince them otherwise. Nadine was furious. She hated him, just as she had hated Pierre's refusal to tell her, or the police, what it was that they had discovered. Sally wanted to call Nadine, but George advised her against it.

"But I was fond of Pierre, and I'd like to go to the funeral," she argued.

"That's quite out of the question. You must stay where you are Sally. In any case, Nadine wouldn't see you. To her, you represent Jo who she blames for Pierre's death and Marie's disappearance."

"But that's just not true!" cried Sally.

"I know, my dear. But promise me you won't call her?"

"All right. I promise. But what about poor Marie, George? Is there no news of her?"

"Apparently not. But I will see what I can find out while I am there. Now I must go, Sally. You take care of yourself, and I'll call you when I return."

"Goodbye, George, and thank you for everything," she said.

Inspector McGregor would be at the house after lunch, which gave Sally time to work out what she had to do before he arrived. If she was to find out where Jo had hidden the secret document, or whatever it was, she would need to have proof of her identity in order to gain access to it; and her birth certificate alone would not give her the right to Jo's estate. She had to find out if Jo had a lawyer, or had made a will, and that meant Minneapolis. If she called the university straight away, she might just catch the professor she had spoken to before, before he went home. She sat down and dialled the number of the university.

Professor McCloud seemed pleased to hear from Sally again.

"I am sorry to bother you, Professor, but I do need a bit of help. Do you know how I could find out if Jo had a lawyer?"

"Of course, Sally. I'm sure I can help you with that. Jo did have a lawyer friend in New York who came up here quite often. If you contact him, I'm sure he would know. I will let you have his phone number."

Thank you, I'll do that," she replied.

"Is there anything else I can help you with, Sally? What about his funeral?"

"Oh dear, I'd forgotten about that, but the police did tell me that they couldn't release his body until they had finished their investigations."

"So what is happening there, Sally? Have they not found Jo's killer yet?"

"No they haven't, and I am in trouble because whoever killed him was looking for something, and they probably think that I have got it. That is why I asked you if you knew what he was working on, because it must have been something terribly important."

"Goodness me, Sally!" exclaimed McCloud. "Why didn't you

tell me? All I know is that when Jo left, he planned to finish a book he was writing, and do some travelling. He never mentioned any further work. This is terrible!"

"Yes it is, and I'm scared stiff, Professor."

"But what are the police doing about it, Sally? I hope you have some sort of protection."

"No, I haven't, but the inspector leading the investigation is coming to see me today, and I intend to ask for his help."

"You be sure you do that, Sally, and please let me know how you get on."

"There is just one more thing, Professor. Jo's friend at the American University in Beirut has been killed."

"Oh, no! Not Professor Soulaya?"

"I'm afraid so."

"But there surely can't be any connection, can there?"

"Oh, yes, Professor. There most certainly is. Pierre was working with Jo on a dig in England last year, and now everyone who was involved in that is in danger."

"Good God! What on earth did they dig up?"

"That's exactly what I want to find out, Professor," she replied.

Sally was eating an omelette when the phone rang.

"Who were you talking to, Sal? The phone's been engaged for ages," complained John.

"Don't exaggerate, John. I called Jo's university to try to find out if he had a lawyer."

"Whatever for?"

"Because, silly, I will have to send some proof of my identity to his lawyer before I can go poking about in his bank strong box, won't I?"

"Ah, I see. It would certainly help. But don't forget you have to get probate first, Sally."

"Yes, of course, I know that. But have you come up with anything at Marlborough?"

"Yes, I have. A man at the morgue told me that the archaeologists took the skeleton up to London."

"That's great!" said Sally.

"Yes, but now we have just got the whole of London to

search," said John wryly. "I'm leaving now, Sal, so I'll be back before the inspector arrives."

Ninety minutes later Inspector McGregor walked into the house, followed by a rosy-faced constable.

"Well, so we've found you at last, Miss Wincott," he remarked.

"I wasn't lost, Inspector. Just away on business," replied Sally.

"If you say so," he replied.

"And where is the lovely Sergeant Jones, Inspector?" Sally couldn't help asking, as McGregor sat down, smiling.

"Now Miss Wincott, what have you got to tell us? Why have you left London, for a start?"

"I left London because I was scared, Inspector. As you know, my father was killed, and my flat broken into."

"Yes, by someone who is looking for something. What I don't understand, Miss Wincott, is why someone who claims to know nothing is so frightened that she decides to leave her job and hide away in the country! Don't you think it's about time you told me the truth?" Sally sighed.

"All right, Inspector. I'll start again. When I went to the hospital to see Dr Jordan, I was convinced that he was mad, and I certainly didn't believe for one moment that he was my father. He was barely conscious and said very little, but he did say that if anyone knew who I was, or that I had been to see him, my life could be in danger! I had absolutely no idea what he was talking about, Inspector."

"Why didn't you tell me this before, Miss Wincott?"

"I didn't think it was important, and, as I said, I thought he was mad."

"What else did he say before that? I must know everything," insisted McGregor.

"I told you. He just said how happy he was to have found me, and how like my mother I was, and he gave me the photo, which you have. That's all."

"I want you to tell me, Miss Wincott, exactly what he said just before he warned you. Come on now, there must have been something?"

"No, there wasn't. There was nothing else, Inspector." Sally was afraid that he could hear how fast her heart was racing.

"All right, let's try something else. Dr Jordan was an anthropologist, was he not?"

"Yes."

"Do you have any idea what he was working on, or what he was doing in London?"

"Now how on earth could I possibly know that! He was a complete stranger to me," retorted Sally, feigning annoyance. "And incidentally Inspector," she said, rising from her chair, "I have now confirmed that he was my father. I obtained a copy of my birth certificate from St Catherine's House."

"Why did you do that, Miss Wincott, if you thought he was mad, and was already dead?"

"Well what would you do Inspector, if you were adopted and someone turned up saying he was your father? Wouldn't you want to know?"

"Point taken. Please sit down, Miss Wincott. Perhaps we could pause for a moment. How about a cup of tea?"

"Good idea," agreed Sally, retreating into the kitchen feeling relieved and quite pleased with herself.

Sally placed a tray with three mugs of tea and a plate of biscuits on a side table, and sat down opposite the inspector.

"What about the hit and run driver, Inspector?" she asked. "Have you not found any witnesses?"

"Nobody has come forward so far," he replied.

"But who took Joseph into the hospital? Surely that person must have seen what happened?"

"He did, but it wasn't much use. He was a porter on his way to work there, but by the time he arrived at the spot, the car was well on its way. He was too concerned for your father to think about getting the registration number."

"Damn! It must have been the people who killed him."

"Possibly," agreed McGregor. "But we may yet get something from the appeal we put out."

"There is something else I should tell you, Inspector," said Sally several minutes later.

"Ah... well, what is it, Miss Wincott?"

"Two suspicious looking men walked into my office the other day and scared my secretary."

"Why ever did you not call me straight away?"

"I don't know, but she phoned me, and I told her to go straight home. I was afraid they might return and smash up my office, like they did my flat, and I dare not risk anything happening to her."

"You did quite right there, but what did they want? Did she speak to them?"

"Of course. They said they wanted to see me on business. She told them that I was away in New York, of course."

"Did she describe them?"

"She said they were dark and well-dressed in business suits, and she thought that the one who spoke had an Italian accent."

"Good! That's something to go on, at last," snapped McGregor. "Now, where can I find your secretary? I need to get a full description from her."

"Of course," agreed Sally. "But please, Inspector, is there any possibility you could put one of your men to keep an eye on the offices? Julie really needs to return to work, with me being away, and she is afraid of losing her job. I must be sure it is safe for her to return."

"I'll see what can be arranged, but first I must talk to her. Now, if there's nothing else you can tell us, Miss Wincott, we'll be on our way. You just call Sergeant Wilson at Petersfield if you have any problems, and he'll send someone over straight away."

John's car drew up in the lane outside as the policemen drove off.

"Damn, I've missed him!" exclaimed John. "How did it go, Sal? Is he going to look for those men?"

"I hope so. Inspector McGregor's going to get a description from Julie, and hopefully will put someone on duty at the office, so if they go back again they'll get them."

"But what about you, Sal? What did he say about that?"

"He just said I was to call Petersfield, if I had any problems."

"Is that all?"

"Well, what can we expect, John?"

Over dinner that evening, John related the day's events at Marlborough.

"Did you go over to Brigstone Down, Darling?" she asked.

"Yes I did, but I had trouble finding the dig site."

"Why? It is still there, isn't it?" she asked.

"Yes, just. I went into the village pub to ask the way and the landlord said that he was disappointed that the foreign researchers had not returned. As far as he knew, the local archaeological society had only been back there once."

"So nobody else has been poking about there then. But what was it like? Did you take any photos?"

"No. I forgot my camera, Sal, but it was quite an anti-climax. It had been raining heavily, and I had to clamber over two half-flooded fields to get to it. The site was roped off, but not at all secure. There was a group of stones round a circle, and some of them were quite big. Some smaller ones were lying all over the place, and it looked as though they might have been moved. My guess is that the local builders have been going up there and helping themselves."

"Oh what a shame! But what about the field where they found the Brigstone Man? Did you see that?"

"No, it was impossible to tell where it was. All the fields around the site are ploughed up, and there was no sign to show where a dig had taken place."

"Oh, dear. That's disappointing, but at least it doesn't look as though anyone else has been trying to find more remains."

"Except perhaps for the local builders," laughed John.

Two days later, John left for Heathrow for a five-day tour of duty. He and Sally had spent a happy time together in the garden, and Sally felt secure that John had got over his anger, and that all was well again between them.

Chapter Sixteen

Sally felt totally relaxed after John had left. It had been wonderful to have him there after the nerve-wracking days she had spent alone, but now she felt almost guilty at the surge of elation which came with the realisation that she was free again to make her own decisions. Does living with a man and accepting his love and protection mean that the woman ceases to be an individual, she wondered. If John expected always to have the upper hand, then their friendship would falter. Love and cherish was one thing, but 'Yes Darling, anything you say Darling', was not for her!

That afternoon Sally called Jo's New York lawyer friend. Mike Steward was in a meeting and his officious-sounding secretary asked her to call back in an hour.

An hour and a half passed before she tried again and, after a five minute wait she was put through to Mike's office.

"Mike Steward; how may I help you?" asked a friendly voice.

"Mr Steward, you don't know me, but my name is Sally Wincott and I am calling from London," announced Sally.

"Yes, Miss Wincott; what can I do for you?"

"Professor McCloud at Minneapolis gave me your number. I am Joseph Jordan's daughter, and I am hoping you can help me with some information."

"Jo's daughter! But Jo didn't have any children," he exclaimed. Here we go again, thought Sally, as she took a deep breath.

"I am Joseph's English daughter, Mr Steward. I was born in London soon after the war."

"Good God! You're not Nancy's daughter, by any chance?"

"Yes I am. How do you know?"

"I met Nancy when I was with Jo in France," he replied.

"Good Heavens! So you knew her?" Now it was Sally's turn to be surprised.

"Only slightly. We spent a wonderful day together, the three of us, driving south and clambering around ruins. She was a lovely girl. But tell me Sally, what can I do for you? I heard about Jo's death. It was a terrible shock."

"Yes, it must have been. I only met him the day before he was killed, and I couldn't believe that he was my father."

"Killed? Did you say he was killed, Sally?"

"Yes. Didn't you know?"

"No I did not. Was it some sort of an accident?"

"No. He was murdered."

"Oh, my God! That's terrible," came the shocked response. "Is that why you are calling me Sally?"

"Not exactly. The police are investigating his death, of course, and Professor McCloud told me that he had no family, and as I have since found out that he was my father, it would appear that I am his next of kin, so I need to contact his lawyer, if he had one."

"I see. You should understand, Sally, that Joseph was not a wealthy man."

"Good Heavens! You don't think that is why I want to contact his lawyer, do you?" asked an indignant Sally. "He was a complete stranger to me, Mr Steward. I am just trying to do the right thing for his family and friends. I am sure there must be someone who should be contacted."

"I understand, Sally. Jo did have a lawyer in Minneapolis. I recommended him to someone when his wife died. If you leave your address with my secretary, I'll write to you with his name."

"Thank you," said Sally, coldly. "But I would prefer it if you would fax it to my office tomorrow, if you don't mind."

"All right, Miss Wincott. I think I can arrange to do that," he agreed.

What a horrible, arrogant American! thought Sally after replacing the receiver. How dare he assume that I'm after Jo's money. Even I know that university professors, even American ones, are not millionaires.

Two days later Sally boarded a NorthWest Airlines 707 bound for Minneapolis. Jo's lawyer had seemed anxious to meet her, and she had asked her solicitor to send her birth certificate over by courier. She had told no one that she was going.

When Sally finally emerged from the long queue at Immigration, she saw a swarm of people waiting to greet their arrivals. How on earth was she going to be able to find Professor McCloud? Moments later, she spotted a large bright notice held aloft, sporting her name in bright red lettering.

"Professor McCloud! Thank goodness. I thought I'd never find you," she laughed, as the tall man turned towards her.

"And you must be Sally. I'm very pleased to meet you," he exclaimed, taking her arm to steer her towards a pretty blonde woman nearby. "This is my wife, Abigail."

"Hello my dear. We are so pleased you could come. Now don't you worry about a thing, we'll take care of everything. Have you been to America before, Sally?" she asked.

"Only a couple of times, on holiday."

"Then you're an old hand," said McCloud.

"Not really, but it is very exciting to be here, and what a stunning airport you have," remarked Sally, gazing around at the vast hall.

"Yes, it is fairly recent," agreed McCloud. "Minneapolis is renowned for its modern architecture, as you will see, Sally."

Abigail took charge as they drove away.

"We're taking you straight home, Sally, so that you can relax until dinner. You must be tired after your long flight."

"Oh no, please!" objected Sally. "I'm staying at the Holiday Inn, and I'd prefer to go straight there, if you don't mind."

"We wouldn't hear of it, my dear. You are staying with us. Don't worry about the hotel, we will cancel it."

"Oh, but I couldn't possibly. You mustn't go to all that trouble, Abigail, really." Sally felt thoroughly embarrassed. She knew about American hospitality, but she was a complete stranger to these people. But the McClouds insisted, and she was too tired to argue.

Jamie and Abigail McCloud lived in a small pseudo-Georgian

house on the outskirts of the town. As soon as Sally had unpacked and showered, she fell asleep on the comfortable four-poster bed.

It was dark when she awoke, wondering where she was. She jumped out of bed and switched on the light. Abigail had put her into a pretty guest room, furnished in traditional colonial style, and Sally felt immediately at home and relaxed. She dressed quickly and went downstairs to find her hosts. The house was quiet and there didn't seem to be anyone around. She opened the door and found herself in a sitting room where a log fire burned in the grate. She was just making a discreet survey of the books on the bookshelves when the door flew open and a tall, handsome man strode into the room.

"Hi! You must be Sally Jordan," he greeted, as he walked towards her, his hand outstretched. "I'm Alex, Jamie and Abigail's son."

"Hello! You quite startled me, but my name is not Jordan. I'm Sally Wincott," replied Sally, avoiding his dark eyes which seemed to be staring at her.

"I apologise. I wasn't thinking. You're Sally Wincott-Jordan by all accounts," he suggested. "My father told me about your phone call. We were all very upset to hear about Jo's death. He was a good friend of the family."

"Thank you," said Sally.

"Would you like a drink before dinner, Sally?" he asked.

"Yes please, that would be very welcome. But where is your mother? I haven't seen her since I arrived."

"Oh, she's in the kitchen, rustling up some fancy dish."

"Could I see her? I'd love to help."

"Oh, no, you just stay here and relax. I want to hear all about you and your mother, and how you met Jo." Sally sat down clutching her glass.

"Oh, no, please. I was hoping I might just forget all that for a while," she pleaded.

"I am sorry, Sally," he apologised again. "I understand. I'm sure it can wait."

"Perhaps tomorrow," said Sally as Abigail came into the room.

"There you are Alex! So you have met Sally."

"Yes, Ma, we are already great friends," he replied, placing a protective arm around Sally's shoulders. Sally felt the blood rushing up to her head, embarrassed at the not unwelcome attention she seemed to be arousing.

"Dinner is ready when you are. Come along, Sally," announced Abigail.

Over dinner that evening Sally learned that Alex lived and worked in Minneapolis as the head of a successful real estate business. He was over six feet tall, dark haired and devastatingly good looking, and judging from the conversation at the dinner table, he was also highly cultivated. By the end of the evening Sally knew that she was fatally attracted to him.

The following morning Alex drove Sally into town for her appointment with Jo's lawyer, promising to pick her up afterwards for lunch. The lawyer's offices were situated in a glass-fronted skyscraper downtown off Nicolett Avenue. Sally was greeted by a bespectacled spinster secretary who showed her into a gloomy waiting room furnished with huge brown leather armchairs and a dark oak table holding a collection of financial magazines. Sally wondered if they had furnished the offices at a hotel sale.

She didn't have long to wait before the door opened to reveal a small, grey haired man.

"Joseph Klein," he announced, advancing towards her. "I am sorry to have kept you waiting, Miss Wincott. Please do come in. What a shock to hear of Joseph's death! I am so sorry. He was a good man, your father."

"Yes, I believe so," agreed Sally, as she sat down on a small armchair at the side of his desk.

"Now Sally… I may call you Sally?" he asked, an impish grin creeping out from under his wiry moustache.

"You may, Mr Klein."

"Your father came to see me just before he left for London, you know."

"Did he really? Was it about something important?"

"It certainly was. He told me that he was going to look for you."

"Oh? I wonder how he knew about me?"

"So what I need to know, Sally, is how you met."

Sally took a deep breath, bracing herself to relate again the story of her meeting with Jo, for what seemed like the hundredth time.

"I have no idea how he found me, Mr Klein. I didn't even know of his existence until I received a phone call from the hospital telling me that my father was there. I thought they must have made a mistake, but Joseph had insisted that they call me. They said that he was dying and that I should see him, so I went."

"That must have been quite a shock for you, Sally."

"It was, not least when I saw what state he was in. He had been knocked down by a hit and run driver, and had suffered a heart attack; but, worst of all, I was convinced that he was mad."

"Why did you think that, Sally?"

"He was rambling on about something, and he said that my life could be in danger if anyone knew who I was or that I had been to see him! Really, Mr Klein, I thought he was a lunatic, and I certainly never believed that he could be my father!"

"My goodness! I hadn't heard about the accident, Sally."

"It wasn't an accident, Mr Klein. Someone was trying to kill him, and they eventually did."

"Yes, Mr Steward told me. So this whole thing is looking quite serious."

"I'm glad you think so. Now you know how I feel, wondering if I am next on the list."

"I see," he murmured, not seeing at all. "So you believe that Joseph's warning may have been serious, Sally?"

"I know it was."

"When did you speak to Mr Steward?" asked Sally, quickly changing the subject.

"Only yesterday, when I rang to tell him that you were coming over."

"Why? Did you think he would be interested!"

"Yes; I was sure he would want to see you. He is coming up for the weekend anyway."

Oh, no! thought Sally, as the lawyer continued.

"What made you decide to find out if Joseph really was your

father, Sally?"

"I don't really know," she lied. "After the police told me that he had been killed I felt terribly confused, and almost guilty. Then, the following week, in my parents' old house, I found my adoption papers quite by chance, and decided to apply for my birth certificate, and there it was. My father's name was given as Joseph William Jordan."

"Yes, the certificate arrived from your solicitor yesterday, Sally, and it seems quite correct," said Klein, as the buzzer on his desk startled them.

Sally glanced nervously at her watch; praying she wouldn't be late for her lunch with Alex, while Klein instructed his secretary on the phone.

"Now Sally, I'll tell you a little about Joseph's affairs. I can confirm that you are his only surviving kin, and that there are no other living relatives. Joseph's wife, Joan, died two years ago, and there were no children. When he came to see me last month, he signed a new will and testament naming you, Sally Wincott, as his daughter and heir."

"I wonder how he found my name?"

"Probably the same way as you found his, Sally."

"I suppose so."

"Joseph was not a wealthy man, but he was comfortably off, Sally. As you know, he held the chair at the Department of Anthropology at the university for a number of years, which gave him a good salary. He lived, during the week, in a small rented apartment near the university, and he did own a chalet out by the lakes where he spent his weekends.

"His friend, Mike Steward, sometimes joined him there for the fishing. This was his only property, Sally, so it will be yours when probate is granted to keep or dispose of as you wish. I believe it is very attractive and is right on the shore of Lake Minnetonka, which is a popular tourist spot."

"That is a pleasant surprise!" said Sally.

"Joseph's only other asset, apart from cash savings, is his life insurance policy which will be released to you as soon as I have registered your claim."

“This is far more than I could have expected. It never occurred to me that my father might leave me something. You have really surprised me, Mr Klein.”

“There is one more thing, Sally. When Joseph came to see me he left a small packet addressed to you, and asked me to ensure that, in the event of his death, it should be forwarded on to you. So as you are here, I will fetch it.”

Oh, not another mystery code, thought Sally, as he left the room.

A few minutes later, the lawyer returned.

“Here we are, Sally,” he said, handing her a small padded envelope. “If you would just sign this chitty to say that you have received it,” he asked, pushing a paper across the desk. “Now I think that is all I can tell you for the moment, Sally. Do you have any questions?”

“None that I can think of, Mr Klein, except that I would like to know when I may have access to my father’s affairs. It is not his money that interests me but, as you know, he was murdered and I need to know why. That is why I am anxious to look at any papers he may have deposited somewhere.”

“Don’t you think it would be better to leave that to the police, Sally?”

“Certainly not. In any case the police would surely not have the right to go looking about in his bank deposit box!”

“Well Sally it will take a while before probate is granted on Joseph’s estate, but I could prepare an affidavit to the effect that you are his daughter and rightful heir, if you think it will help.”

“Thank you, Mr Klein, that would be useful.”

“Now if there isn’t anything else I can help you with, Sally?” he said, rising from his chair to close the meeting.

“No. I think you have covered everything, Mr Klein. I am very grateful for your help.”

“It was past eleven o’clock when Sally stepped out into the street, which gave her just over an hour for some sightseeing. Professor McCloud had been right when he had mentioned the architecture in Minneapolis. Sally thought it was stunning, and the shops lining Micolett Mall were amazing too. It wasn’t long before she found her way up to the first level covered walkways, known as the 'skyway system' which ran almost right around the town centre.

She was so intrigued with one particular gift shop that she was nearly late for her meeting with Alex McCloud, and arrived back at the lawyer's building to bump right into him, flushed and breathless.

"Goodness Sally! What did he do to you?" he asked, catching hold of her arm to lead her into a terribly chic-looking restaurant.

"Nothing thank God," she laughed. "I was window shopping and nearly got carried away. My goodness Alex, aren't the shops here amazing!"

"I guess so, but we think your London stores are pretty fabulous, Sally."

Over lunch, Sally learned that Alex was divorced and had no children. He had started his working life in banking, but had found it terribly boring and had switched into real estate some five years earlier. His firm specialised in the highly lucrative management of corporate property portfolios, and he travelled extensively to meet with clients.

Sally was fascinated listening to Alex, and she could hardly take her eyes off him. Not only was he incredibly good looking, but he also had the smoothest speaking voice she had ever heard. No wonder he had made such a success of his business, she thought. He literally oozed charisma. Struggling to keep her composure and think clearly, she became aware that apart from his intelligence and obvious confidence, what impressed her the most was his lack of arrogance. He appeared to be entirely unaware of the effect he had on those around him. Hurrah, thought Sally, at last a *real* man!

Alex in his turn was eager to know all about Sally, and how she had met her father, but she was determined to steer clear of the subject of Joseph during their lunch. Instead, she had him laughing at her stories of some of the crazy days and frequent panics at the advertising agency. When the subject of boyfriends came up she told him about John, suddenly thinking how angry he would be when he heard that she had been to Minneapolis without telling him!

Their lunch ended all too soon for Sally as Alex kissed her fondly on the cheek before dashing back to his office. Sally felt bewildered. What was happening? How could she feel such a pull towards someone she had just met? I am in love with John, she told herself, as she made her way down the road towards the river.

On her return to the McClouds' house, Sally remembered the small packet that the lawyer had given her. She pulled it from her handbag and sat down to open it. Wrapped carefully in what looked like paper handkerchiefs were two small chunky keys and a piece of paper. The biro writing on the paper was barely legible, but she made out:

> Dear Sally, take great care of these.
> I know you will make the right decision.
>
> Your father, Jo

Then I was right, she thought. Jo did hide something in a bank, and these must be the keys. But where is it?

Over dinner that evening, the McClouds were anxious to hear about Sally's visit to the lawyer.

"I had a pleasant surprise," she told them. "As well as his estate, Jo left me a chalet by a lake somewhere."

"Yes. Jo's house at Minnetonka. It's very pretty," said Abigail.

"I'll drive you over there tomorrow, Sally," added Jamie.

"Oh, thank you Jamie, that's very kind of you, but Alex has promised to take me to see it in the morning."

"Has he indeed! He doesn't waste much time, our Alex," remarked Jamie. Sally blushed.

"I met him for lunch today, and I found him to be wonderful company."

"Yes, he is rather a lady killer, Sally. Be careful or he'll have you falling in love with him," warned Abigail.

"Oh, that won't happen," laughed Sally. "I've got my man back in London."

The following morning Alex called for Sally at ten o'clock. It was Saturday and, after looking over the cabin Sally had planned to spend the afternoon shopping.

Clambering into the low, open-top sport car, Sally noticed that the back seat was packed with food and wine. What was she letting herself in for, she wondered, shaking off a slight feeling of unease as Alex roared off down the road.

Was she not just going to look at the cabin she had inherited, or was she perhaps an unsuspecting weekend conquest? Half an hour later, as Alex pulled up under some trees with the lake glistening before them she really didn't care.

"How can you call it a cabin? It's gorgeous!" cried Sally, unconsciously grabbing Alex's hand.

"Yes, it is attractive," he agreed as he unlocked the door. "I understand that it was a small fishing lodge when Jo bought it, and he and Joan did most of the work themselves." Sally stepped into the large, comfortably furnished living room and looked around. A huge stone fireplace with a built-in barbeque stood commanding the room. A small door led into a large fitted oak kitchen whose windows looked out onto a copse of green oaks and maple trees. A second door led into a study, the walls lined with maple panelling and hundreds of books. Upstairs, Sally found three double bedroom suites and a spacious bathroom furnished with an old-fashioned iron bath and a huge walk-in shower.

"I love it! I love it!" she cried, before skipping downstairs to find Alex piling logs into the fireplace.

"Come on, give us a hand, Sally! Get the stuff out of the car," he ordered.

"Just a minute, Alex. What are you doing? I've come to see my house – not to move in!"

"Well, why not?" he asked, as he swung round, dropping a log onto the floor. "After all we've got the whole weekend ahead of us. You don't want to go back now, do you?" Sally felt the blood rushing to her face.

"Now look, it was very kind of you to drive me down here Alex, but as soon as I have had a good look round and taken some photos, I'd like you to drive me back."

"Oh, come on, Sally. You know as well as I do that you'd love to stay."

"You don't know anything of the sort, Alex." Sally felt more than a little annoyed. Oh, don't say that I was wrong about him, she thought, struggling to control her anger. The smile had left Alex's face.

"I'm sorry Sally. That was a bit strong wasn't it? Perhaps we should just have some lunch and then I'll take you back, if you really want to go, but I can assure you that Jamie and Abigail are not expecting you back today."

"That's as may be, Alex. But I do think you might have asked me before we left. After all, we are complete strangers."

"I apologise, Sally. You are right, of course. But I really don't feel that we are strangers at all." Sally's legs gave way as she sank down into a large leather armchair. She felt totally disarmed. Then she started to giggle.

"What are you laughing at, Sally?" asked Alex, now embarrassed. "Have I said something funny?"

"No, it's not you Alex. It just struck me as such a silly situation. I mean, here's me, behaving like some naïve young girl who's never been alone with a man, when it must be obvious to you that I like you!"

"Well what the hell was that all about?" he demanded, throwing his arms around her.

"Because you can't just assume that someone you have just met is going to agree to spend a weekend with you," she replied, making a vague effort to push him away.

"But, my dear Sally, it isn't just someone, it's you, and you know as well as I do that we have been making love ever since we met."

"Oh, God!" sighed Sally. "I give up."

"Good. Let's have some champagne, shall we?" And he went out to fetch it from the car.

Later that evening, Alex drove Sally to a well-known restaurant at the other side of the lake. It was crowded but that didn't seem to worry them, as they sat unaware of everyone around them. As they were drinking their coffee, they were interrupted by a fellow diner.

"Good evening, Sally!" she turned round, startled.

"Oh, Mr Klein! Hello again."

"Good evening, Alexander!" said Klein, reaching across to shake Alex by the hand. "I'm dining with Mr Steward. He's here for the weekend."

"Do you mean Mike Steward from New York?" asked Sally.

"That's right, and he would very much like to meet you, Sally."

"Oh, Lord!" she mumbled.

"Who is he? Do you know him?" asked Alex, sensing Sally's unease.

"No I don't, but he was a friend of my father, and I don't particularly want to meet him."

"Why ever not?" asked Alex.

"I think you should, Sally," said Klein. "May I bring him over?"

"I suppose I should meet him."

"Is there a problem with this man, Sally?" asked Alex looking puzzled as Klein returned to his table to fetch his guest.

"I've only spoken to him on the phone, Alex, and he gave me the impression that he thought I was after Jo's money."

"That's ridiculous, isn't it?"

"Of course it is."

As Alex signalled the waiter to bring more coffee, Joseph Klein returned with a distinguished-looking, silver-haired man.

"Sally, I'd like you to meet Mike Steward."

"How do you do," said Sally, turning to greet the handsome man.

"Sally I'm so pleased to meet you, and how like Nancy you are!" said Mike. "This takes me right back to the day I met her with Jo in France. They were sitting at a table, just as you are now, and when Jo introduced me she said 'how do you do', exactly like you!"

Sally felt embarrassed. "Do join us for coffee Mr Steward. Do you know Alex McCloud?" she asked.

"Yes. I believe we have met previously with Jo. I won't disturb you now Sally, but I would very much like to have a talk with you before you leave. Perhaps you and Alex would care to join me for a cocktail tomorrow evening?"

"That would be fine, wouldn't it Sally?" asked Alex.

"Yes, of course," she agreed.

"Good. I have something for you, Sally, from your mother, which I think you would like to have."

"Really?" Sally was suddenly interested. "Then I shall look forward to that, Mr Steward."

On their return to the cabin, Alex busied himself stoking up the fire while Sally went upstairs to change. When she returned to the living room, she found candles lit all round the room, and Frank Sinatra singing *Strangers in the Night*.

"Oh, Alex, isn't this crazy!" she cried.

"Crazy like you, Sally Wincott-Jordan," he replied as he took her in his arms. "That's why I'm falling in love with you."

The following evening Alex and Sally drove over to Joseph Klein's lakeside cabin to meet Mike Steward. As with Sally's 'cabin', Klein's was more of a house. In fact it was *Nouveau-riche* luxurious, with fitted shag carpets and crystal chandeliers everywhere.

Having been seated by an enormous re-constituted stone fireplace with its imitation gas-fired logs, Sally and Alex were offered cocktails of every conceivable colour and trays of professionally prepared canapés. Joseph Klein was obviously determined to live up to the sophisticated tastes of his friend from New York.

Mike Steward was charming, and it wasn't long before Sally realised how wrong her impression of him had been. He told her about the day he had spent with Jo and Nancy, and then, having returned to his room to fetch it, he presented her with the letter that Nancy had sent him twenty-seven years earlier.

"Nancy wrote to me from Paris," he told her. "And I intended to tell Jo about it, but, at that time, I was sitting my final exams, and somehow it was forgotten." Sally's eyes filled with tears as she scanned through the faded writing on the notepaper.

"When I met Jo in London last year, and we talked about our time in France after the war, I suddenly remembered Nancy's letter, and that was when I told him about it," continued Mike. "I thought I had thrown it away years ago, but when I moved house recently, I found it, so when I heard that you were coming over, I thought you would like to have it."

"So when she wrote that she was pregnant, she was expecting me?" asked Sally. "Oh, how sad! But why on earth did she leave Jo?"

"I suppose she was just afraid that he wouldn't understand about her past. After all she was a very insecure girl, abandoned by her husband's family, and totally lacking in self-confidence."

"But do you think that Jo would have married her, or was it just a wartime fling for him?" she asked.

"I believe he would have married her, if he had found her. At least, that is what he told me last year."

"That's difficult to believe. Surely he could have traced her?"

"Perhaps. But I believe that he did love her, Sally. Please don't feel bad about it. I know that Jo had always wanted a family, and I am sure that he would have made a good and loving father."

"But Mike, what about the other child that she had? Who adopted it, and where is it now?"

"I've no idea, Sally. I suppose that he or she is still in France."

"So I have a half-brother or sister somewhere. I wonder what he's like?" Alex placed a protective arm around Sally's shoulder.

"I wouldn't worry about that now, Sally. At least you do now know a little more about your family."

"I know, and I am grateful to you Mike for giving me the letter. I shall treasure it. But I can't help wondering about the other child."

Sally and Alex returned to Minneapolis the next morning, Alex to his work and Sally to the McClouds. Abigail was reading in the living room when Sally walked in.

"Sally my dear! How was your weekend?"

"Oh, Abigail, I'm so sorry. I wanted to call you, but Alex insisted that you knew I would be staying up at the lake."

"Of course I did, Sally. Now tell me, how did you get on? Did my naughty Alex behave himself?"

"Yes he did. He behaved impeccably," laughed Sally.

"And what did you think of your cabin, Sally?"

"I love it. It's a lovely house, and I wish I could live there instead of my flat in the middle of London!"

"Well now that it's yours Sally, you must come over as often as you can. You know we will always be delighted to see you."

That evening Jamie and Abigail drove Sally to the airport for her flight back to London. Sally felt sad to be leaving, but knew in her heart that if she had stayed any longer, she would have become inextricably involved with Alex. She was going home to John, and although determined to put Alex right out of her mind, she knew that in the years ahead, the memory of their weekend together would always be there.

Having said farewell to her hosts, Sally was about to go through the control, when she heard her name called over the public address system. Fearful that something might had happened to John or Julie, she hurriedly sought out the information desk. As she approached it she noticed a huge cellophane-wrapped bouquet of orchids and red roses held upright by someone hidden behind it.

"I am Miss Wincott," she said breathlessly to the girl behind the desk. "Is there a problem?"

"That's for you to decide, Miss Wincott," replied the pretty uniformed girl, laughing as the rustling bouquet suddenly dropped in front of her to reveal Alex.

"Oh, Alex!" she cried. "What on earth are you doing here? We said goodbye this morning. You are crazy!"

"I know I am," he replied, as he embraced her fondly. "You must know that I couldn't let you go, just like that, my darling." All Sally's determined resolutions flew away as they embraced passionately in the middle of the passing throngs of people.

Half an hour later, Sally dashed through into the departure lounge as the gates closed. Her heart was racing and she felt as though she was about to collapse.

"Damn you, Alex!" she muttered, as she sank down onto a seat, her eyes filling with tears. "Why, oh why did you have to come?"

Dawn was breaking as Sally awoke form a fitful sleep. A cup of coffee and a muffin lay on the tray in front of her. It was all a dream, she told herself. It never really happened. Drinking her coffee she looked out of the window to watch the clouds open up as the plane started its descent towards Gatwick.

Chapter Seventeen

On her way back to the house, Sally stopped to collect Felix. He was not at all happy to have been suddenly dumped, and decided to ignore her. There was a message on the answerphone, but she decided to get some sleep before facing whatever problem may have arisen during her absence.

The phone woke her later that afternoon. It was John calling from the flat.

"Sally! Where on earth have you been? I've been calling you for two days," he cried.

"Why? You only got back today, didn't you?"

"Yes, but I was worried about you, Sal."

"I'm fine John, really I am," she replied.

"But didn't you get my messages?"

"I really haven't checked. I decided to keep clear of problems for a day or two, and try to relax."

"That's fine, Sal, but it really is very worrying when you don't answer my calls." John was sounding annoyed.

"I'm sorry."

"Now look Sal, I'll be with you this evening. I've been sorting things out in the flat and it's looking almost back to normal again."

"That's great John. Thank you so much. What time will you be here?"

"About seven thirty I should think," he replied.

"Good. I'll have dinner ready for you, Darling."

Sally checked her messages. The first one was from Julie with the news that a stranger had been found in her office. She had called the police who had nabbed the man as he left the building. Shocked, Sally called Julie straight away. Inspector McGregor had shown her some photographs, none of which she had recognised as the man in the office. The second call was from the Inspector. He confirmed that the intruder had been detained, but that his accomplice, who had been parked outside the building, had got away. They were trying to trace the owner of the car.

Sally felt relieved that at least something was being done. Perhaps she would be able to return to work soon if the police caught Jo's killers. She busied herself unpacking and hiding away the traces of her Minneapolis trip. She had bought John a cashmere sweater, and left it in its carrier bag at the bottom of her side of the wardrobe thinking it would make a good Christmas gift.

Sally awoke the following morning feeling relaxed and happy to be home and lying on John's strong arms again. She felt she had succeeded in pushing Alex McCloud completely from her thoughts.

Later, as Sally and John were just setting off for a walk, Inspector McGregor rang, sounding rather grim.

"Good morning Inspector!" greeted Sally. "Do you have some good news about that man you arrested?"

"I'm afraid not, Miss Wincott. We had to let him go."

"Oh, no! Why?"

"Our friend has an Italian passport, Miss Wincott, and when his lawyer arrived at the station, he confirmed that he had diplomatic immunity, and we had to let him go."

"But that's ridiculous! He may be a murderer!" cried Sally.

"According to his lawyer, the man was acting as a Diplomatic Emissary attached to the Vatican."

"The *Vatican*?" cried Sally.

"What?" yelled John, who was standing next to her.

"That man the police arrested was a Diplomatic Emissary from the *Vatican*, John!" cried Sally, sinking down onto a chair, her heart crashing against her chest. John took the receiver from her hand.

"Inspector, are you quite sure about this?" he asked.

"Absolutely, Mr Taylor," replied McGregor.

"But what about the lawyer? Are you sure he's genuine?"

"There can be no doubt about that, sir. He is a well-known

defence lawyer, and I have known him personally for a number of years."

"Then what about the other man, Inspector? The one who got away?"

"I'm afraid that is a dead end too. The car is owned by the Italian Embassy, and the driver is a Trade Attaché with Diplomatic Immunity."

"But there must be something you can do, Inspector? Is there no way you can connect them to the break-in at the flat? What about their fingerprints?" John wasn't giving in.

"No sir, we cannot touch them."

"Are you saying then that you are back to square one, Inspector?"

"It would seem so, sir," snapped McGregor, "unless Miss Wincott can come up with some explanation for the religious connection."

"I'm sure she has no idea what it could be," said John.

Sally sat up to take the receiver back from John.

"Inspector McGregor, my secretary has returned to work and now you're telling me that you have let the men go. How can I be sure that she will be safe now? Don't you think it likely that they will try to get into my office again?"

"Try not to worry about that, Miss Wincott. Now that we have some idea of what we are up against we will keep a close eye on your offices and flat. Now, if you have anything else to tell me, I suggest that you get in touch with me as quickly as possible."

"I will Inspector, and thank you for your help," she said, and hung up.

"This is getting really tricky John. Now the inspector knows there is a religious connection, it won't be long before he guesses that Jo must have found something really important, and I don't think I can go on pretending to know nothing for much longer. What on earth can we do?"

That evening, as Sally prepared dinner, John went into the bedroom to change and shower. She was just taking the potatoes out of the microwave ready to be sautéed, when John stalked into the kitchen carrying the cashmere sweater she had bought him in one hand, and its carrier bag in the other.

"Sal, what is this?" he asked.

"What?"

"This shopping bag, Sally. What's it doing in the wardrobe?"

"Oh no!" she exclaimed, turning around. "You were not supposed to see that. It was for your Christmas present."

"But what's this bag, Sally? 'The Cashmere Store, City Centre Shopping Mall, Minneapolis'? How did it get here?"

Sally's heart lurched as she felt the blood rush to her face. Damn, now I'm for it. How am I going to get out of this?

"I don't know. Somebody must have given it to me," she murmured.

John threw the sweater and the bag down onto the table.

"For God's sake Sally! What the hell are you playing at?" he yelled, grabbing her arm to turn her to face him. "Look at me! You've been over there, haven't you? That's why I couldn't get you on the phone. Answer me!"

"Over where?" retorted Sally defiantly. John raised his arm as if to hit her. Sally had never seen him so furious.

She threw the potatoes down and turned on him. "Don't you shout at me, John. I'll do what I bloody well like. If you think I'm going to ask your permission every time I want to do something, you're very much mistaken." And she marched into the living room, shaking with anger.

"Well, that's great, isn't it?" shouted John, as he followed her. "You can just take off to America without a word to me? That's some fine partnership we've got, isn't it?"

"Yes, I bloody well can if I want to. Isn't that what you do all the time, and do I ask you where you are or what you are doing when you are away?"

"That's different. It's my job," he retorted.

"Balls! If you think I am going to sit around waiting for you to come back from your trips before I can make any decisions, then you'd better find somebody else. And for your information, I went to Minneapolis to see my father's lawyer because he asked me to."

John sank down onto the sofa, his anger fading into despair.

"Sally, I just don't understand you anymore. I thought we had a good partnership, but now I'm not sure. Did it never occur to you that I might be worrying about you? All I ask is that you are honest with me, but just lately you seem determined to come up with all sorts of stories, anything to avoid telling the truth. I can't cope with it, Sally."

"And all I ask, John, is the right to make my own decisions and to lead my life without feeling constantly obliged to seek your approval."

"In that case, Sally, I suggest we have a break. You are obviously totally oblivious of my needs, and seem determined to live and act as though I don't exist."

"Oh, well if that's what you think, John, then fine. All that I have done for you has obviously meant nothing. Just get out of my hair. I can manage perfectly well without you. And you can remove your things from my flat. Goodbye!" And she rushed from the room, struggling to hold back the choking sobs which were forcing their way into her throat.

Sally threw herself sobbing onto her bed. John knew she was a capable, independent girl. Why did he have to be so bloody bossy? Surely he knew her well enough by now to realise how his over-protective attitude could annoy her? She had thought it would be wonderful to have someone like him to look after her, but now she could see that perhaps she had been mistaken and she felt guilty. John loved her, she was sure, and she loved him. So why couldn't they understand each other?

"Oh, God, John, I never wanted to hurt you. Please forgive me," she sobbed into her duvet.

Sally awoke startled with Felix curled up beside her. A car drove off. She sat up listening. The house was silent. John had gone.

Sally lay back in the double bed, but it was impossible to sleep. She padded downstairs and poured herself a large glass of whisky.

"John's gone," she told Felix, who was mewing at the door. She let him out and then decided to follow him. Outside it was cold, but she sat down on the wooden bench hugging her dressing gown around her. As Felix jumped up beside her, the owl from the barn next door flew over her head hooting.

"Hello owl," she said, gazing up to admire the huge white shape. "We're all alone now, and I'm glad."

Sally awoke late the next day. She felt wiped out, but she had made a decision. She would go to London and collect Jo's note from the solicitors. Following a quick call to Julie to arrange to meet for lunch, she set off in her car.

Sally parked her car at the far end of the road, away from her office, before walking carefully into the building to be greeted by the welcome sight of a policeman. Her group were delighted to see her, and offered their condolences on her father's death.

"I hope I will be able to start back again soon; I really miss you all," she replied. Julie seemed happy and relaxed to be back at work, assuring Sally that she felt quite safe now with the policeman downstairs.

After lunch, Sally drove to the city. Old Mr Smithers seemed surprised to see her again so soon, but happily returned the envelope containing Jo's note.

Having thanked the old man, Sally returned to her car where she hid the envelope under the carpet, just in case those men spot me, she thought.

It was late afternoon when Sally got back to the house. She put the kettle on to make some tea before settling down to deal with Jo's note. She remembered that her mother had left her a small Victorian locket, holding photographs of herself and her father, and went upstairs to look for it. Then she took Jo's note and copied the numbers with an indelible pen onto a tiny scrap of paper, while at the same time, repeating them over and over again. She just managed to fit the tiny scrap into one side of the locket and covered it with the faded picture of her mother. She would destroy it as soon as she was confident she had the number firmly in her head.

"There now," she said to Felix, who was busy tearing up Jo's original note; "they can smash up my flat, this house, or whatever they want, but they'll have to kill me before they get their hands on Jo's numbers."

That evening Sally began to feel lonely again, and wished she could talk to Pierre. Wondering whether she should call George, the telephone rang. She hesitated. Suppose it was John? What would she say to him? Much as she longed to hear his voice, she just couldn't face anymore quarrelling. She picked up the receiver without answering. It was George.

"George!" she cried. "I was just thinking about you. How are you?"

"I'm not too good, Sally. I'm in hospital."

"Oh, no! What's happened? Nothing serious, I hope?"

"It could be worse. I had a slight accident in Beirut, after Pierre's funeral."

"Oh my God! It wasn't those people, was it, George?"

"No, I was driving a hire car up to Zahleh, when it suddenly skidded off the road. Luckily there was no one coming down, but I ended up on the road below with a broken arm and a slight neck injury."

"I'm so sorry George, but what did the police say? Are they sure it was an accident?"

"Of course," he laughed. "Everything's an accident to them!"

"Now tell me Sally, what are you up to? Are you and John still in Hampshire?"

"I am, but John has left. He has had enough of my stories; we had another terrible row."

"Oh, dear, I am sorry, Sally," he said.

"I went over to Minneapolis without telling him. I saw Jo's lawyer, and he confirmed that I am his only heir. But something has happened over here, George," she continued.

"Oh, Sally, are you all right?" he asked.

"I'm fine, but my flat was ransacked and some strange men got into my office."

"Great Heavens! What happened Sally?"

"I was so afraid for my secretary, that I sent her home and called the police."

"The police! Oh Sally, no!"

"I had to, George, and anyway they are already investigating the break-in at my flat; but don't worry, I didn't mention anything about the dig. They realise that whoever killed Jo was looking for something and have agreed to put a man on duty at the office building."

"But what about you, Sally? Have they offered you any protection?"

"Only that if I should have any problems to call the local police. But George, listen to this: one of the men got into my office a second time and the police arrested him."

"That's wonderful news, Sally!"

"No it's not. They were both Italians with Diplomatic Immunity, and worse, the one they arrested was an Emissary attached to the *Vatican*!"

"What?" yelled George. "My God, that means they know *everything*! No wonder they are trying to kill us!"

"Oh, George, now you are really scaring me." Sally was shaking so that she almost dropped the receiver.

"And you say that the police let the man go, Sally?"

"Yes, they said they had no choice. But George, are you sure that your car hadn't been tampered with?" she asked, suddenly concerned.

"After what you have just told me, Sally, I would think it quite likely."

"Oh George, please be careful. You mustn't go back to Beirut."

"I won't. But don't worry, Sally. I can look after myself," he replied.

"What about Pierre's funeral, George?" asked Sally. "I have been thinking about it so much. Was it terribly sad?"

"Of course. Pierre was very popular at the university, and had many friends. Nadine was wonderful and got through the day very well, but it was Aurora who worried me. Nadine is quite beside herself with worry over her. She seems to have become obsessed with the Wiltshire dig and her father's finds on Delos. She refuses to work and spends all her days searching for Marie, and every night scouring through Pierre's papers."

"Oh dear, but what of Marie, George? Was there any news of her?"

"I'm afraid not. They have found no trace of her. She seems to have just disappeared."

"That's terrible, but do you really think she was kidnapped?"

"I did, but I'm not so sure. The strange thing is that no one has demanded a ransom, which would be the usual thing over there."

Sally felt frightened after her talk with George but determined to be practical. She was sure no one could have traced her to the house, unless they had followed her from London.

The next few days passed quickly for Sally as she busied herself in the garden and went into Petersfield to buy paint for the house. If she was going to have to stay there a bit longer, she might as well do a bit of decorating. It surprised her how little she thought about John, although, one evening, remembering Minneapolis, she found herself wondering about Alex. Was he thinking of her? Could she hope that she might hear from him?

George called again at the end of the week. Aurora Soulaya had phoned him saying that she wanted to reopen her father's dig at Brigstone Down, and wanted his approval. George had done his utmost to dissuade her, but it was no good. Aurora was determined to continue with Pierre's work, and to find out more about the Brigstone Man. He had given her Sally's phone number and hoped that she would be willing to meet her. Sally jumped at the idea.

"Of course I will George. I could meet her at the airport, and she could stay with me here. It would be company for me."

"That would be very kind of you, Sally," he replied.

"What is she like? Does she speak any English?"

"Of course. She speaks fluently, like her mother. I'm sure you will get on very well together. She is about the same age as you, Sally."

"That's great! I shall look forward to that, George. Will you ask her to let me know what flight she will be on?"

"I am sure you will be hearing from her very soon, Sally, and thank you again."

Sally felt quite excited at the prospect of meeting Pierre's daughter. She hurried upstairs to the guest bedroom and started planning what it needed to make it more welcoming. By the end of the day, she had thoroughly cleaned the room, turned over the old carpet, changed the curtains, made up the bed and placed vases of flowers on the mantelpiece and dressing table. She stood back to admire her work, hoping that her guest would appreciate it as a pretty room in a typically English country cottage.

That evening Aurora phoned. She would be arriving the following afternoon.

Chapter Eighteen

Sally drove up to Heathrow to meet Aurora. The Middle East Airlines flight arrived on time and she started to panic that she might not be able to find her visitor, but George had described Aurora perfectly.

"Aurora?" she enquired as the beautiful, dark haired girl in leather jacket and designer jeans emerged from the barrier.

"Sally, hello! It's so good to meet you," replied Aurora breathlessly.

"Here, let me take that trolley. You've brought a lot of stuff with you." Aurora laughed.

"I know. I wasn't sure how long I would be staying. It is very kind of you to meet me, Sally. I don't know London very well."

"Don't worry about that, Aurora. I'm going to take you to the house first, then we can think about Wiltshire later."

"Oh, no, Sally, please don't. I have booked a hotel for tonight and I shall take a train tomorrow."

"No, you won't," said Sally. "I promised George that I would look after you, and you are staying with me, for tonight anyway. My house is only an hour's drive from the dig site, so we can decide what is best to do tomorrow."

"All right, Sally. I will come quietly," laughed Aurora. "But I am quite a capable person you know."

"So I have heard. Come on then. It's this way to the car park." And, linking arms, the two girls left the airport.

Aurora was delighted with Sally's house, and with the whole village.

"I have seen pretty English villages in films, and yours looks just the same."

"Yes, I suppose it does."

After she had unpacked, Aurora joined Sally in the living room. Sally offered her a drink, unsure whether or not she should offer alcohol.

"I would love a glass of wine, if you have some," replied Aurora.

"Of course I have; red or white?"

"I only drink red wine. We have some wonderful wines in the Lebanon, Sally."

"I have read about that. So we have that in common to start with, don't we, Aurora?"

"And a lot of other things too, I am sure," said Aurora, as she handed Sally a beautifully wrapped small packet.

"But you shouldn't bring me anything," muttered Sally, embarrassed. "I'm just happy that you are here."

"It seems such a shame to spoil such a pretty parcel," remarked Sally, as she untied the ribbons and opened the box. She gasped as she carefully lifted out a heavy chunk of polished rose granite, glistening with embedded quartz crystals.

"Oh Aurora, how beautiful!"

"Do you see what it is? The little fish-like creature there is at least two thousand years old."

"How wonderful! I love it. Oh Aurora, you couldn't have picked a better gift."

"I dug it up in the Bekka Valley last year and took it home to polish it."

"How clever you are," said Sally, as she carefully placed it on the oak mantelpiece over the fireplace.

"I shall think of you and Pierre whenever I look at it. Thank you so much, Aurora."

Sally turned to her guest.

"Aurora, you may not want to talk about it, but I must tell you how terribly upset I was to hear of your father's death. I only met him a few times, but I became fond of him. He was so very kind and understanding. The news came as a real shock, and I hope you can accept my most sincere sympathy. I have been thinking about you and your mother ever since it happened."

"Thank you, Sally. He told me all about you, and he liked you a lot. I think he hoped that we would meet one day."

"I am sure that we will be great friends," said Sally, clasping Aurora's hands in hers as her eyes filled with tears.

"I am not the only one to suffer, Sally," said Aurora softly. "Your father was killed too, and all over this secret they dug up."

"I know, Aurora, but that was different; he was a total stranger to me, and ever since I have been trying to find out exactly what it was that they found."

"Sally that is precisely what I intend to do."

"Then we must work together. Did your father tell you about the note Jo gave me?"

"He did, but not what it represented."

"Me too. Pierre and George were adamant that I shouldn't know more, except that it concerned the names of the Hyperboreans."

"Then we are both in the same boat, Sally. Both of our fathers have been killed, Marie is missing, and George has just had a narrow escape. We must find out what it is before anything else happens."

"I think I know how."

"Really? That's wonderful, Sally. Let's drink a toast to our partnership."

An hour later the two girls sat down to the dinner that Sally had carefully prepared. Aurora was impressed.

"That was delicious, Sally. I can't even make Hommos! I'm not in the least interested in domestic things, much to my mother's disappointment. She thinks I should have married years ago.

"How is your mother, Aurora? Will she be all right with your coming away so soon?"

"She is staying in the house at Zahleh with my aunt and uncle, and is probably glad to have me out of the way."

"That's difficult to believe."

Later as the girls relaxed by the log fire, Aurora turned to Sally.

"Sally, you said you thought you might know a way of finding out what this terrible secret is."

"Yes, it was Jo's note, Aurora. Your father and I both thought the numbers on it must be the code of a bank deposit box somewhere."

"He did tell me that. But how can we find out which bank it is and then get access to it?"

"I don't know, but I think I can get to his estate now. I went over to Minneapolis last week to see Jo's lawyer, and he confirmed that Jo has left me everything in his will."

"OK, but you surely can't get to his papers until probate is granted, Sally?"

"Perhaps, but I do have a written affidavit stating that I am Jo's daughter and rightful heir, and I shall use it to try to get into his bank, wherever that is."

"So you'll have to go back to Minneapolis."

"No. Your father seemed to think that Jo had a bank account in Beirut, and that he may have deposited something there."

"Good Heavens! So are you thinking of going there?"

"Yes, I hope so, and now that we have met, perhaps we could go together?"

"Of course, Sally. This sounds quite exciting. But surely he would have left something in his home bank?"

"I don't think that is likely, Aurora. He was in London examining the Brigstone Man when he discovered something important, and he flew straight to Beirut to show your father. That is why we think he must have left something there."

"But what about London, Sally? Has he got a bank there?"

"I suppose that's possible too," agreed Sally. "He could perhaps have just taken some photos to show your father. In any case, your father thought he might know which bank in Beirut Jo used, so that is the first place I would like to look."

"I see," said Aurora, sounding not altogether convinced. "As soon as I have made arrangements to reopen the dig at Brigstone, I could return home and you could come with me, Sally. What do you think?"

"But I thought you were going to start work here straight away, Aurora."

"I had hoped to, but it looks as though I will have to wait for the permit. Rather than hang around sightseeing, Sally, we could fly to Beirut and start our search, then I could return afterwards."

"Well, if that's all right with you, Aurora, I'd love to go."

"Fine, that's settled then," said Aurora. "Now I am rather tired, Sally. I think I should get to sleep."

"Oh, I'm sorry. I wasn't thinking. You must be exhausted. We'll have a quiet morning here tomorrow, then I'll drive you over to Brigstone Down after lunch. I haven't seen it yet, so I shall look forward to that."

Aurora awoke late the following morning. "I had a lovely sleep, Sally, but goodness me, look at the time!"

"That's fine," laughed Sally. "I'm sure you needed it. Come on I've made some strong coffee."

"Wonderful! But Sally, I've been thinking. Are you sure you should go to the dig site? Papa told me that you had to stay out of sight."

"I know, but frankly I am fed up with being cooped up down here with nothing to do, so unless those men know where I am, or what I plan to do, how could they possibly know that I will be there today?"

"You may be right, but all the same, we will have to keep our eyes open."

"I'm sure there is absolutely nothing to worry about, and you will be with me, Aurora."

"I certainly will," agreed her new friend.

After an early lunch, the two girls set off for Marlborough, where they stopped to enquire about the local archaeological society who had provided their fathers with a team of helpers for the excavation the year before. Unhappily, all that they learned was that the majority of its members had been students, most of whom had left the area. Sally told Aurora that John had found out that Jo had taken the skeleton up to London.

"That is how I know that Jo examined him, and the flying boat there."

"Yes, and then he flew straight to Beirut to tell my father what he had found," said Aurora. "I knew about that because my mother told me that it must have been something really important because

Jo seemed so shocked."

"Did you hear anything about their meeting that day, Aurora?"

"No such luck. I was out, but I do know that George was there too."

As they left Marlborough to drive over to Brigstone Down, Sally asked, "Did you father ever say anything about a religious connection, Aurora?"

"No, he didn't why?"

"Well it seems pretty obvious now that whatever they dug up must have had some strong religious significance."

"Do you mean that it was some sort of divine relic, like the Holy shroud, or some saint's bones?"

"Exactly, and whatever it was was so important that George warned me that if its discovery was ever made public, it could cause chaos or even war!"

"My God! Papa never told me that."

"I expect he thought it better that you didn't know, just as they refused to tell me."

"Now I think I am beginning to understand, Sally."

"Did George tell you that my flat was broken into?" asked Sally.

"He did and I can understand how that must have frightened you. I don't blame you for leaving London."

"But that's not all, Aurora. Afterwards two men tried to get into my office, and when the police arrested one of them, it turned out he was Italian and had diplomatic immunity."

"Oh no. Not the Mafia!" exclaimed Aurora. "So does that mean that they are still at large?"

"I'm afraid so. But it's worse than that, Aurora. The man they caught was an emissary from the *Vatican*!"

"What?" yelled Aurora, turning shocked towards her. "Do you mean that the Vatican has sent people to kill our fathers to stop them from publishing news of their find? This is just too incredible! We all know what the Catholic Church was capable of in the past, but to send out hit men in this day and age is surely not possible!"

"I agree, but supposing that what they found posed a threat to the whole Christian faith, perhaps even made a mockery of it all, then they would feel obliged to stop it in order to protect the church, would they not?"

"I suppose, in theory, it is possible. But really Sally, it surely couldn't be that, could it?"

"The fact remains," continued Sally, "that someone tried to kill Jo in the road, then got into the hospital and searched through his things before finally poisoning him, then, guessing that he had given me something, ransacked my flat and tried to get into my office. It must have been the same man that the police arrested."

"Oh, Sally, I hadn't realised quite how involved you were," said Aurora, now concerned for her friend.

"That was why I contacted your father and George because I was frightened, and didn't know what it was all about."

"I am so sorry, Sally. I had no idea you had been through such a terrible time!"

"It wasn't so bad, Aurora."

"Well whether George likes it or not, Sally, we are going to find out. Right?"

"Right," agreed Sally as she parked the car in the centre of the village. "This is Brigstone, and all we have to do is find the dig site. Let's ask at the pub." But the pub, of course, was closed.

"Let's just go over there."

"I think I will recognise the road," said Aurora.

"How on earth? You're not psychic, are you?"

"No, but I've been here before."

"What? I had no idea. When was that?"

"It was last year, during the dig. I was in London with my mother, and I came down one day by train. That was the last time I saw Marie."

Sally soon found the road to Brigstone Down, and with Aurora's help soon arrived at the dig site.

"Is this it?" she asked, scanning the desolate field. "There's not much to see, is there?"

"There never is, once a site has been closed," said Aurora. "Come on, I'll show you where the platform is." And striding over the muddy field she led Sally to the place where the scattered and broken boulders lay. The granite platform was covered with grass and weeds." Aurora scraped some away to reveal the surface of the ancient landing pad below.

"Gosh, it's enormous!" said Sally. "But where are the buildings that surrounded it?"

"I don't think they finished excavating them, but these stones must be part of them and the conduit that ran around the platform. But I'd love to have seen the tower. That would have been interesting."

"Wasn't the Brigstone Man found in another field?" asked Sally.

"I've no idea where they found him. That is the main reason that I want to reopen the excavation. There must be someone here who knows where it was."

An hour later the girls arrived back in the village, tired and muddy. The lights in the Cock and Bull came on just as Sally pulled up outside.

"Let's just hope that there is someone in the pub who can tell us something," said Sally. A fire had been lit in the lounge bar, and they sat down at a table beside it. "How about some wine to warm us up," she suggested.

"Good idea," laughed Aurora, looking around admiringly at the pretty oak-beamed room. "There is nothing like this in the Lebanon, not where a woman can go unescorted. I think it's great!"

The landlord was quite a young man and seemed happy to see them.

"It's funny you coming in like this today," he remarked. "Two gentlemen were asking about the find on the Down this morning."

"Really? I wonder who they were. Did they look like policemen?" asked Sally.

"Oh no. They were foreigners. They were asking all sorts of questions, and wanted to know if the archaeologists were coming back."

"Oh, no!" exclaimed Sally and Aurora in unison. "What time was this?" asked Aurora, as Sally clutched hold of her arm.

"It must have been about quarter to twelve. Why? Do you

know them?" he asked.

"I think we may do," muttered Sally.

"Do you know if they are staying in the area?" asked Aurora.

"I have no idea. They came in a large Mercedes and roared off towards the London road."

"Jesus! I hope they've gone," said Sally, peering anxiously out of the window. "I don't suppose you could describe them, could you?" she asked.

"I'm not sure," replied the landlord. "It was busy at the time, but I think they may have been Spanish or something, judging by the accent of the one I spoke to."

"Then it was *them*!"

"Yes it must have been." Sally started to panic.

"What on earth are we going to do now, Aurora? They could be hanging around somewhere. What if they saw my car? They could follow us back to the house!"

"Then we'll just have to make sure they don't," said Aurora resolutely.

"If you have a problem, ladies, you are very welcome to stay here," said the landlord.

"That's very kind of you, but we have to get home," said Sally. "Are you sure there is nothing else you can tell us?"

"Do you mean about the archaeological dig?" he asked.

"Of course."

He was disappointed that the archaeologists hadn't returned to continue with the work because it was good for trade, and a lot of his summer customers had been interested.

"Could you show us the field where the skeleton was found?" asked Aurora, unfolding a local map on the table.

"As far as I can remember, it must have been in the West Field," he said, pointing to a place on the map. "But you should ask Mr Easton, the farmer. He'll be able to show you exactly where it was."

"Thank you, I will," said Aurora. "You have been a great help, but before we go, can you tell me if there is anywhere nearby where we can hire a car?"

"There's only Fred's garage down the road. He may be able to find you something, but it won't be a new model. You'd be better to try in Marlborough."

"Thank you. You've been very kind," said Aurora, rising to take Sally by the arm.

"Why on earth did you ask him that?" whispered Sally as they left the pub.

"Isn't that obvious? If those men are still around, they just might spot your car, but they are hardly likely to take any notice of two women in headscarves driving some tatty car with local number plates, are they?"

"What? I haven't got a headscarf," objected Sally, laughing.

"I have," said Aurora, as she led Sally cautiously out into the road.

Some forty-five minutes later, two grey-faced women in headscarves drove slowly out of the village in a rusty old Morris Minor before speeding off towards Andover.

It was dark by the time the girls got back to the house. Felix growled when they walked in to the living room, barely able to recognise his mistress in her weird disguise.

"Wasn't that great!" exclaimed Aurora. "I haven't had as much fun for ages."

"That's all very well," moaned Sally, "but what about my car? How am I going to get it back?"

"Don't worry about that, Sally. I'll pop back and fetch it in a couple of days."

When Sally went downstairs the next morning, she found a fax on the machine from John.

> Dear Sally, I have taken a small furnished flat near Heathrow and have moved my things from your flat. I hope you will be happy. Please don't hesitate to call me if you have any problems. I shall worry about you.
>
> John

Aurora found Sally in tears in the kitchen, holding her hand under the cold tap.

"Whatever is the matter, Sally? Are you all right?"

"I'm fine," she answered bravely. "I just spilt boiling hot coffee on my hand – and there's this," she added, handing Aurora the crumpled fax.

"So this is the boyfriend," remarked Aurora as she read it. "It sounds pretty final to me. Are you happy about it?"

"Well of course I'm not," said Sally.

"Are you still in love with him?"

"I don't know if I ever really was. Sometimes I hate him for being so masterful and confident, and sometimes I wonder how on earth I ever managed without him. Perhaps I had just got used to having him around, and now that he's gone, I feel a bit lost."

"Well if that's all it is Sally, the sooner you put him out of your mind, the better."

"I suppose you are right, of course, and anyway, I've got enough to worry about at the moment. I'm just so glad that you are here, Aurora."

Later, after they returned from a long walk, they sat down to discuss the previous day's excursion.

"Sally, I've been thinking: why don't I drive back to Brigstone this evening to get your car? That way it will be done and we can make our plans for Bcirut."

"Oh no, Aurora! It's quite a long way. I'll have to come with you."

"Certainly not. Nobody knows me, and anyway, I love driving at night. I will be back in a couple of hours."

"Well, if you insist, Aurora. But I do feel guilty letting you go off on your own in a strange country." Aurora laughed.

"Don't be silly. I've driven all over the world Sally. I shall enjoy it."

After dinner that evening, Aurora prepared to leave.

"Don't you think you should call your mother, Aurora?" asked Sally. "You haven't spoken to her since you arrived. She may be worried."

"Oh, dear, I forgot. Yes, you are right, Sally. I'll just give her a quick call, if you don't mind."

Sally was in the kitchen when a white-faced Aurora walked in slowly. "What it is, Aurora? Is your mother all right?" she asked, as her friend sank down onto a chair.

"It's Marie," muttered Aurora. "They've found her."

"Oh no!" exclaimed Sally. "She's not…?"

"They've killed her," said Aurora, breaking down. "They found her body in a builder's skip. She had been dead for some time." Sally turned to throw her arms around her sobbing friend.

An hour later the two horrified girls were still sitting, stunned in the living room.

"What are we going to do?" asked Sally.

"What can we do, except just carry on and find out what these bastards are looking for," replied Aurora, grimly. "But first, Sally, I am going to get your car back."

"Don't be ridiculous," objected Sally, grabbing Aurora's arm as she stood up. "You're not going anywhere like that. It's nearly eleven o'clock, and you are in shock. My car can wait. I'm going to call George. Perhaps he hasn't heard, and we should warn him."

George had received a call from Nadine earlier. She had been more furious than sad and he was worried that she seemed to have declared war on the police, blaming them for the death of Marie as well as Pierre. He advised Aurora to get back home as soon as possible to look after her mother.

"Well, at least George is all right," she said. "I think we should try to get some sleep now, Sally. We can decide what to do in the morning."

"I'm going to make you a hot toddy, Aurora, and put a hot water bottle in your bed."

"Oh, no, Sally," laughed Aurora. "I'm all right, really."

"Stop arguing, silly. You've had a nasty shock. Come on now; up to bed with you," and she pushed her friend up the stairs.

The next day the sun was shining as the girls got up,

"I feel much better today," said Aurora, bravely.

"So do I," agreed Sally. "Let's get out into the garden this morning. Do you know anything about shrubs, Aurora?"

"Shrubs? What are they?" was the response.

After lunch they drove over to Petersfield in the cranky old car to buy some plants for the garden. On the way back Aurora turned suddenly to Sally.

"I'm going to ring the airport. I think I should go home to my mother." Sally was surprised.

"When are you thinking of going?"

"We'll go tomorrow, if you like."

"We?"

"Of course. You're not afraid, are you, Sally?"

"Of course I am, but I'd love to go."

"That's settled then," said Aurora. "I'll book a flight for tomorrow."

That evening Aurora left Sally in the house while she drove off towards Marlborough in the old car. It was after midnight when an anxious Sally saw her car draw up outside.

"Thank God you're back!" she cried. "I've been worried sick."

"Whatever for?" laughed Aurora. "It was a doddle. I'll go and pack now," she said, striding purposefully up the stairs.

At eleven o'clock the next morning, a BOAC DC10 took off for Beirut, carrying the two girls.

Chapter Nineteen

Four and a half hours later, Sally and Aurora stepped onto the tarmac at Beirut. The sky was blue and the sun was shining fiercely down. Sally felt as though she was arriving on a Spanish holiday in July, but, as they entered the crowded terminal, she realised that this was different. It was packed with burqa-robed women, some with their faces hidden behind yashmaks, waiting to greet their menfolk returning home from contract work in Europe.

There were tour operators' representatives of all nationalities hunting down their charges; page boys from the luxury hotels holding up placards; and irascible taxi drivers shouting each other down in their competition to grab the most affluent-looking visitors. The smartly dressed officer at Passport control seemed more interested in chatting up Sally than in checking her passport, and the two young customs officials with film star looks were far too busy panning over the arrivals for young blonde girls to bother with anyone's luggage.

"Is it always like this?" asked the bewildered Sally as Aurora led her through the clamouring masses towards the exit.

"Oh, yes, always," laughed Aurora. "Come on, it's this way. I left my car here so I hope it hasn't been stolen."

"Is that likely?"

"Who knows, but it's really too old to interest anyone," she replied.

Half an hour later they were driving down the wide, palm tree-lined boulevard leading from the airport in Aurora's open-topped white Buick.

"Isn't this super!" remarked Sally. "It's just like the Riviera."

"Just you wait, Sally. Beirut isn't all like this by any means.

The new Khalde Airport was only built about ten years ago."

It wasn't long before they turned off onto an older road, running between banana plantations. Sally thought that Aurora was driving rather too fast, but they were continually passed by battered Mercedes, their windscreens obscured by hanging worry beads and mascots, and Arab music blasting out through the open windows.

A little further on Sally noticed a sort of shantytown under the trees, with dozens of wooden shacks with tin roofs. Small children were running barefoot among tethered animals and discarded rubbish.

"What's that?" she asked, staring shocked at the squalor.

"It's Bourj al-Baranjneh refugee camp," replied Aurora grimly.

"Where are they from?"

"They are Palestinians, and the sooner they leave Beirut, the better."

"But where will they go?" asked Sally, surprised by Aurora's apparent callousness.

"I really don't care, anymore," said Aurora, her face hardening. "They have caused us enough problems, and now the Israelis are bombing our villages in the south. If we don't get rid of them soon there will be another war and we will all have to leave!" Sally would have liked to pursue the subject of the Palestinians, but thought it may be wiser not to press her host into political arguments. They continued their drive into the city in silence, with Sally staring amazed at the number of modern tower blocks and at the construction work going on everywhere.

Aurora drove slowly down the main shopping street at Hamra before turning off into Lyon Street, where the family apartment was.

"Here we are," she announced. "Mother will be surprised."

"Is she here?" asked Sally.

"No. I didn't want her to dash back here for us, so we'll drive up to Zahleh to see her tomorrow. You will enjoy that, Sally."

That evening Aurora took Sally to a well-known restaurant for dinner.

"*Ahlan-Wa-Sahlan*," greeted the manager, who obviously

knew Aurora.

"Would you bring us a full Mezze?" she asked, as the waiter placed glasses of iced water and Arak on the table.

Sally could hardly believe her eyes as she watched the table gradually fill with the most amazing variety of small dishes.

There was Tabbuleh, Kubbeh, Mtabbal, stuffed vine leaves, fried aubergines with yoghurt, Hommos and Labna and the waiter kept coming with warm, freshly baked pitta bread. After that came a delicious chicken stuffed with lemon and pine nuts. When a large dish of rosewater-flavoured pastries topped with honey and pistachio nuts appeared, Sally had to decline.

"That was fantastic, Aurora!" she cried. "I don't think I have ever enjoyed a meal so much. It was absolutely delicious."

"It was a pleasure, Sally. It is always such a treat to watch visitors' faces when they see a real Mezze for the first time. Let's skip coffee here. I will make you a good Turkish coffee at home."

Back at the apartment, Aurora telephoned her mother.

"We won't need to go up to Zahleh tomorrow, Sally," she announced. "My mother is coming back in the morning."

"I hope she hasn't shortened her stay for us."

"No. She is miserable up there, and as her sister is returning tomorrow, she may as well come with her."

"That's all right then. I shall look forward to meeting her," said Sally.

"Now that we are not going, I know what I must do tomorrow, Sally. I really must go to Marie's family. They'll be wondering why I haven't contacted them."

"Of course you must," agreed Sally, "and while you are out, perhaps I can make a start on trying to find out which bank Jo had an account with."

"How are you going to do that?"

"I really don't know, but I'll think of something," replied Sally hopefully.

Sally slept well that night and awoke early with the sun streaming in through the venetian blinds. It was seven o'clock and already the traffic was building up. She opened the wide picture window and leaned out over the balcony to hear the Muezzin calling from the mosques all over the city.

After a quick shower, Sally sat down with her notepad to try to work out how she could find her father's bank. She remembered that Pierre had told her that it was probably in a road near an airline office, so all she had to do was to find a bank in that road. The problem was that she couldn't remember the name of the road. She thought of looking up the addresses of airline offices in the telephone directory, but then remembered that it would be in Arabic! She was going to have to ask Aurora.

Over a light breakfast of orange juice, French-style croissants, fresh figs and coffee, she asked for Aurora's help. It didn't take her friend long to find that the main MEA offices were situated in Bab Edriss, after which she found that there were branches of four different banks in the same road.

Sally was eager to dash out and call at each of the banks.

"You can't just go rushing off around Beirut on your own, Sally," warned Aurora. "In any case, even if you do find out which bank it is, don't forget you will have to bluff your way in there again to get to the safe deposit room, and if you have asked about Jo's account before, somebody may remember you."

"Oh Lord! I hadn't thought about that. You are right, of course," said Sally. "But how on earth am I to find which bank it is, Aurora?"

"Let's try telephoning, and if that doesn't work then I'll do the footwork." Aurora was hoping she sounded confident.

"You are wonderful! You make me feel such an idiot. What would I do without you?"

"Of course you're not an idiot, Sally. You're just over anxious. I must see Marie's parents this morning, so while I am out, try phoning the banks, Sally. They all speak French, if not English, but please don't think about going there on your own, will you? Beirut is perfectly safe once you know your way around, but until you do, you must rely on me."

"All right, Aurora, I won't go out, but I can't see what you are so worried about. Those Vatican men can't possibly know that I am here."

"Maybe not, but someone may be keeping an eye on the

building, and if they see a blonde girl going in and out, we could have problems."

"Why? They were in London, Aurora."

"They broke into your flat, didn't they?"

"Yes."

"Then they may have found a photograph of you. You must have had some pictures somewhere, Sally."

"Oh Lord, I hadn't thought of that!"

Aurora's mother arrived back at the apartment at midday to find Sally in the kitchen.

"Hello! You must be Sally, Aurora told me you were here."

"How do you do, Madam," replied Sally in English. "I hope you don't mind; I thought I would prepare a light lunch. Aurora should be back at any time now."

"That's very kind of you, my dear, but I think I will just unpack and have a rest."

Nadine Soulaya was a tall, handsome woman, and very slim. Sally thought she looked exhausted. She longed to speak of Pierre and to demonstrate her sympathy over his death, but she was afraid to broach the subject.

"Where is Aurora?" asked Nadine. "Has she abandoned you?"

"Oh, no. she has gone to see Marie's parents, Madam."

"So you know all about that, Sally?"

"Yes, Madam. Aurora was terribly upset when she heard."

"Please do call me Nadine, Sally, everyone else does. Now has Aurora made you comfortable?"

"Yes perfectly, thank you, and I love your apartment, Nadine."

"Yes, it is pleasant. Now I shall leave you, if you don't mind Sally. I must rest a little."

By two o'clock Aurora had still not returned and Sally started to worry. Nadine was still in her bedroom and Sally was not sure if she was awake or sleeping. She decided to take her some lunch on a tray and knocked on the door. There was no reply. She knocked again then carefully turned the glass door handle and tiptoed in. Nadine was lying fully dressed on the bed, her face a deathly white. A sudden panic gripped Sally. What if she had taken some pills? She carefully set the tray down on the bedside table and leant over Nadine. Was she breathing?

"Sally!" Nadine cried, suddenly awake. She sat up, staring at Sally. "Is everything all right?"

When Aurora returned that afternoon she found Sally and her mother deep in conversation in her bedroom.

"Hello Mother. How are you?"

"And where have you been, Aurora, going off like that and leaving your guest alone?"

"That's all right," laughed Sally. "I'm enjoying myself immensely. Your mother has been telling me all about the Lebanon, Aurora."

"Good, then I won't have to bother," was the response.

"Is she always like this?" asked Sally.

"Invariably," replied Nadine wryly. "Goodness knows where she learned such terrible manners; certainly not from me!"

"Did you have any luck with the banks?" asked Aurora, as Sally joined her in the kitchen.

"Yes, I hope so," said Sally. "It was quite easy. First I rang the British Bank of the Middle East, and then the Chase Manhattan, as I thought they would be the most likely. I told them that I wanted to open an account and that I would need to have a safe deposit box. Three of the banks in the road have them, but only two have boxes available; the Bank Union National and the British Bank of the Middle East. The Holland Bank's boxes were all taken."

"So that means it could be any one of those three."

"That's right, but don't forget Aurora that it was the British Bank that your father mentioned."

"Fine. Then we shall try that one first," said Aurora.

"But I first have to find out if Jo had an account there, so how will I do that?"

"Your name is Jordan, is it not?"

"Yes, sort of."

"Then let's just play it by ear," said the confident Aurora.

"Gosh I'm scared. What if they think we are bank robbers casing the place?"

"Come off it, Sally! Just stop worrying, will you. We will probably just walk straight in with no problems."

"But what if there's a guard in the strong room watching while I am fiddling about trying to find which key it is?"

"Then you'll just have to look and act as though you are terrible rich and have two boxes and can't remember which one it is. In which case we'd better fit you out with some of mother's model clothes, because in your jeans you would never be accepted as one of the international set staying at the St George."

"Oh, come on, Aurora," objected Sally. "I'm not going to start dressing up again!"

Sally lay awake almost the entire night, picturing the scenario for gaining access to the safe deposit boxes. The most important thing, she told herself, is to appear totally confident, and for that I must work out exactly what I am going to say.

At five o'clock the next morning, having finally fallen into a light slumber, she awoke shivering with the duvet on the floor. She crawled out of bed and padded silently into the kitchen to fetch a glass of water. Aurora was sitting red-eyed at the table, a glass of tisane in front of her.

"Aurora! Are you all right?"

"I suppose so, but what are you doing up at this hour, Sally? Couldn't you sleep either?"

"No. I'm just so scared about the bank. I've been having nightmares about what might go wrong. We could end up in prison, Aurora! But what about you? You haven't been crying, have you?" she asked, taking her friend's hand in hers.

"It's just all too much," muttered Aurora. "First my darling papa, and now dear Marie. I just can't take it in, Sally." And the strong confident Aurora broke into heaving sobs in Sally's arms.

It was past eleven by the time Aurora phoned for a taxi to take them to the bank, which left them very little time before the banks closed at midday.

"Come on Sally," she urged, as they dashed out into the street. "With any luck they will be too busy just before lunchtime to worry about us."

The streets of West Beirut were thick with traffic, the spectacle of which so fascinated Sally, that she almost forgot to be nervous. At eleven thirty the taxi dropped them off outside the bank.

Aurora opened the cab door and, after looking carefully up and down the street, took Sally's arm and hustled her into the building.

"This is what you must always do, Sally. Never get into a strange car, even if it has a taxi sign. Always use the driver I know, and ask him to wait for you. It isn't expensive."

"All right, I'll try to remember," agreed Sally.

"Have you got Jo's code numbers, Sally?" whispered Aurora, as they walked into the banking hall.

"Yes, of course. I've written them on my arm."

"And you have got the keys, haven't you?" Aurora was now sounding more nervous than Sally.

"Shut up!" hissed Sally. "Of course I have."

Sally approached a counter manned by a young Indian woman.

"*Bon Jour*!" she said.

"*Bon Jour Madame*. How may I help you?" replied the young woman.

"*Ah – vous parlez Anglais*?"

"Yes Madame, we have a number of American clients."

"I'm sure you do," said Sally, smiling sweetly. Then, taking a deep breath, she said, "I would like to go to my safe deposit box please."

"Of course, Madame. You do have an account with us?"

"Oh yes," replied Sally, holding her fingers crossed behind her back. "Do you need to see some identification?"

"I'm sure that will not be necessary," replied the girl, smiling back at Sally with her brilliant white teeth. "You know the way? It's the staircase over there," she said pointing across the hall.

"Yes, of course. Thank you," said Sally, turning to join Aurora with a wink. "So far so good," she whispered as she led the way down the stairs.

Moments later they reached the entrance to the strong rooms to be greeted by a uniformed commissionaire.

"*Bon Jour Mesdames. Vous avez la cle*?" he asked.

"*Évidement*," replied Sally.

"*Le premier numero, s'il vous plait*?" he asked.

"*Numero trois*," replied Sally, her heart beating in her chest.

"*Suivez-moi, Mesdames*," he said as he swung open a heavy

iron door. "*Voila*!"

"*Merci*," said Sally and Aurora in unison.

"Phew!" exclaimed Sally, as they found themselves alone in a room lined with metal boxes.

"That wasn't so bad, was it? You were great," said Aurora. "Well done."

"It was all right for you, Aurora. I nearly had a heart attack! I mean, what if that girl had asked to see my cheque book or something."

"Well she didn't did she. She just wanted to get away for her lunch. Now come on Sally, let's get cracking with the keys."

One of the keys had a cedar tree embossed on the barrel and Sally thought it would be the most likely one. Rolling up her sleeves to read the numbers on her arm, she worked her way along the wall of boxes until she found a match.

"It's here!" she cried excitedly, as she held the key in her trembling hand. "Pray," she hissed, as she slid it into the keyhole and turned it. Nothing happened. "Hell!"

"Turn it the other way," said Aurora at her side. Sally turned the key twice and heard a soft click.

"That's it!" she cried. "It's open!"

"Well hurry up, for heaven's sake, or the bank will be closing. It's gone quarter to twelve," urged Aurora.

Sally carefully slid out the long heavy box and laid it on the table. It was half full of papers. A blue folder lay on top marked:

Report of an examination of two skeletal remains found on Delos in May 1965 (by Dr Joseph Jordan; August 1971).

Tucked into the five page report was a photograph of a flying boat and a small envelope containing two more photos. Lying underneath was a large DHL envelope, addressed to Jo in London containing a letter from Pierre.

"Quick!" urged Aurora, as she pulled up two chairs and sat down to study the contents. "I'll read through the report while you look at the photos and the letter."

Sally looked first at the photo of the flying boat. It was quite faint and had obviously been taken with an instant Polaroid camera. She was just able to make out some lettering on the side of the vehicle but it looked like some ancient language.

"There's a word here, and I suppose it could be a name, but I can't read it, Aurora."

"Never mind. Try the others."

Sally took out the other two photos from the envelope.

"Oh look! It's a picture of a woman."

"That's interesting, and doesn't she look biblical with that robe around her face. Is there anything else?"

"Only a picture of some writing," replied Sally, passing it to Aurora.

"My goodness! It's some sort of an inscription," said Aurora. "It's not Greek. It could be ancient Assyrian. How extraordinary on Delos! Yes, and the letters on the flying boat may be the same."

"Oh Lord, we're not doing very well, are we?" remarked Sally.

"Quick, read the letter," urged Aurora. "That must surely tell us something. There's nothing much in Jo's report so far." Pierre's letter appeared to be questioning George and Jo's find in Athens, and was laid out in numbered paragraphs.

"You weren't far wrong, Aurora," said Sally after a few minutes. "The lettering is Aramaic, and the name on the flying boat is 'Apolanus'."

"What about the inscription with the picture? Does he say what it was?" asked Aurora.

"Just a minute," said Sally, scanning through Pierre's small writing. "Here it is. He asks George to confirm the age of the papyrus. Can he be sure that a reed papyrus could survive in metal for over two thousand years?"

"But what does he say about the lettering?" again urged Aurora. "Quick, we are running out of time."

"He asks if they can be sure of their translation."

"But what did it *say*, Sally?" insisted Aurora, nervously jumping up from her seat.

"I'm looking," said Sally. "Yes – *Oh my God*!"

"*What*?" yelled Aurora.

"Look, Aurora," said Sally, holding the page up for her to see.

On it Pierre had quoted George and Jo's interpretation of the letting, it read:

Mary of Nazareth, beloved of Apolanus
Blessed of all women.

"Mary of Nazareth!" cried the girls in unison.

"*Merde*!" swore Aurora. "It *can't* be the Virgin Mary! That's outrageous!"

"But why does it say, 'Blessed of all women'?" asked Sally.

"I don't know, but she's not our Lady."

"Beloved of Apolanus," Sally continued. "That means that Apolanus, the Hyperborean, was intimate with a girl called Mary from Nazareth. But what was he doing on Delos? None of it makes sense, does it?"

"I'm totally confused. I just don't know what to think. What else is there in the letter, Sally?"

"You take the last three pages, Aurora, and I'll finish going through these," said Sally, as there was a knock on the door and the Commissionaire came in.

"Oh, no!" muttered Aurora.

"The bank will be closing in three minutes, Ladies, but you may have a few minutes longer until the hall is cleared of clients. I will let you know in good time," he said.

"Thank you. That's very good of you," said Aurora, exchanging a fearful glance with Sally.

The girls skimmed through the remainder of Pierre's letter, but it offered no further revelations, and many of his questions were similar to those now running through their heads.

As Jo's report on the skeletons revealed nothing that they hadn't already been told, they reluctantly folded the papers back into the box and returned it to its hiding place.

"I wasn't expecting anything like this," remarked Aurora, as they left the strong room.

"But what if it was a picture of the Virgin Mary, and she did have a lover?" whispered Sally.

"You mustn't think that, Sally. It's too wicked," admonished

Aurora. "It must be another Mary. There may have been several Marys in Nazareth, and anyway, we don't have an exact date."

"But what about the Brigstone Man?" asked Sally. "There was nothing there about him, and I thought he was supposed to be the important one. I remember now that when I told George about the man from the Vatican, he said that meant that they must know everything. So perhaps whatever Jo found on the Brigstone Man was connected with this Apolanus and Mary."

"You could be right, Sally, and Jo must have hidden his report about that somewhere else."

Aurora took Sally's arm as they approached the bank's door.

"You wait here while I check if our taxi is there, and don't come out till I call you. We must be on our guard all the time while you are here."

"I know," sighed Sally. "What a bore."

Back at the apartment, the girls sat down to review the morning's adventure.

"We must talk to George. Now he will have to tell us exactly what he and Jo found," said Sally.

"I agree, but I am not at all happy about that picture."

"Do you mean the one of Mary?" asked Sally.

"Of course. You do realise that I am a Christian, Sally?"

"Yes. George told me that your father was a Maronite Christian. Are you of the same faith, Aurora?"

"I am, and I can never accept that our Lady was an adulteress."

"I understand, but it may not have been her."

"The whole thing was probably some horrible hoax," suggested Aurora, hopefully.

"Pierre's letter was sent to Jo in London, questioning what George had told him, was it not?" said Sally, changing the subject.

"Yes."

"So George wouldn't have told him anything on the telephone, would he? He must have written to him, probably also sending the letter by courier. So what did Pierre do with it?"

"Now that I do not know," said Aurora. "I have searched right through papa's papers, and I have found nothing at all about either of the digs, or their post mortem reports."

"So do you think he may have destroyed it?" asked Sally.

"I suppose it is possible, but I will have another good look in his room at the university," said Aurora, as Nadine came into the room.

"There you are," she remarked. "Why don't you take Sally to the beach this afternoon, Aurora? It's a lovely day."

"I thought we might drive south to Tyre, before the Israelis start bombing it again," said Aurora.

"Good Heavens Aurora! You don't really think it will come to that, do you?"

"Inevitably," retorted Aurora, as she left the room. Sally turned shocked to Nadine.

"Is it really going to be bad now in the Lebanon?"

"I sincerely hope not," replied Nadine. "Aurora follows the news more closely than I do, but she could be right, and it is obvious that the Israelis will continue to retaliate to the PLO raids into Israel."

After a quick lunch Aurora put through a call to George in Athens. He was just leaving his office for the lecture room when she got through.

"Aurora! What a pleasant surprise. Are you calling from England?"

"No George, I'm back in Beirut, and there is somebody here who would like to speak to you."

"Hello, George!" said Sally, as she took the receiver.

"Good Heavens Sally! You are not in Beirut, are you?"

"Yes George. I came with Aurora."

"But, my dear girl, you are taking a terrible risk after all that has happened!" George sounded genuinely concerned.

"Perhaps I am, but I just couldn't go on sitting at home doing nothing, and as Aurora was returning, I decided to come with her."

"I suppose you are going to tell me that you are hoping to find Jo's bank?"

"I already have," she replied.

"What? And did he have a safe deposit box, Sally?"

"He did, and that is what we want to talk to you about, George."

"Oh, dear," mumbled George, with what sounded remarkably like a sigh. "Are you telling me that you have found something, Sally?" he ventured.

"Indeed I am, and we need to talk to you urgently, George," said Sally, enjoying his apparent discomfort. "Aurora and I plan to come over to Athens, so I hope you will be willing to provide us with some answers."

"I shall be delighted to see you both, of course. But tell me Sally. What exactly did you find at the bank?"

"You know I can't discuss it on the phone, George, but rest assured that we have studied Jo's papers and now need to discuss what we saw with you."

"I see. Then so be it. Let me know when you will be arriving, Sally, and I will meet you at the airport."

"Oh, please don't worry, George. Your arm must still be in plaster."

"I'm perfectly well, Sally, thank you, and I can drive again… Greek fashion at least."

"How did he sound?" asked Aurora, after Sally hung up.

"Worried, and very surprised. I'll bet he never imagined that I would come, or that I would get to Jo's bank."

"Then he underestimated you, didn't he?" laughed Aurora. "Now, do you fancy a drive down to Sidon and Tyre, Sally?" she asked.

"I certainly do, if you are sure that it is safe."

"Of course it is," replied the ever confident Aurora; "and tomorrow I'll take you to see Baalbek and the Bekka Valley where our famous wine comes from, and half of Europe's supply of Hashish too."

"Wow! I can't wait," exclaimed Sally.

A couple of days later, after a lightning tour of some of Lebanon's well-known tourist spots, the two girls were eager to move on to Athens to tackle George.

"I'll book our flight," said Aurora.

"Thank goodness I have paid holidays," remarked Sally. "I've already used almost all of this year's allowance, and if I don't get back to work soon I shall be completely broke."

"Don't worry, I have friends who work for air Liban, and they'll get us on stand-by for next to nothing."

"That's a relief. But before I leave Beirut, Aurora, I really would like to do a bit of shopping. Couldn't we go to the souhks? I'd love to see them."

"We could, but it may not be a very good idea, Sally. We could be spotted by Marie's friends, and it's not the safest of places at the best of times."

"Oh do let's try. I'm sure the two of us can look after ourselves."

"Well, all right," agreed Aurora, reluctantly. "We had better go early in the morning, before the usual tourists, and I'll get our taxi driver to take us there and back."

Early the next morning, Sally and Aurora left the apartment and drove to the huge central Place des Canons. Sally's eyes were as wide as a child's seeing fireworks for the first time as they alighted at the top end of the square which housed the gold and silversmiths and dozens of jewellery shops.

"Wow!" she exclaimed, staring in disbelief at the dazzling displays in the packed windows. "Look at that! Is all this stuff real?"

"Of course it is," laughed Aurora.

"But it's so cheap!"

"It's tax free here, and it's all made by individual craftsmen."

"Oh, I must buy something, but what?" said Sally.

"Come on, I'll take you to an Armenian jeweller I know. He will give you a fair price, but don't forget to bargain. You must never agree to pay the asking price."

Almost an hour passed before Aurora was able to drag Sally away from the jewellery quarter.

"I know a shortcut through to the flower market," she said, as she led Sally into a narrow lane.

"Oh, how lovely!" exclaimed Sally, pointing to the banks of brightly coloured flowers massed against the walls ahead of them.

"You wait. The fruit and vegetables souhks are just as spectacular," said Aurora, as they approached the end of the alleyway.

"What was that?" cried Sally, turning to look back as they were suddenly startled by gunshots, shouting and car horns blaring behind them. "What is it?" she hissed as Aurora grabbed hold of her arm.

The shouting was coming nearer, when suddenly, they saw a terrified mule dragging a broken, heavy cart galloping down the alleyway towards them.

"*Merde*!" It's coming straight at us!" yelled Aurora pushing the frightened Sally ahead of her. "Run Sally, *run*!" she yelled.

"*Where*?" screamed Sally. "We'll never make it!"

A loud shot rang out and a bullet whistled over their heads. Aurora threw herself at Sally, sending them both sprawling heavily against a wooden door as the crazed animal passed within inches of their legs.

"My God, we could have been killed!" cried Sally, as they looked up to see the cart smash into the end of the alley.

"For God's sake, let's get out of here," urged Aurora, as a crowd of men and boys came screaming towards them, and grabbing hold of each other, they hauled themselves up and limped as fast as they could into the flower market.

Dodging behind displays of Hibiscus, Bougainvillea and Oleander bushes, Aurora quickly led Sally back to the square where their taxi was waiting.

"What was all the shooting? I can't stop shaking," said Sally, as they sped back to the apartment.

"It may just have been to warn people, or perhaps they were trying to shoot the mule. We hear gunshots all the time now. It's nothing unusual."

"So it wasn't intended for us then?" asked a fearful Sally.

"I don't think so," replied Aurora.

"You don't *think* so?" Sally repeated, aghast at Aurora's apparent calm.

"All the same, Sally, I think it is time we moved on, don't you? I'll ask my friend if he can get us on the Athens flight tomorrow."

The following day, having said goodbye to Nadine, Sally left for the airport with Aurora.

“There are so many more places I would love to have seen,” she said, “but I have really enjoyed my stay, thanks to you Aurora.”

“Then you must come back again,” said Aurora, as they turned onto the wide boulevard leading to the airport.

A heavily-loaded lorry chugged along in front of them, and just as Aurora approached to overtake it, a black Mercedes shot past the two of them, his horn blaring obnoxiously.

“Stupid idiot!” muttered Aurora as she pulled back behind the lorry.

“*Look out*!” yelled Sally suddenly, as a heavy pallet of bricks started to roll off the side of the lorry, right in their path. Aurora braked and swung the wheel round to accelerate past on the inside lane, the car’s tyres screaming against the edge of the ditch.

“Jesus!” she yelled, while Sally sat white-faced, hanging onto the sides of her seat with her eyes shut tight.

“Please stop, Aurora. I think I’m going to be sick.”

“Nonsense,” snapped Aurora. “That’s the last thing we should do. We must keep going. I’ll drive round to the staff car park, and we can get into the airport that way. Don’t worry, Sally. Just keep your eyes peeled and yell if you see that car again.”

“You don’t think it was them do you?”

“It could have been.”

“Oh, Lord!” sighed Sally. “Let’s get out of here!”

Chapter Twenty

Three hours later Sally and Aurora arrived in Athens. George was waiting at the airport and drove them straight to their hotel.

"Thank God you are all right, Sally. I was worried when you told me you were in Beirut. You didn't have any problems there, did you?"

"Not really; just a runaway mule nearly ran us down and we nearly got smashed up by a load of bricks."

"Good Heavens! You weren't hurt, were you?"

"Of course not," said Aurora.

Over dinner that evening the girls told George about their find in Jo's safe deposit box.

"Now that we've seen the stuff about the Delos find, surely you can now explain what it all means?" asked Sally.

"To start with," interrupted Aurora, "who was the Mary in the picture? You translated the inscription as 'Mary of Nazareth', but there must have been more than one Mary living there. She couldn't possibly have been the Virgin Mary." George was looking thoroughly uncomfortable as he struggled to find the right answer.

"You are right, Aurora. There was no way of knowing exactly who she was at the time."

"At the time?" queried Sally. "Do you mean that you found out who she was later?"

"Perhaps," admitted George.

The two girls glanced at each other. It was obvious that George was struggling to keep something from them.

"But what about the Hyperborean, Apolanus?" asked Sally, trying a new tack. "Did 'Beloved of Apolanus' mean that he was her lover? Who was he, and what was he doing on Delos? It's all very confusing, George."

"Now there I may be able to help you, Sally," he said. "There is an ancient manuscript in a monastery on Delos telling of the Hyperboreans flying, and I believe you may find something there about Apolanus. I started to look through it last year, but didn't have time to finish it."

"But George, about this Mary. Are you sure you can't tell us anything about her?" Aurora was not giving up.

"Well girls, if you insist, but all I can say is that after further research, we were able to agree that the woman in the picture was Mary of Nazareth, the wife, or betrothed of Joseph the carpenter."

"Oh, no!" cried Aurora, her hands covering her face as George continued.

"We were so shocked by what we found that we were convinced that it must all be some gigantic hoax. But, after having weighed up all the evidence of the two digs, the one on Delos and the one in England, we realised that it would have been virtually impossible for anyone to carry out such a complicated operation. If it was a hoax, then it must have been planned by someone who hated the Church so vehemently that he was determined to destroy it… perhaps the Anti-Christ, or the Devil himself!"

"So, if it wasn't a hoax, and it was the Virgin Mary, why can't you tell us the rest of the story?" said Sally. "Surely now that we know this much, George, you can tell us what my father found about the Brigstone Man? There was obviously something there to connect the two finds."

"I am very sorry, Sally, but I can tell you nothing more." Sally was losing patience.

"But that's ridiculous! Look, George, my father, and Aurora's father and Marie have all been killed, and you and I are in danger. We have every right to know. I insist that you tell us!" George shook his head as Aurora took over.

"Sally will search her father's papers in London, George, until she finds his report on the Brigstone Man, so you might as well tell us now." But it was no good.

"I wouldn't put too much faith in Jo's records," he said. "Don't forget that the three of us agreed that no one else should ever know what we had found, and we have no way of knowing if Jo ever really intended to break his word."

"I give up," said Sally, angrily.

"Good," replied George.

"There is just one more thing puzzling me, George," said Aurora, attempting to break the growing enmity between the other two.

"What is it, Aurora?" he asked.

"Can you now explain the reason why you and my father were not allowed to continue with the research on the Delos two? I remember that papa was furious at the time, and he never could explain it."

"I'm afraid that is a bit of a mystery," said George, "but I believe there may be a very simple explanation."

"Like what?"

"Jealously, for one," said George. "The director of the Athens Archaeological Institute at the time was a very frustrated man. As an archaeologist he had never directed any significant excavations, and to have Pierre and I uncover something so important on his own doorstop would have been totally unacceptable."

"That doesn't sound very plausible," remarked Aurora.

"I agree, but I can come up with no other reasonable explanation."

"Are your Delos two still hidden away in the museum, George?" asked Sally.

"As far as I am aware, they are," he said. "I am sure that the director would have informed me if he had any intention of moving them."

"Well, girls, thank you for the dinner," said George, as they stood up to leave the restaurant. "It is good to see you both again, but if there is nothing else I can help you with, I must get home. I have a heavy day in front of me tomorrow."

Sally cast a disappointed look towards Aurora as they took their leave.

"Thank you for talking to us, George. I can't pretend that I am not disappointed, but as you seem determined to keep us in the dark, there is not much we can do."

"Try to understand, Sally my dear," he said, taking her arm. "It really is best that you don't know everything."

"Goodbye, George. Do take care of yourself, won't you," she said.

"Well that's that then. We seem to be getting nowhere fast," said Sally to Aurora. "Perhaps I should have tried to find Jo's bank in London first, instead of coming here."

"No, I don't think so. After all, we do now know about Apolanus and Mary, however impossible it may seem. Why don't we go over to Delos, as we are here, Sally? You never know, we may find something about Apolanus at the monastery that George mentioned."

"Oh, yes, why not?" agreed Sally. "I would love to see the place where they found him."

Early the next morning the two girls took a taxi to Piraeus to catch the boat to Delos. The weather was stormy but they were lucky, and the ferry left on time.

On their arrival, they found a man on the quay with scooters for hire and, as George had told them how to find the monastery, they set off eagerly to the northern part of the island. They found the village quite easily, but there was nothing to indicate the whereabouts of a monastery, and the whole place seemed deserted.

"Let's try that way," suggested Sally, pointing to a dirt track leading uphill. "Aren't monasteries usually built on high ground?"

"You may be right," agreed Aurora.

Turning a corner, they came suddenly upon an enormous heard of goats of all colours and, following them, an old woman in black, bent double so that she was almost walking on all fours.

"Oh look! She must be at least a hundred years old!" exclaimed Sally, as they pulled up in front of her. She hadn't heard the scooters, but her wrinkled face lit up with a toothless grin when she saw the girls.

"*Kaleespere*," said Aurora into her ear. The old women uttered a greeting, waving a gnarled hand in the air.

"*Tha boroosateh na moo peetwe poo eeneh to monasteeree, parahkalo*?" asked Aurora.

"*Tee*?" the woman grunted, holding her shaking head to one

side.

"*Monasteeree*?" bellowed Aurora.

"*Ah... Eeneh eepahrk*," she shrieked loudly, waving her arms upwards.

"What does she mean?" asked Sally, trying not to laugh.

"I think she said it's up there," said Aurora, pointing up the hill ahead of them.

"*Ne ne*," screamed the crone, grabbing hold of Aurora's arm.

"*Parakalo Madame*," said Aurora, touching her hand.

"*Kaleespera*," added Sally, as they remounted their scooters.

"That's the only Greek I know," she said, as they sped off up the hill. "I didn't know you spoke Greek, Aurora?"

"I don't really. Just the usual tourist phrases I picked up working here. Oh, look! That must be the monastery up there," she said, pointing to some white buildings glimpsed through the trees ahead.

"Isn't this fun! I do hope we can find something interesting there," said Sally.

"I have a feeling that we will," said Aurora, as they turned off onto a pathway.

Christian was by now a studious twenty-nine year old, and had been at the monastery for several months, working in the library. On his return to France from London, he had sought out his friend, the local priest, who had helped and tutored him. A year later he had joined the Dominican Order at Prouille as a novice before returning to England to complete his studies at a college near London.

When Sally and Aurora were shown into the monastery library by one of the senior fathers, Christian was seated at a table, carefully cleaning the worn binding of an old book.

"Here we are ladies," said the elderly monk, as he beckoned towards Christian. "Brother Christian will help you. I believe he speaks a little English. I hope your Greek and Latin are up to scratch."

"Oh Lord! How are we going to be able to read anything at all?" whispered Sally to Aurora.

"I'm sure we will manage," replied the always confident

Aurora, as the monk left them to their search.

Christian looked up from his work as the girls approached.

"Hello! I believe you speak English?" said Sally.

"Just a little," he replied with a strong French accent. "I worked in London for a short time."

"But you're not Greek, are you?" Christian laughed.

"Very few of us are. I am French," he said, smiling. "Now, how may I help you?"

"We are interested in the Hyperboreans who settled in Britain from Anatolia," said Aurora.

"Or the Trojans who were enslaved by the Mycenaeans," added Sally. Christian looked startled.

"They Hyperboreans? What period are we talking about?"

"About one thousand to two thousands BC," replied Aurora.

"What is your interest in the Hyperboreans?" he asked. "It is rather an unusual request."

"I am an archaeologist, and I have recently been studying them at the British Museum," said Aurora.

"How interesting. I worked on a dig once, when I was a student in England," said Christian.

The girls exchanged glances.

"I believe you have a manuscript here concerning them, and as we were in Athens, we decided to come to see you," said Aurora.

"Then I think I can help you. There are several old volumes that I know of, but if you can be more specific about exactly what you are looking for, it would save a lot of time." Sally became suddenly aware of the need to step carefully, willing Aurora to say no more.

"I have read a little about the Hyperboreans being able to fly," suggested Aurora. "Do you have anything on that?"

"Yes, of course. Do sit down and I will fetch the manuscripts."

Sally breathed a sigh of relief as Christian climbed up the library steps to the top level of the shelves.

"You don't think he knows something, do you? He seems awfully wary of us," she whispered to Aurora.

"I don't see how. He probably just thinks it is an unusual request."

"Well don't say anything more, for goodness sake."

"Of course I won't," snapped Aurora, as Christian appeared carrying three leather-bound volumes and placed them on the table.

"There, I think you will find what you are seeking. If you need any help with Latin, let me know. Good luck!" he added, as he returned to his work at the far end of the library.

"Gosh, where do we start?" whispered Sally, as she carefully opened up a leather-bound manuscript.

"First just look for an index. Most of the old manuscripts have one," said Aurora. "You should be able to recognise some of the letters. If you spot something that rings a bell, pass it to me."

"I'll try, but I feel pretty useless, and it's going to take hours to look through these."

"Never mind. If we have to stay for the night, we will. Now, let's get cracking."

It was late afternoon by the time Aurora had satisfied herself that there was nothing of interest in the first big volume Christian had brought them.

"We're never going to find anything at this rate," moaned Sally despairingly.

"Yes we will. Quick! Pass me that slimmer book over there. Wasn't there something in the index about Delphi and Delos?"

"Yes, but how can that help?"

"Haven't you heard of the legend about Hyperboreans sending offerings there from Britain, Sally? We don't yet know how they travelled, do we? There may be something about them flying there."

"Perhaps, but what about Apolanus? I thought we wanted to find something about him?"

"You just keep looking for a name beginning with a… alfa and p… ro," said Aurora.

"All right, I'll try," said Sally.

"How are you getting on?" asked Christian as he approached their table.

"Very slowly," said Sally.

"Please do call me if you have difficulties," he said.

"We may have to take you up on that," said Aurora, as Sally

gave her a sharp kick under the table.

An hour later Sally found a name beginning with 'ap…' and excitedly passed it to Aurora.

"It's him!" whispered Aurora, carefully skimming over the wording. Minutes later she found the word 'Nazareth' half a page further on. "This is wonderful! It proves that he visited Nazareth," she cried.

"So the inscription with Mary's pictures was true then. He really was Mary's lover!"

"Yes," said Aurora. "But which Mary?"

"What about the flying? Is there nothing about that?" asked Sally.

"I haven't found anything yet, but I think we can be satisfied with this, don't you, Sally? It is getting rather late. Let's call it a day, shall we?"

"I agree. You have done wonderfully well, Aurora. It couldn't have been easy."

Christian, aware of their excitement, left his table and walked over to them.

"Have you found anything interesting?" he asked.

"We have found one useful reference, Brother, but unfortunately we do not have time to search any longer," said Aurora.

"You are welcome to stay and continue tomorrow," he said.

"That is very kind, but it will not be necessary. We must catch the morning ferry back to Athens."

"We are very grateful for your help, Brother Christian," added Sally.

"I am always happy to meet English visitors," said Christian, as the girls rose to leave. "My mother was English, you see."

"Oh was she?" remarked Sally.

"Yes. Her name was Nancy."

"Fancy that! My mother was called Nancy too. Did your father marry her in France?"

"Yes, but he was killed in the war," said Christian.

"How sad. Do you still keep in touch with your mother?"

"Oh, no. she died a long time ago. I never knew her."

"I'm sorry," said Sally, embarrassed for having questioned him so far. "Thank you for your help, Brother," she said, taking his outstretched hand. "We have enjoyed our visit."

"Good luck with the renovation work," said Aurora, as they left the library.

"That wasn't a bad afternoon's work, was it?" remarked Aurora, as they sped away downhill. "We must get back to the town before it gets dark, or we will be too late to find a room for the night."

That evening the girls ate in a small friendly taverna down by the harbour.

"Let's give George a ring and tell him what we found," suggested Sally, but she soon returned to the table disappointed. "He wasn't there. There was no reply."

"Never mind. We can try tomorrow," said Aurora.

The following morning Sally and Aurora awoke early, the autumn sun streaming in through their window.

"We've got hours before the ferry leaves, and we haven't seen anything of the island, Aurora. Couldn't we just see the place where they found the skeletons? It won't take very long, surely?"

"The ferry leaves at eleven o'clock, which gives us about three hours, so we could just about do it, but we will have to hurry."

"Oh come on, do let's go!" urged Sally. "We may never get another chance."

It was a quarter past ten when the girls mounted their scooters at the foot of Mount Cynthus for the return ride back to the town. Driving as fast as they could they sped through desolate scenery, disappointed with all that they had seen. The island was dotted with ruined buildings and broken statues, as though it had all been blown away by a hurricane. Everything was grey and brown, even the trees, and there seemed to be no water or green undergrowth anywhere.

Rounding a sharp bend in the road, they found themselves blocked by an old lorry, creaking under a heavy load of stones.

"Oh, not again!" cried Sally, fearful that the load was about to crash down onto the road. For precious minutes it was impossible to pass the lorry, with both girls shouting and waving at the driver in vain.

"We'll miss the ferry if we don't get past!" yelled Aurora, as Sally leaped from her scooter and ran up to the front of the lorry, waving frantically. The old driver suddenly woke up jamming on his screeching brakes, a blank expression on his palsied face. Signalling their thanks, the girls carefully manoeuvred themselves between the lorry and the road edge, then sped off again, singing loudly.

They were just approaching the town when a herd of unattended goats suddenly jumped down onto the road from the hillside.

"Oh, no, I don't believe it!" yelled Sally, again. This time, they had no choice but to weave slowly between the lazy, munching animals.

As they skidded to a halt on the harbour quay, they saw the Athens ferry halfway out in the bay.

"Well, that's just great," muttered Aurora. "We've nearly killed ourselves for nothing, and now we will have to wait around until the next one."

"When will that be?" asked a dishevelled Sally.

"I don't know. We'll have to ask."

"Let's go to the taverna. I could do with a drink," said Sally.

"Good idea," replied her friend.

Luck was with them as there was a ferry sailing from Mykonos at three o'clock that afternoon, so the girls settled down to a long Greek lunch.

They were just finishing their meal, when they heard a commotion outside on the quay, and a woman came rushing into the taverna shouting and waving her arms in the air.

"What's going on?" asked Sally, turning around to see the other diners rush to the door.

"Let's go and see," said Aurora, as they joined the excited crowd outside.

"*Vahrkah, Vahrkah*!" they seemed to be shouting.

"*Pleeo... Boom!*" yelled a young boy standing nearby.

"What is it?" asked Sally.

"I'm not sure. I think something's blown up. I'll try to find out," said Aurora, as she marched over to the ticket office.

Moments later, Aurora returned, her face drained of blood. Sally grabbed her arm.

"What is it? You look terrible." Aurora sunk down onto a low wall.

"It's the ferry, Sally. It has sunk!"

"Sunk? You don't mean *our* ferry that we missed?"

"Yes, the morning ferry to Athens. It's gone!"

"Oh, my God!" cried Sally. "Whatever happened?"

"I don't know. All I do know is that we weren't on it. That's all that matters, isn't it?"

"No, it's not," shouted Sally. "What about all the people who were? Have they been rescued?"

"How should I know. Go and ask somebody."

"I'm sorry, Aurora. It's just such a shock, I can't believe it. Let's go inside and calm down," said Sally, placing an arm around her equally horrified friend.

Back in the taverna, Aurora turned to Sally. "Listen Sally; the people are talking about an explosion."

"Oh no!"

"Didn't you hear that boy shouting 'Boom'?"

"Yes I did. Was that it?"

"The ferry was blown up, Sally, and we were supposed to be on it." Sally turned to Aurora, her eyes wide with fright.

"You are not suggesting that somebody put a bomb on the ferry to kill us, are you? But that's outrageous! You can't be serious, Aurora!"

"I am," replied her grim-faced friend.

"But if they wanted to kill us here, why didn't they try before? Why blow up a boat full of people? I'm sorry Aurora, but I think your imagination has gone too far. In any case, George is the only person who knew we were coming here, and no one knew what ferry we would be on."

"Somebody did."

"Who?"

"The monk in the library knew. Remember, I told him we were catching the morning ferry?"

"Oh, my God!" exclaimed Sally suddenly. "It was *him*!"

"Who?"

"The French monk. It must have been him!" Sally was almost shouting.

"For heaven's sake, Sally, what are you talking about?"

"Didn't he say he had been on a dig when he was a student in England?"

"Yes, he did."

"Listen, Aurora. Pierre and George told me that they were trying to contact all the people who had been involved in the Brigstone dig, because it was obvious that there had been a leak. Someone had found out that they had discovered something important."

"Yes? So what has this got to do with the monk?" asked Aurora.

"Before they left England they had managed to find nearly all of the students who had worked there, all except one, that is."

"Go on," urged Aurora.

"The only one they hadn't found was a French theological student."

"Good Lord, Sally. You could be right! That Brother Christian did seem quite shaken when we mentioned the Hyperboreans. But surely a man who has taken holy orders could never have carried out such a terrible thing?"

"Oh, I don't know. I read somewhere that it was a Dominican monk who started the slave trade!"

"I am beginning to feel as though I have stepped back into the religious wars of the Middle Ages," said Aurora. "As if our problems in the Lebanon were not enough, with Iranian-backed Muslims fighting the Christian Phalange, and the Israelis bombing the Palestinians as well as the Syrians; we now have hit men from the Vatican killing archaeologists, and monks on Greek islands blowing up ferry boats! Am I dreaming, or is all this really happening?"

"It is. But what can we do now? How are we going to get away from here? I'm not getting on any more boats."

"You'll have to, unless you happen to know Onassis, in which case we could borrow his helicopter."

"Oh, shut up Aurora. I'm going to call George again. We'd better warn him."

"Good idea, and I'll see if I can find a boat going to Rhenia. I think that would be the safest way back."

When all the excitement over the sinking of the ferry had died down, Aurora managed to find out from the fat lady in the taverna that her brother, Spiros, had a boat, and was going to Mykonos that evening. Spiros was more than happy to be approached by a beautiful young woman who offered to pay him a generous fare to keep him company on the crossing.

On her return, Aurora found Sally still on the phone.

"I can't get hold of George," she whispered. "I called the university and they said he hadn't been in today, then I called the laboratory, and they said the same thing. I'm worried Aurora."

"Well, don't be," said Aurora. "George is a tough character. Now listen, Sally, I've fixed for us to go to Mykonos tonight, and I suggest we separate there."

"Oh, must we?"

"Yes. It's a much better idea. I am sure you will be able to find a direct flight to London from there, and that way you will avoid Athens. I can take the ferry from there and then fly home."

"I suppose you are right. It does seem the most sensible solution, but I shall miss you, Aurora. I would never have got through all this without you."

"Nonsense. You have been a great support to me, Sally. I shall be back in England for the dig in a few weeks, but until then, I must spend some time with my mother."

"Of course you must," agreed Sally.

It was late evening when Sally and Aurora left Delos behind them. Stepping onto the rickety fishing boat, they were welcomed with a roar of laughter from the fat-bellied Spiros, his eyes bulging like an owl at the sight of the two attractive young women.

"Are you sure we are doing the right thing?" whispered Sally as Spiros opened up the throttle, lurching around the helm, a bottle of Ouzo clutched in one hand.

"Don't worry," laughed Aurora. "He's just enjoying himself.

Let's sit down and try to relax."

It was a short run across the strait to Mykonos, and the girls were soon caught in the spell of a magical Greek night.

The sea was smooth as a sheet of black glass as the little boat cut a path across it. Sally closed her eyes, aware only of the throbbing of the engine. She realised how tired she was after all the excitement of the past weeks. At last she could let go and try to empty her mind of all that had happened. Pulling her legs up onto the hard bench she rested her head against Aurora's shoulder and fell into a light sleep.

Moments later she was startled by Aurora's sharp intake of breath.

"Oh, look, Sally!" she cried, leaping to her feet to lean over the side railing. "How beautiful!" The moon was not yet very high in the star studded navy-blue sky, but it's dazzling rays shot down onto the water catching the leaping backs of a school of dolphins as they raced alongside the little boat.

Having thanked the ogling Spiros, the two girls parted company on the quay. Sally embraced Aurora tearfully then climbed into a creaky old taxi to take her to the airport. She was lucky. Although it was almost the end of the season, there was still an English charter plane operating and, a couple of hours later, she was given a seat which had not been taken up.

It was past midnight when Sally landed in Luton to find herself stuck there until the first morning train for London. The restaurant was closed, but she found a machine holding a few dried-up sandwiches, and another dispensing lukewarm coffee. And so with her appetising supper, she settled down for the night.

Christian knocked on the door of the senior monk's office.

"Enter," called Father Ignatius, looking up from his desk. "Ah, Brother Christian, do sit down. You look quite pale. Are you not well?"

"Oh yes. Thank you," muttered Christian, clutching hold of the arms of the chair with shaking hands. "I need some help, Father," he added, his voice trembling. "Something terrible has happened, and it's all my fault."

"Dear me. What can it be that has upset you so?"

"Have you not heard the news, Father?" asked Christian, his eyes filling with tears. "The ferry sank this morning, and the two girls were on it, and lots of other people," he said, his shoulders heaving with sobs.

"Yes I do know about it, Brother, and it is terrible, but you mustn't take on so."

"But you don't understand, Father," sobbed Christian. "Somebody put a bomb on the boat and killed all the people, and it's my fault. I killed them!"

Father Ignatius' mouth fell open as he rose from his chair to take Christian in his arms.

"Come now Brother, you are not yourself. This accident can have nothing to do with you. It was God's will. Come with me and tell me why you are so upset." And he led the distraught young man down the corridor to the chapel.

Father Ignatius listened patiently on the other side of the confessional while Christian blurted out his story.

"I told Father John that the English girl and her friend were catching the ferry yesterday," he sobbed.

"What English girl?"

"They came to the library to look for information about the Hyperboreans."

"Did they indeed?" mused Ignatius.

"They were so nice, and now they are dead!"

"Come now, Brother, calm yourself. What are you trying to tell me?"

Then Christian told of his friendship with Father John, the elderly monk who had preceded him as keeper of the ancient manuscripts, and with whom he shared an interest in archaeology. The old monk had told Christian that if the discovery of the two Hyperboreans on Delos ever came to light, it could bring disaster to the church. Christian had not hesitated to tell his friend about the dig he had worked on in England, and about the discovery of the Brigstone Hyperborean, whereupon Father John had pressed him for more information about the archaeologists carrying out the excavation.

"Don't you see, Father, those girls in the library were talking about the Brigstone Man, and it was the dig at Brigstone that I worked on. I felt sure that they knew about the two found here."

"And what did you know about that?" Father Ignatius sounded shocked.

"I only knew what Father John told me, and a little about the Hyperboreans from one of the manuscripts."

"Then you must put it right out of your mind, Brother Christian. Whatever you may have told Father John could have absolutely no connection with the sinking of the ferry."

"But if somebody thought those girls knew something, then surely he may have decided it was his duty to tell someone, Father?"

"What nonsense!" retorted Father Ignatius, now openly irritated. Come now Brother Christian, you must pull yourself together and try to forget all about it."

Then, with the usual blessing, he dismissed the troubled young man.

Christian returned to the library. He felt helpless and defeated. He was sure that Father Ignatius knew something, but was at a loss to work out what it might be. He knew he couldn't think badly of Father John, but, at the back of his mind was the niggling suspicion that he must have told someone else about the girls. Could it perhaps have been the Brother he had often talked about, the one who had been sent to Rome?

Christian tried hard to push it from his mind, but the doubts persisted. He wished he could go to the town to find out if the girls were among the victims, but he couldn't leave the monastery. There was nothing he could do to appease his guilt.

Later that morning, Sally picked up a newspaper at Paddington to read on the train. Glancing over the titles as she made her way to the platform, she noticed a small heading near the bottom of the page:

GREEK ISLAND FERRY TRAGEDY
Few survivors
57 People reported missing after a holiday ferry returning to Athens from Mykonos sank following an explosion on board.

Sally's heart was thumping, and her eyes filled with blinding tears as she boarded the train for Petersfield. An elderly lady was already seated by the door, and Sally fell over her walking stick in her distraction.

"I'm, so sorry," she muttered, as she staggered to her seat.

"Are you all right, my dear," asked the old lady.

"Oh, yes," said Sally, blushing. "I am sorry, I just had rather a shock." And tossing the newspaper to one side, she sat with her eyes shut tight, determined to blot out the memory of the ferry.

Chapter Twenty-One

It was late afternoon by the time Sally arrived back at the house, having stopped off at the cattery to collect a very angry Felix. As soon as she released him from his travel case, he shot upstairs to the bedroom where he ensconced himself on top of the wardrobe. She knew it would be useless to try to persuade him to come down, and resigned herself to a few more catless days. Then, arming herself with a mug of strong tea, she sat down to deal with the messages left on her answerphone.

The first call was from Julie, wondering where she was. The second was from Alex. He was coming over to London on business in two days' time, and very much hoped that they could meet.

"Oh Lord!" muttered Sally in a sudden panic. She had tried to forget him, and now she would have to decide if she should see him again. There was no message from John, and she realised that she hadn't thought about him at all since Aurora's arrival in London. She would postpone her answer to Alex until the following day.

The one person Sally did want to speak to was George, and later that evening, she dialled the number of his apartment. There was no reply. It was the third time she had tried to contact him and she was becoming concerned. She rang Aurora in Beirut, but Nadine told her that Aurora was in the shower and would call her back. Sally began to feel totally frustrated, and quite alone again. Even Felix had deserted her! Pulling herself together, she went into the kitchen to make an omelette.

Half an hour later, Aurora called back.

"I still can't get hold of George," Sally told her. "I tried his apartment and there was no answer again. "I'm sure something must have happened to him, Aurora."

"Don't worry, Sally. I'll try from here, and if I can't get to him at home, I'll call the university in the morning. He must be around somewhere. Is everything all right with you?"

"Yes fine, but I miss you, Aurora."

"Me too. What are you planning to do now?"

"I think I'll go up to London in a couple of days."

"Oh, do be careful, Sally. Are you going to try to find Jo's bank there?"

"Of course. I think I'll try the Chase Manhattan Bank first."

"Well, good luck. I'll be thinking of you, Sally, and please keep in touch, won't you? I'll call as soon as I have spoken to George."

Sally awoke early the next morning to hear the phone ringing. It was Inspector McGregor.

"Do you have anything else to tell me, Miss Wincott?" he asked.

"About what, Inspector?"

"About your father and his work."

"No, inspector, I do not. But I can tell you that someone is trying to kill me!"

"What has happened, Miss Wincott? Why have you not contacted us?"

"Because I have been in Greece, Inspector, and somebody blew up the ferry that I should have been on."

"Good God!" exclaimed McGregor. "Not the Mykonos ferry?"

"The very one," said Sally.

"But what on earth were you doing on Mykonos, if you don't mind me asking, Miss Wincott?"

Sally realised that she had already said too much.

"I was with a friend, taking a short break away from all the problems here," she lied.

"I do believe you are not being absolutely honest with me, Miss Wincott."

"You may believe what you like, Inspector," said Sally, defensively.

"I believe you know about your father's involvement in

something of religious significance, and that you are trying to solve the problem for yourself," he said.

"Do you really?" remarked Sally.

"The trouble is…" continued McGregor, "I cannot quite see why you took off to a Greek island without letting me know you were going away."

"Well that's just it, Inspector. I just wanted to get away."

"Miss Wincott, if you are determined to play cat and mouse I can't stop you, but please don't expect me to protect you if you fail to let me know where you are!"

"I'm sorry, Inspector. I just didn't think. I have no intention of going away again, but if I do, I promise to let you know."

"Thank you," said McGregor, curtly, before ringing off.

I must watch my tongue, thought Sally as she dished out some Whiskers onto the cat's dish in the kitchen.

"Fee-eeelix," she called up the stairs, but there was no response. "Silly cat," she muttered as she went up to the bedroom. Felix glared down at her through one half-opened eye.

"All right, you can stay up there all day if you like. I don't care," she said, as she went back down the stairs.

Sally sat at her desk, munching a piece of toast, and before she had even given it a thought, found herself searching for Alex's fax number. His reply came back an hour later. He would be arriving in London the following day and would be staying at Grosvenor House. Would she meet him for lunch at the Caprice? She faxed back immediately, confirming that she would be there at twelve thirty.

That afternoon Sally could think of nothing other than what she would wear, would he still like her, or would she still like him? She could hardly eat anything that evening as she packed an overnight bag ready for a stay of several days. Then she phoned the Bankside Police Station and left a message for Inspector McGregor.

Lying awake in bed that night, Sally tried to picture her flat. What sort of state would it be in after the police had been over it and John had removed his things? What had he left her, she wondered, and what would happen with Alex? Would they spend the night together, and if so, where? She was just dropping off to sleep when she was startled by a heavy thud as Felix landed on her bed from the top of the wardrobe.

"Thank you, Felix," she muttered. "Now I'll never get to sleep!"

Early the next morning, Sally awoke in a sweat. She had been dreaming. She was on a hill on Delos, the sun burning down on her, when suddenly she heard a motorbike behind her. It was coming straight for her down a rocky hill, and she started to run. She tripped on a boulder and fell heavily, unable to get up. The bike was almost on top of her and, as she looked up, she saw that the rider's face was a dead man's skull, laughing at her, and he was wearing a red robe, like a cardinal. She screamed and blacked-out. Then she saw a young monk in a brown cowl, staring at her, and a voice was saying: "My mother was English. Her name was Nancy… Nancy… Naaa… ncy." Sally leaped up her heart beating faster.

"He didn't do it! He couldn't have done," she yelled aloud. "He was my brother. I know he was!"

Two hours later, Sally was on her way to Petersfield to catch the train for London.

Round her neck she wore her mother's locket bearing Jo's code numbers. This time she had left Felix with his friend, the retired army major who lived down the lane.

Sally took a taxi from Paddington to Green Park and walked into the Chase Manhattan Bank on Piccadilly where she asked to see the manager.

"Do you have an account, Madam?" asked the young man on the counter.

"I'm afraid not, but it is quite important," she said.

"Just one moment, Madam," he said, as he disappeared through a door.

Sally glanced around the banking hall, but could see nothing indicating access to the safe deposit vaults. The young man returned.

"I'm very sorry, Madam, but without an appointment, Mr Smith cannot see you today."

"Then you may be able to help me," said Sally. "I want to open an account, but I do also need some information. Can you tell me if it is at this branch that my father has an account?"

"I should be able to do that," he replied. "What is his name?"

"Dr Jordan," replied Sally. "Dr Joseph Jordan from Minneapolis. He had a Sterling account for use on his frequent visits to London."

"Just one moment," said the clerk, tapping into the keyboard at his side. "Yes, it is this branch, but his account has been dormant for some time."

"Yes, I understand. Thank you," said Sally, thinking that all she had to do now was to find out if he had a safe deposit box there. "Do you think I could see the manager tomorrow morning? I am only in London for a couple of days, so I don't have a lot of time."

"I will just check with his secretary," said the clerk, disappearing through the door again.

Minutes later, Sally had her appointment with the manager and was on her way to meet Alex at the restaurant.

Alex was waiting for Sally in the entrance foyer of the Caprice.

"Sally! You look marvellous," he exclaimed, planting a tentative kiss on her cheek.

"Hello Alex," she said, blushing. "You haven't been waiting long, have you?"

"No honey, I just arrived," he replied as he took her arm and led her into the restaurant.

"I am so pleased that you could come, Sally. I haven't stopped thinking about you ever since you left," he said, as the waiter held their chairs for them. Sally's legs were shaking as she sat down.

"It is lovely to see you again so soon, Alex. How are Jamie and Abigail?" she asked, attempting to keep the conversation less intimate.

"Oh, they are just fine, but it's you I want to talk about," he replied, as the waiter handed Sally a large menu which she thankfully hid behind.

"I've been away in the Middle East," said Sally.

"Goodness! And I've been thinking of you slaving away at the agency. Why did you go there, Sally?" asked Alex.

"I can't return to work until I've cleared up the mystery of Jo's murder," said Sally. "I went to Beirut with the daughter of Jo's friend, Pierre Soulaya."

"Oh yes, I remember him coming over to see Jo."

"He's been killed too," Sally announced.

"My God! Do you mean that he was murdered, like Jo?"

"Exactly, and so too was Marie, his student at the university."

"Jesus! What the hell have you gotten yourself into, Sally?" cried Alex.

Sally reached over to take Alex's hand in hers.

"I don't know how much you know about all of this, Alex."

"My father told me that Jo seems to have been involved in some secret archaeological discovery, and that he was killed because of it."

"That's more or less right," said Sally. "But it's more complicated than that, and very frightening."

"But my dear, you mustn't go rushing off trying to sort it out yourself. You could get into terrible trouble! You must leave it to the police." Sally smiled at his obvious concern.

"It's far too late for that, Alex. I'm in it up to the neck, and have been from the start."

"Oh, my poor crazy Sally. What am I going to do with you?"

"Help me," said Sally. "I need to talk to someone, and I trust you Alex. I am going to tell you all about it from the beginning; but first, let's just enjoy our lunch."

"Good. I'm glad, Sally. I can free myself this afternoon and we will go to my hotel."

Alex had reserved a small suite in the hotel, and as Sally removed her coat, she was amused to see a large bouquet of red roses and a bottle of Taitinger champagne in an ice bucket on the centre table. Alex, however, who had been struggling to control his desire to throw himself at her ever since their meeting, was now more concerned with the story that she was about to unfold.

"Would you like some champagne, Sally?" he asked gently, as they sank down onto a huge sofa.

"I'd rather have another coffee," she replied.

"Of course, Darling," he said, as he picked up the phone to order it.

"Alex, I can't tell you how much it means to me to have someone I can confide in. I have been struggling with this bloody secret ever since I met Jo in hospital, and the only real support I have had was from Aurora. I don't know how I would have survived Beirut and Greece without her. We were nearly killed there!"

"Oh, no!" he exclaimed, placing a protective arm around her shoulders. "But what about your boyfriend, John? Has he not been helping you?"

"Not really," said Sally. "We had an awful row over it, and I haven't seen him for a while."

"I'm sorry," said Alex.

As soon as the waiter had left a pot of coffee, Sally steeled herself to tell Alex all that had happened over the past few weeks.

It was almost an hour later by the time Sally recounted her adventure on Delos, and the explosion on the ferry. Alex had been sitting quietly taking it all in, a deep frown on his forehead.

"This is absolutely incredible, Sally! I can hardly believe it's true."

"I know, but it is real, believe me," laughed Sally, nervously. "And it really isn't funny."

"Come here, my Darling," he said, now allowing herself to throw his arms around her. "I think you deserve a drink after all that, don't you? And I think you are just amazing!"

"No, I'm not," said Sally, blushing. "Aurora was the strong one. She was fantastic."

As they sipped their champagne, Alex turned to Sally.

"What about this monk in the library, Sally? You don't really think he blew up the boat, do you?"

"I do not, not now," she said. "I had a strange dream last night, Alex, and it suddenly came to me who he was."

"Who he was? What do you mean?"

"He told us that his mother was English, and that her name was Nancy."

"Nancy? Wasn't that your mother's name, Sally?"

"Yes, it was. Remember when we went to Mr Klein's house to meet Mike Steward?"

"Yes, and he gave you a letter your mother had written to him."

"That's right. He also told me that she had been married to a Frenchman and had a baby, and that he had been killed in the war."

"So?" queried Alex.

"The monk in the library said that his father had been killed in the war too."

"So the monk's mother was an English woman called Nancy, and his father was killed in the war. What does that prove?"

"When I asked him if he stayed in touch with his mother, he told me that she had died a long time ago, and that he never knew her," said Sally. "My mother died a long time ago… when I was born!"

"Well I agree that is quite coincidental, but I can't see that it proves any connection," said Alex.

"But don't you see?" cried Sally. "I dreamed about him. Why did I dream about him if he wasn't my brother?"

"Oh, come now, Darling," sighed Alex. "You probably dreamed about him because you wanted him to be your brother. It doesn't prove that he was."

"He *was* my brother, Alex. I'm sure of it. And I am also sure that it couldn't have been him who blew up the ferry."

"Why not?"

"Because he was in an enclosed monastery," she said.

"Well whoever did it, Sally, the only thing that matters is that you are alive. I'm sure the Greek police will take care of the culprit."

That evening over dinner, Alex broached the subject of Jo's secret again.

"What do you intend to do now, Sally?" he asked.

"I should have thought that was obvious," she replied. "I'm going to find out if Jo had a safe deposit box here. As I told you, all that we found in Beirut was his report of the Delos skeletons and, as he examined the Brigstone Man in London, he may have hidden that report here."

"I don't see why," remarked Alex. "After all, he was an American, attached to a university. Surely he would have kept his papers there?"

"I disagree. Don't forget that he was so shocked by what he found, that he flew immediately to Beirut to tell the others."

"In that case, what proof did he take to Beirut, and why was it not with the papers you found there?"

"I don't really know, but he probably took some photos with him, and Aurora has promised to have another search through her father's papers at the university."

"All right," said Alex. "So how are you going to go about finding if Jo had a bank in London, Sally? Do you have any idea which one it might be?"

"Oh, yes, I did all that this morning. He had an account with the Chase Manhattan Bank in Piccadilly, and I have an appointment with the manager in the morning!"

"Well I take my hat off to you, Sally. You certainly don't waste any time, do you?"

"Of course not," laughed Sally. "You don't really think I'm a complete idiot, do you Alex?"

"That I most certainly do not! You surprise me more and more, my Darling."

"Good," said Sally.

Alex had ordered breakfast for two in his suite, and as Sally emerged from the bathroom the following morning, he threw his arms around her and led her to the table.

"Oh Alex," she sighed. "I don't know what I am doing here. It's madness! I must go over to my flat this morning before I go to the bank."

"Whatever for, Darling? You are here with me now and that's all that matters. I have moved my meeting to this afternoon, and I will come with you to the bank. So stop fretting and drink your coffee like a good girl."

"You don't really want to come with me, do you Alex?"

"Of course I do. You don't really think I am going to let you go off on some treasure hunt without me, do you?"

"It is not a treasure hunt, Alex. It is extremely important; three people have been killed, and if you can't understand that, then I would prefer it if you would allow me to continue on my own."

"I am sorry, Sally. I was just trying to be helpful," he said, aware that his choice of words had annoyed her. "This whole affair must have worn you down."

"Of course it has, but you don't think I am going to stop now, do you? My God! You men are all the same!"

"Wow – there, steady on Alex," he said, chiding himself. "We've only just met, and already the war of the sexes is breaking out! I think I'll just go and shave before I get accused of being a rough colonial!"

Sally and Alex arrived at the bank at five minutes to ten, and despite Alex's reticence, Sally was feeling quite confident. Alex waited in the banking hall while she went in to see the manager.

Twenty minutes later, she emerged, having opened an account for herself, and reserved a safe deposit box.

"How did you get on?" he asked.

"Fine. No trouble at all," she replied. "I've got myself a safe deposit box and shall come back tomorrow with my jewellery!"

"Your jewellery?"

"Of course! My Russian tiara," she joked. "I just told the manager that I had inherited some valuable pieces, and needed to deposit them. It was easy." Alex shook his head.

"But Sally, I don't see how you are going to get into Jo's box, or even if he had one."

"Oh Alex, I just asked the manager, and he told me that he did."

"But what about the code numbers, and the key, Sally?"

"Oh, I've got all that, Alex," she said, as they walked, arm in arm, out of the bank.

After lunch Sally took a taxi to her flat. She went in by the side entrance, hoping to see Bill, the porter, but he was not in his lodge. Avoiding the lift, she walked up the service stairs. She thought it highly unlikely that the Vatican men would still be hanging around but, with an obvious lack of police presence, she couldn't help feeling nervous as she turned the key in the door.

The flat felt cold and unwelcoming without either John or

Felix there. It no longer felt like home, although everything appeared to be in place and nothing was missing. She picked up a pile of mail and sat down to make a few phone calls.

Sally first called her office.

"Oh Sally, I'm so glad you have called. I have been worried. Have you been away again?" asked Julie.

"Yes, but I'm back now. Is everything all right?"

"I'm not sure," said Julie. "Personnel have called twice, wanting to know when you will be back. I think you should talk to them, Sally."

"I will. But how's work going, Julie. Are you busy?"

"Not really, that's why I'm worried. I think you should get back now, Sally. There are several new accounts coming in and nothing coming our way at all."

Sally suddenly realised that she risked losing her job if she didn't get back to the agency very soon.

"I'll call personnel now, Julie, and tell them I hope to be back in the office on Monday."

"Oh Sally, that would be great!" cried Julie.

Switching her mind back to Delos and the ferry, Sally dialled Aurora's home number, remembering that she had promised to call George.

"Sally! Where on earth have you been? I've been trying to get you." Aurora sounded upset.

"I'm in London. I told you I would be."

"God, I forgot," said Aurora.

"Have you spoken to George?"

"No Sally. I can't speak to him. He's dead."

"*What*!" yelled Sally, almost dropping the receiver. "What do you mean? He can't be!"

"He is," replied Aurora, calmly.

Clutching the phone tightly, Sally asked, "Please Aurora… please say it's not true. They can't have killed George too."

"They have," replied Aurora in a matter-of-fact voice. "They have killed all the four people who directed the Brigstone dig, Sally."

"But are you sure it was them? Perhaps he had a heart attack, or something."

"No Sally. The Athens police are investigating his murder. He was shot in the head outside his apartment. I suppose you do realised where that leaves you, Sally?"

Sally couldn't answer. Her mind began to race, one question screaming through her head.

What am I to do?

I'm the only one left!

Sally was shaking all over. She had never felt so frightened in her life.

"What shall I do, Aurora? *They are going to kill me now*!" she was almost screaming down the phone to Beirut.

"No they won't," said Aurora firmly. "Not if you get out of London *now*, Sally! You must be mad going there."

"But I've found Jo's bank, and I'm going to get into his safe deposit box tomorrow, Aurora."

"For God's sake, Sally, leave it. You'll get yourself killed! It simply is not worth it."

"But I thought you wanted to know what they found as much as I do."

"Of course I do, but not at the expense of getting you killed! Go back to the house, Sally, *please*. Jo's secret can wait where it is."

"I know you are right, Aurora, but after all that we have been through, and now that I am so close, how can I give up? I'm going back to work on Monday, anyway. I've got to, or I will lose my job."

"Then at least promise me that you will ask the police for some protection," insisted her friend.

"I told the inspector that the bomb on the ferry was intended for us, so I might as well tell him that three people have been killed because of Jo's secret."

"Good, but remember that you still don't know what Jo found."

"If I call him today, that'll be the truth," said Sally.

"What do you mean?"

"I mean that I don't know today, but by tomorrow I may know

everything!"

"*For God's sake, Sally*," yelled Aurora down the phone. "don't be a fool. Just get out of London as quick as you can, and forget about Jo's bloody bank!"

With the shock of hearing about George's death, Sally forgot to tell Aurora about Alex. She longed to call him, but remembered that he would be with his client. She would tell him that evening.

Sally thought back to George and all that he had told her. He was a strange man, but she had grown to like him, although she was not able to weep for him as she had for Pierre. Aurora's warning suddenly brought her to her senses. What was she doing sitting in her flat when the killers could still be watching it? Then she started to panic again.

After filling a suitcase with some warmer clothes and a few books, Sally locked up the flat and left. She had arranged to meet Alex at six thirty, so she took a taxi to the hotel and waited for him in the lobby. She ordered a drink and bought a newspaper. Disappointed that there was no further mention of the ferry disaster, she started to think about Christian, the young monk. Why was she so certain that he was her half-brother? It must have been something in her subconscious, but she was sure that he must have been at Brigstone Down. Could he really have somehow been involved in the blowing-up of the ferry? She was just wondering how she could find out more about him when Alex arrived.

Up in Alex's suite, Sally told him about George's murder, and Aurora's insistence that she should leave London. Alex was aghast.

"Is that three people who have been murdered, Sally?" he asked.

"No, four. Don't forget poor Marie, Pierre's student."

"No wonder Aurora wants you to leave town, Sally," he said. "I quite agree… you shouldn't have come, my Darling."

"But Alex, George was killed in Athens, and they tried to kill us on Delos, so surely they can't be in London now, can they?"

"If they really were sent by the Vatican, Sally, they could have other agents over here. After all, your father was killed here, wasn't he?"

"Oh, I don't know what to think any more. Do you think they are all over the place then?" asked Sally.

"It is possible, I suppose. If this thing is so vital to the Church, they will stop at nothing. We'd better call the police, Sally."

"I've already spoken to the inspector. Alex. He knows everything, or almost everything."

"That's all right then, Darling," said Alex.

That evening Alex asked Sally if she really wanted to leave.

"Of course I don't! Now that I'm here, I intend to finish what I started."

"But do you really still want to go to the bank tomorrow, Sally?"

"Yes Alex. I do. And I would like you to come with me."

"Are you sure you are doing the right thing, Darling? I will come with you, of course, but we will have to be very careful."

"I know, but I'm not afraid, are you? And anyway, if there is something terrible in Jo's safe, then I will need somebody with me to help me decide what to do with it."

Chapter Twenty-Two

Forgive them Lord
For they know not What they doeth

Sally opened her mother's locket and took out the slip of paper showing Jo's numbers. The first of the three rows started with the number 'Three', which had matched the safe in Beirut. The other two rows started with the number 'Five', which was the same as her own newly-allocated number. With her biro, she carefully copied the numbers onto her arm, while Alex rang down to the reception desk for a taxi.

At eleven o'clock Sally and Alex walked into the Chase Manhattan Bank on Piccadilly.

"I have arranged for a safe deposit box," said Sally to the clerk on the counter.

"Of course, Madam," said the girl, recognising her from the previous day. "The Commissionaire will show you the way," she said, beckoning to a uniformed man near the entrance.

Several minutes later Sally and Alex found themselves alone in a large room lined with safe deposit boxes.

"Here we go, Darling," said Alex, squeezing Sally's arms. "Are you sure you are ready for this?"

"Ready as I will ever be," she replied nervously, as she walked slowly along checking the numbers on the boxes.

"Five seven nine, five six two, five five three… that's it!" she cried, stopping in front of one.

Fumbling in her bag for the key she hesitated, then handed the key to Alex.

"You open it, Alex. I'm scared."

"I doubt if Jo would have put a bomb in it," he joked, as he turned the key.

Sally stood with her eyes shut, her heart beating wildly, as Alex pulled out the long box and laid it on the table.

"There we are… that wasn't so bad, was it? Now let's just see what all the fuss is about, shall we?"

Lying squashed against the sides of the metal box was a package wrapped in newspaper. Alex carefully lifted it out and handed it to Sally.

"Gosh, it's quite flat! Whatever can it be?"

Underneath lay a blue folder, labelled **Report on the examination of a Hyperborean found on Brigstone Down, Wiltshire, England. (By Dr Joseph Jordan, September 1971).**

As Alex lifted out the folder, three sealed envelopes fell from between the cover. On was addressed to 'The Editor of The Times', one to 'The Jerusalem Post', and one to 'The Curator of the Natural History Museum' in London.

"These must be the letters Jo asked me to send if anything happened to him. I wonder if we should look at them?" said Sally.

"No. Open the package."

"Should I?" she asked, gingerly running her fingers over it.

"Of course, you must, Sally. Isn't that what you have been waiting for?"

Sally began to tear away at the layers of newspapers.

"I think we need some scissors, it's covered with Sellotape. You haven't got a penknife, have you Alex?"

"No I haven't. You must have something in your handbag, Sally. How about a nail file?" Sally tipped her bag out onto the table.

"This should do it," she said, grabbing her metal keyring.

A scraping noise startled them as the last of the newspaper fell away from a square piece of glass.

"Take it easy, Sally, you'll cut yourself. What is it?"

"There's something shiny between two bits of glass," she said as she lifted off the top piece to reveal a scrap of metallic skin suit covering the precious papyrus.

"Oh look!" she cried, peeling back the protective layer. "It's a sort of manuscript."

"A very ancient one, I would say," said Alex, peering down at it. "There's some writing on it, Sally. Can you read it?"

"Of course not. It's some strange alphabet, or hieroglyphics, like Egyptian or something. I don't think it's Greek."

"Well it must be something important," said Alex. "Let's hope that Jo has explained it in his report."

Sally carefully rewrapped the papyrus in the torn newspaper while Alex opened the file. In his report, Jo had detailed the progress of the dig at Brigstone Down, and how he and Pierre had found the Hyperborean in an adjoining field. He had taken the skeleton up to London where he had the use of a room at the Natural History Museum in South Kensington.

"So that's where he took it!" exclaimed Sally, grabbing the file from Alex.

"What?"

"The Brigstone Man. He left it in the museum in London."

"But I thought that no one was supposed to know about it."

"Perhaps it was just another ancient skeleton to the museum," said Sally.

"What else is there in the report? There must be something about the piece of parchment, Sally."

"I'm looking," she said, as she scanned through the pages. "Ah, I think this is it. He describes how he was scraping off something from the man's ribs when he found a piece of ancient papyrus."

"Yes? Come on Sally. Don't keep me in suspense," urged Alex.

"He says that, written on the papyrus were seven lines of Aramaic script," continued Sally. "But when he had translated them he was so shocked that he was convinced that it could only be some elaborate hoax, Alex."

"But what did it say, Sally?" urged Alex.

"Just a minute," she said, frowning, as she stared down at the page in front of her. "I'm reading it. *Oh my God*!" she yelled. "*It can't be… I don't believe it*!"

"Whatever is it, Sally?" asked Alex, grabbing hold of her as she slumped over the table, her head in her hands.

"Look!" she whispered, pushing the page towards him.

"*My God*!" he exclaimed, his jaw dropping open.

There in front of them was Jo's translation of the writing on the papyrus. It read:

I AM JESHUA OF NAZARETH SON OF APOLANUS AND MARY
WHO CAME TO SAVE THE WORLD FROM MANS INIQUITIES.
BLESSED BE ANDREW ABOVE ALL MEN
WHOSE LOVE TRANSCENDED ALL IN ATONEMENT
FOR THE SINS OF PETER HIS BROTHER AND JUDAS.
HE BORE MY CROSS AND GAVE HIMSELF UP
TO THE LORD GOD MY FATHER AT GOLGOTHA
WHEN HE SPAKETH THESE WORDS
FORGIVE THEM LORD FOR THEY KNOW NOT WHAT THEY DOETH.

"I don't know what to say, Sally," said Alex. "I don't believe any of this. It's got to be a joke."

"Don't say anything. Let's just go home," said Sally. "I can't think about this at all. Put it all back in the box, Alex. I've seen enough."

Sally and Alex left the bank in silence. Alex hailed a taxi and ordered the cabby to drive around Hyde Park, while Sally sat, pale and silent, with tears running down her face.

"Buck up, Darling," he said, giving her an encouraging hug as they passed Marble Arch for the third time.

"I'll try, Alex," she replied, struggling to find a tissue to wipe her eyes. "It is silly to be so upset, but after all this time, it was such an anti-climax to find that it was probably just some ridiculous hoax after all."

"We don't know that, Sally. I agree that was my initial reaction when I saw what Jo had written, but didn't you say that was exactly what Jo, Pierre and George thought too?"

"Yes, but I must admit that when we spoke to George in Athens, he said that they had eventually had to admit that what they found was genuine, and that was just days before he was killed. But listen, Alex," she continued, "if it was a hoax, and that papyrus thing wasn't real, why have four people been killed?"

"Let's go back to my hotel and talk about it there, Sally. I can't think straight at the moment."

"Good idea," agreed Sally.

"When are you going back, Alex?" she asked, as the taxi turned down Park Lane.

"My flight is booked for the day after tomorrow, Darling, but I can always change it," he replied.

"I would like you to come back to the house with me, if you are free, Alex," said Sally. "I don't want to stay away any longer, I am worried about Felix."

"Who on earth is Felix? Not another airline captain, I hope?"

"No, silly. Felix is my cat."

"Oh, that's all right then," laughed Alex. "We must get back to Felix!"

Back in the hotel, Sally and Alex settled down to discuss the morning's discovery.

"What is interesting is that the wording on the papyrus ties up so well with what Aurora and I saw in Beirut," said Sally.

"Did it? Remind me," said Alex.

"There was a picture of a woman and a photo of some writing, which Jo had translated as saying that she was Mary of Nazareth, beloved of Apolanus."

"And now," interrupted Alex, "we have another one saying that Jeshua was the son of Apolanus and Mary!"

"Exactly. Which would mean, if it is true, that he was the son of Mary's liaison with Apolanus, the Hyperborean!"

"And Mary was not a virgin visited by an angel," added Alex.

"That's right!" laughed Sally. "The 'visitor' was Apolanus!"

"No wonder the Church wants to hush it up," said Alex. "If it is true, then it's dynamite!"

"But that's not all," Sally continued, "what about the crucifixion, Alex? If he, or Jeshua was forty-five years old, as Jo said he was when he crash-landed in Wiltshire, then it must mean that he really did rise from the dead!"

"No, silly!" exclaimed Alex. "Didn't you read what it said? It was Andrew, Peter's brother who took his place and was crucified! But the bit I like best is when he said: 'Forgive them Lord, for they know not what they doeth'!"

"Yes, that is funny," agreed Sally. "Just imagine all those people looking up at the poor man hanging there, thinking it was 'you-know-who', when all the time it was Andrew!"

"Good Lord, Sally, I hadn't realised you were an agnostic."

"I'm not, at least, I wasn't," she said. "I don't know what to believe now."

After Alex had left for his meeting, Sally sat thinking for a while. She longed to tell Aurora what they had found, but decided to call her later that evening. She left Alex's suite and went downstairs to order some tea, and as she sat in the lounge, she suddenly knew what she wanted to do.

Sally's taxi dropped her outside the Chase Manhattan Bank in Piccadilly. Carrying her briefcase, she walked briskly down the stairs to the safe deposit vaults, then she opened her father's box and removed the blue folder, the three letters and the package containing the precious papyrus.

Stepping out into the street with her bulging briefcase, she took another taxi straight to Paddington Station, where she deposited the case in a left luggage locker before returning to the hotel.

Later that evening, carrying the precious evidence, Sally boarded the train for Petersfield with Alex. They found an empty carriage and sat down opposite each other.

"What a funny little train," remarked Alex.

"Yes, I suppose it does look quaint to you. I suppose your trains are enormous, like everything else in America."

"Well yes, and they are a lot more comfortable than this!" he remarked.

"That's probably because they travel far greater distances."

"You don't look very comfortable, Sally. Why on earth are you sitting on your briefcase? Have you got something valuable in it?"

"Don't be silly, Alex," she laughed, blushing. Then, before she realised what she was saying, added, "It's something far more valuable than my jewellery."

Alex turned to stare, astounded across the carriage at Sally. "My God, Sally!" he cried. "You haven't… you didn't go back to the bank, did you?"

"Shush… somebody will hear you," she whispered. Alex jumped up from his seat and sat down beside her.

"Sally, you must be mad! Do you realise what you have done?"

"Of course I do. And I know exactly what I am going to do as soon as I get back to the house."

"But you silly girl!" he cried. "Can't you see that you have placed us both in danger?"

"It was a risk that I had to take," she said. "And anyway, did you notice any foreign-looking men following us onto the train, Alex?"

"No I didn't Sally. But why? Just tell me why you did it. What do you intend to do now?"

"I should have thought that was obvious," she said. "I'm going to destroy everything!"

"What?" he cried, as Sally continued.

"I don't care if Jo was right or not, I just couldn't live with the knowledge that his report was lying there, waiting for the day, perhaps a hundred years from now, when the bank may be demolished, and some ignorant person will find it."

"All right, I understand your reasoning, Sally. But are you sure this is the right thing to do? After all, if it is all true, then we are holding the knowledge of something that could completely change the history of mankind! It's not just a question of Mary's virginity, or the crucifixion, is it?"

"I know, but I just can't live with the responsibility of something so shocking… I just can't. It's too heavy a burden."

Alex took her hands in his.

"Look Sally, don't you think it would be better to just wait and think it over, at least until tomorrow. You have had a shock today, and after all you have been through, it is not surprising that you should want to get shot of it all. Let's just spend a quiet evening together and have another talk about it tomorrow."

"I suppose you are right, Alex, but once I have made my mind up to do something, then that's it. But now that you are here, it would be lovely to spend some time together and just forget about it."

"That's settled then," said Alex. "Come here and kiss me, you crazy girl!" And as the train slowed down, a group of soldiers passing along the corridor, whistled and hollered at the sight of Sally and Alex locked together in a passionate embrace.

It was almost dark by the time they arrived at the house and, as Sally parked the car, she saw Felix perched on the gatepost.

"Fee…lix," she called, scooping him up into her arms. "Good boy! Were you waiting for me?"

"I can see that I am going to have trouble with that one," remarked Alex, laughing.

"You are not jealous, are you?" asked Sally.

"It has been known," he replied. "But at least it's not a poodle!"

Sally was in the kitchen preparing dinner that evening when Alex walked in carrying her bulging briefcase.

"Sally, I hate to bring up the subject again, but don't you think we should try to find somewhere to hide this stuff?"

"Oh, Lord, I nearly forgot. There must be a good place somewhere here."

"Is there an attic?"

"Yes, but that would be too obvious, wouldn't it? If those men did trace me to the house, they'd be bound to look up there."

"They're not likely to find you here, are they?" he asked, concerned.

"No, but now that I'm returning to work, there is always the possibility that I could be followed back from London."

"You didn't tell me that, Sally!" exclaimed Alex.

"Tell you what?"

"That you are going back to work. Oh Darling, you mustn't. It's too dangerous."

"But I have to Alex, or I will lost my job, I have already been away far too long, but don't worry. I will stay here and commute by train."

Alex looked suddenly quite stricken. "Come here my Darling," he said, wrapping his arms around her. "You must know by now how important you are to me, Sally. I simply couldn't bear it if anything happened to you."

"I know, Alex," she murmured, resting her head on his shoulder. "I feel the same about you, but I don't have any choice. I have to get back to the agency."

"But don't you see, my Darling, I want you to come home with me. I want to marry you, Sally." Now it was Sally's turn to look stricken.

"Marry you?" she cried. "You want to marry me?"

"Of course I do. Is that so outrageous?"

"Oh, Alex, I'm sorry. It was such a shock. I don't know what to say."

"Just say 'yes' Darling," he said, pulling her towards him again.

"But we hardly know each other," said Sally, recovering her composure.

"Oh, you mean you haven't seen the bad side of me yet?" he asked.

"Well there is that, Alex," she said.

"I know you well enough, Sally, to be sure that I want you to be my wife and the mother of my children." Sally sat down.

"This is crazy Alex."

"Maybe it is, Darling, but I don't know how I can leave until I am sure that we will spend the rest of our lives together."

"Oh, please, Alex, don't push me," said Sally. "I have fallen for you, although I tried not to, but to talk of marriage so soon is not fair. You are going back to America, and I am going back to my job, which I love. Why can't we just keep in touch for a while, and meet again in a couple of months?"

"Oh, Sally, you are a hard woman. You are breaking my heart."

"Rubbish, I'm just trying to be practical. Please try to understand, Alex. My career is important to me, and I can't just chuck it in and move to Minneapolis; and apart from that, I am simply not ready for another commitment."

"Come here, my Darling," said Alex pulling her to her feet. "I understand, of course. It is a big thing to ask, but I wanted you to know how I feel. You take as much time as you need, and we will meet as often as possible. I have several clients in London, so shall be coming over quite often."

As they were finishing their dinner, Sally had an idea.

"I know where I can hide the papyrus for the time being Alex, but I still intend to burn everything."

"Burn it. Oh, no, Sally!"

"Of course. That was why I had to bring it here," she said. "I could hardly burn it in London, could I?"

"But I thought we had agreed that it would be better to wait for a while, Sally."

"Yes, I know, and I promise I won't destroy anything until I have spoken to Aurora."

"Promise to call me before you do anything drastic, won't you, Sally?"

"Of course I will, Alex."

"Now, where is this hiding place?"

"I'll show you," said Sally, jumping up from the table. "Follow me!"

Leading off from the kitchen was a small outhouse where the lawnmower and garden tools were kept. There were shelves fixed to one of the walls, and several small windowpanes were propped up on the top shelf.

Sally opened her briefcase and carefully lifted out the pieces of glass enclosing the papyrus. Then she slid it behind the windowpanes and placed some flower pots in front of them.

"That's a good idea, Sally," said Alex. "Even if somebody did look up there they would think it was just old bits of glass. Now, what about Jo's file and the letters?"

"Look," she said, turning to pull the lawnmower out from the corner. She lifted off the grass box and placed the blue folder and the three letters in it. Then she replaced the grass box and pushed the mower back into the corner. "There, that should be OK, shouldn't it?" she asked.

"Well, that's brilliant, Sally," he said. "I would never have thought of that. I would probably have put them in the oven and forgotten they were there!" Sally laughed.

"Now perhaps we can relax," she said. "Let's go back inside by the fire."

Lying in Alex's arms on the old sofa, Sally's thoughts turned to Aurora.

"Oh, dear, I can't call Aurora now, Alex. It must be about four in the morning there. It'll have to wait until tomorrow. She will be going spare, wondering why I haven't called."

"Never mind, Darling, it can wait. Can't you forget all that and just concentrate on us?"

"You are right, Alex. We have so little time left before you leave. These last two days have been wonderful, and I am going to miss you terribly."

"Then let's go to bed, Darling," he urged.

"Mmmm let's," she laughed, leaping up to start up the stairs, doggy fashion on all fours, chased by Alex. He threw himself on her as they reached the landing to collapse in a heap on the floor.

The next morning, Sally took Alex breakfast in bed.

"Come on, wake up! I intend to make the most of today if you are leaving tomorrow," she said.

"Then come back to bed, Darling," he pleaded, pulling her down beside him.

Sally woke up to hear a bell ringing. It was the telephone. She looked at the bedside clock. It was half past one in the afternoon. She jumped out of bed and stumbled down the stairs, but the phone stopped ringing as she grabbed it.

"Damn!" she muttered. She was halfway back up the stairs when it rang again, and this time she got it.

"Sally! Where on earth have you been? I've been going mad waiting to hear from you!"

"I'm so sorry, Aurora," replied Sally. "We got back from London too late to call you last night."

"Well for Heaven's sake, tell me what's happened," urged Aurora. "Did you get to Jo's bank?"

"I certainly did, and everything else too," replied Sally.

"Oh, my God, that's great!" cried her friend.

"It isn't really," said Sally, "in fact it's quite terrifying."

"Terrifying?" exclaimed Aurora. "Why, what was it?"

"You know I can't explain on the phone, Aurora, but believe me, what we found was an awful shock."

"So Jo did have a safe deposit box there as well, and you saw the contents, Sally?"

"Yes, and you won't like it at all when you know what it is."

"Oh, Lord, now my imagination will run riot, Sally. It's driving me mad not being there. What are you going to do now? You won't do anything silly, will you? I hope you have left it where it is, if it is so awful."

"Don't worry, Aurora. It's quite safe."

"Well that's a relief. I can be back in England in a couple of weeks, so we can decide what to do then, although I don't know how I'll be able to wait that long! By the way, Sally, you said 'we'. Does that mean that John has come back to help you?"

"No, Aurora. I am with Alex McCloud."

"Who on earth is Alex McCloud? You haven't told him about it, have you?"

"That's all right," said Sally, laughing. "I met him in Minneapolis. He is the son of Jo's successor at the university there, and I think I'm going to marry him."

"What?" yelled Aurora down the phone. "You don't waste any time, do you, you crafty bitch!"

"You're not jealous, are you, Aurora?" joked Sally.

"Maybe I am. What's he like?"

"Wonderful!"

"What's going on Sally?" asked Alex as he came down the stairs.

"It's Aurora, Alex. She's been going spare wondering what we found."

"She sounds an interesting person," said Alex, after Sally had hung up.

"She is and she's very clever. She's an archaeologist, like her father. She and her mother are so brave, wondering if and when another war will break out in Beirut."

"I hope I shall be able to meet her one day," he said.

The next morning, Sally and Alex left the house early for the drive to the airport. Alex was insistent that Sally should drop him at Departures and leave.

"But Alex, why can't I come in with you?" she begged.

"No, you mustn't. I can't stand farewells, Sally. I want to remember you in your little house, not standing forlorn in the airport."

"Remember me? That sounds as though you really are saying goodbye!" Alex laughed.

"Don't be silly, Darling. I'll be back in a few weeks. You know that, don't you?"

"Of course," she said. "All right, I'll just drop you off."

Driving back to the house, Sally felt a strange mixture of loneliness and elation. She wanted to laugh and cry at the same time. She was in love with Alex, and she knew that whatever heartache may lay ahead, she really didn't care. She had never felt like that when John went away, but maybe that was because she was so used to it.

Pausing at some traffic lights, Sally began to sing loudly. A young man driving a battered Vauxhall pulled down his window to yell insults at her, then, as the lights changed, she put her foot down and shot off ahead of him, responding with an uncharacteristic 'V' sign.

By the time she got back to the house she had calmed down considerably, steeling herself for her first day back at work the following day.

Chapter Twenty-Three

When Sally returned to the house the following evening she felt exhausted. She had never imagined just how tiring commuting could be. She couldn't be bothered to get herself something to eat, so she sat down to write to Aurora.

Unsure about what, if anything, she should say about her shock discovery at Jo's bank, she started to relate her certainty that the French monk on Delos was her brother, when a stray thought crossed her mind. She must check that the papyrus was safe before she did anything else. And what if the lawnmower was damp? Perhaps she should have wrapped the report in a plastic bag before putting it in the grass box. She jumped up and went into the kitchen to fetch a rubbish bag before unlocking the door leading to the outhouse.

She switched on the light and glanced up at the top shelf. Something was wrong. There were two small pieces of glass in front of the flower pots. These were not the windowpanes that she had put there. Sally's heart missed a beat as she reached up to move the pots. The windowpanes were still there, but leaning against the wall. That was all. She stared down at the two pieces of glass in her hands. It was the same laboratory glass that had held the precious papyrus. The papyrus was gone!

Sally stood there, her legs glued to the ground.

"It can't be true!" she cried. "It's not possible. Who could have found it here?"

Then, remembering the grass box, she pulled the lawnmower out from the corner and lifted the box off. It was empty.

"Oh no! What on earth am I to do now?" she cried. "My God, I must find them! They must be here somewhere." Panic stricken, she threw aside the garden tools and umbrella. She screamed as a deckchair fell on her foot. This was crazy. She must calm down, and try to work out what could have happened. She relocked the outhouse and limped back into the house.

Sally threw herself onto the sofa beside Felix, fear suddenly taking over.

"My God they've been here!" she cried, jumping up again. She rushed over to the front door and double-locked it. Then she ran upstairs and bolted the sash windows in the bedrooms. Downstairs again she picked up the phone to call the police, then changed her mind and decided to call Aurora before remembering that it would be after two in the morning in Beirut.

"Oh Felix, what are we to do?" she asked the cat. "Calm down you fool. Think!" The only other person who knew where she had hidden the papyrus and Jo's report was Alex. Of course! He must have moved them and forgotten to tell her. Those men couldn't have been here. They'd have ransacked the house before they found them.

Sally dialled the number of Alex's office, but he was not there. His secretary sounded rather odd when she asked if he would be in later. She wasn't at all helpful.

Half an hour was as long as she dared wait, but when she called again there was no answer. Surely they didn't close for lunch in Minneapolis, did they? Her anger mounting she called the number of his flat.

"Alex McCloud. I'm sorry I can't take you call. Please leave your name and I'll call you back shortly."

"Damn you Alex!" she cried. "Where the hell are you?"

Sally paced up and down the room, waves of despair sweeping through her. Grabbing the phone again, she dialled the McCloud's number. A woman answered. It didn't sound like Abigail.

"Hello. Abigail? It's Sally Wincott. I'm sorry to bother you, but I need to contact Alex urgently. Do you…"

"Yes hello? I'm sorry Mrs McCloud isn't at home. May I take a message?"

"Oh, but I am calling from England and I really need to contact Alex McCloud urgently. Is Professor McCloud there by any chance?"

"I am sorry, the professor and Mrs McCloud are not available at present. Perhaps, in the circumstances, you may care to write. I take it you are a friend of the family?"

"Yes I am a friend, but what circumstances? Has something happened?"

"Oh, dear. You haven't heard?"

"Haven't heard what? It's not something to do with Alex, is it?" cried Sally.

"I am sorry, Miss Wincott. I really can't help you. I am sure the family will be in touch if there is something you should know."

"But what is it? I must know. Is it Alex? Has he had an accident? I don't know who you are, but surely you can tell me something?"

"Professor and Mrs McCloud are at the airport, waiting for news Miss Wincott. You must have heard about the plane. It was all over the news."

Sally's heart stopped beating.

"*Oh no*!" Not the one missing over the Atlantic yesterday?"

"I'm afraid so. The professor's son was flying back from London…" but her reply was cut short.

"Oh my God! *It can't be*!" yelled Sally as the receiver fell from her hand.